BLOOD OF GEMINI

Mischievous Malamute Mystery Series Book 3

HARLEY CHRISTENSEN

For Maxine

PROLOGUE

It was a perfect day for a picnic. One of those lazy southwestern days where the sun warms your shoulders as the gentle breeze lulls you to sleep. Ramirez had selected a remote location where the only sound was from a nearby fountain that burbled as plumes of water danced to a synchronized but silent symphony.

A blanket had been carefully smoothed across an even patch of ground. On top he had meticulously arranged a simple but mouth-watering meal. Even Nicoh was happily gnawing on a gargantuan-sized dog bone. Peanut butter-flavored, of course.

Ramirez laughed, tugging on a long strand of my hair as I moaned over the first bite of peanut butter and pickle sandwich he'd made, just for me. It was only after I'd polished off one half and was well into the second I realized he'd been watching me.

"What?" I mumbled, my mouth still partially full as I self-consciously batted the tip of my nose. "Do not tell me I've had peanut butter on my face this entire time." When he chuckled and shook his head, I added, "Okay, you're awed by my freakish, yet masterful sandwich-eating abilities?"

Once again, he shook his head. "Just trying to decide something."

Intrigued, I gently placed the sandwich on its wax paper wrapper. "Um…you and your poker buddies aren't going to start placing bets on how many of these babies I can put away, are you? Because I'll have you know, I have a very important professional reputation to uphold."

His voice was quiet when he replied, his eyes searching mine, "I was just wondering if you thought you could ever like me as much as you do those sandwiches." A smile tugged the corner of his mouth but there was a hint of seriousness in his eyes. And a question.

"Well…" I could feel the heat rising in my cheeks, "these are pretty good sandwiches."

"Uh huh."

"And you did make them."

"I did."

"I suppose…in time…I could like you both equally."

"Equally, as in fifty-fifty?"

"I might be able to manage that."

"Oh?"

"There's just one thing."

"What's that?"

"Don't think you can ply me with sandwiches to improve your odds."

"I wouldn't dream of it." He leaned closer, smiling.

I placed a hand firmly on his chest. "I wasn't done yet."

"Oh? Sorry. What else?"

"Don't ever think about sharing your sandwiches with anyone but me."

"It's a deal." Our lips met just as his phone buzzed, causing us both to shift back in surprise.

"Better get that." I started to reach for the remainder of the sandwich.

Ramirez smiled. "Still aren't sure about that fifty-fifty, are you?" Before I could answer, he stood and moved a short distance away to take the call.

"What are you looking at?" I grumbled at Nicoh, whose tongue flopped lazily as he zeroed in on my sandwich. Having missed his opportunity, he emitted his own rumble before crossing his paws, continuing his destruction of the monster bone.

Ramirez returned moments later, his happy mood gone.

"What?" I struggled to get out, nearly choking in the process. "What is it?"

"That was my contact with the FBI."

"Okay…"

"Winslow Clark escaped. Three weeks ago."

Horror washed over me as I digested the news. "Is he…is he coming to get me?"

He shook his head, looking me straight in the eye. "Worse. They believe he's already here."

Couldn't a peanut butter and pickle sandwich ever just be a peanut butter and pickle sandwich? I groaned as Nicoh engulfed the rest of my half in one noisy bite.

Nope. Life is never that simple.

CHAPTER ONE

"AJ, did you hear what I said?"

Oh, I'd heard him. Right up to the point he'd told me the monster who had killed my parents and sister was on the beeline express to yours truly—provided he hadn't already trained his sharp little eyes on me. I placed my bet on the latter. Clark was antsy to finish the job he'd failed to complete months earlier—to witness my last breath as he ended my existence in this world.

One might wonder what would make a twenty-something photographer so enticing. With Clark, it was all about exacting a revenge long overdue, though I had been responsible for no part. And yet, like my insatiable need for the elusive peanut butter and pickle concoction, Clark's need was rooted in the execution—the completion—of his mission. So he'd returned to destroy me.

Rather than serve myself up as a sitting duck or waste time formulating a response for Ramirez, I bid farewell to the picnic I'd barely started to share with the hunky detective. It only added to the irony that my ninety-eight pound Alaskan Malamute had already had his way with it. I hastily collected the remains; then bitterly snatched his dog bone and tossed it into my bag. I wasn't in the mood to talk about Clark or his current whereabouts, much less his agenda for me. All I cared about was getting out of the park and safely to my home.

Mind you, I had no intention of hiding from him. I simply needed time alone. Time to think. Perhaps I should have been frightened out of my gourd and maybe if I was honest with myself, somewhere deep down I was...frightened. For the moment, I had eclipsed the fear and replaced it with something far more visceral—rage.

It was not an emotion I revered but it was hard to forget the mark Clark had left in the wake of his previous visit. After killing my loved ones, he'd terrorized me and kidnapped my best friend. And now he had the audacity to return. I smirked, my lips forming a vicious snarl. This time, Clark had another thing coming. I wasn't going down without a fight and he sure as heck wouldn't be leaving with what he'd returned for...if he left at all.

Ramirez didn't need to be a mind reader or a detective to register my mood, or my intentions. "Let us—and the Feds— handle this, AJ. I promise, we'll get him," he yelled at my back after I'd rebuked his attempt to grab my arm.

I stormed on, muttering to myself, "That line's been over-played, Detective."

* * *

Camouflaged by a crop of trees, he observed their heated interaction. Once the cop returned from taking his phone call, their conversation had taken on a strained, agitated vibe, almost forcing him to smile.

Almost.

After all these years, he was one step closer to getting what he wanted. What he deserved. He wasn't about to get sidetracked now. Arianna had enjoyed her peace for long enough.

He looked at the old, tattered photograph—a memory of what

had been—promises of what could have been. Tracing the silhouettes with his thumb ignited emotions he'd long tucked away. He shook his head, setting the memories free. The past couldn't be altered or reversed, but the present and the future—that he could control.

And this time, no one—not even Arianna Jackson—would stop him.

CHAPTER TWO

Of course Ramirez was waiting for me when I got home, leaning against his police cruiser with his legs crossed. I gritted my teeth, hoping he hadn't violated any laws while zigzagging through the back streets of Phoenix. One of the perks of being a cop, I huffed to myself, biting my tongue in the process.

Ramirez smirked as he took in my sour welcome. "We hadn't finished our discussion or our picnic, for that matter."

"Winslow Clark makes for bad conversation, not to mention, poor digestion." Ramirez chuckled, forcing me to cock my head to one side. "I hardly think this is the appropriate time for your amusement, Detective."

"I didn't say it was." He continued to peruse my expression, lingering on my body language before frowning. "So we're reverting back to 'Detective' now, are we?"

I shifted under the weight of his scrutiny. "I don't make the rules, *Detective*, I just roll with them as they come."

"Says the girl hell-bent on going after a killer by herself."

I was irritated he had my number and managed to get my goat at the same time. Baaah. "I'd hardly be alone."

Ramirez snorted. "Oh yeah, drag your best friend and canine into it. That's worked out well for you in the past."

I didn't appreciate his haughty tone and threw a few less than ladylike adjectives out before adding, "If memory serves, we managed all right."

Immune to my colorful language, Ramirez shook his head. "And nearly got yourselves killed in the process. Next time, you may not be so lucky. Before you go bounding off like a woman obsessed, I suggest you give that some serious thought."

"I'll take your *suggestions* under advisement." Ramirez scowled but kept his thoughts and own bounty of adjectives to himself. "In the meantime, I'd still like to know how Clark managed to worm his miserable way out of round-the-clock monitoring in a facility supposedly locked down like the Loop 101 during rush hour." He nodded, noting my sarcasm was a special gift reserved for the Feds. There had been no love lost where they were concerned.

"And I would have gladly shared what I had learned, had you not shoved me off and stormed away." Summoning every ounce of maturity I could muster, I responded by sticking my tongue out. "Now that you've had your moment, can we go inside and finish our conversation?"

"Hmph...I don't suppose you'd have any of those sandwiches left, would you?"

Ramirez laughed and shook his head. "You'd have to ask Nicoh about that."

I looked at the massive canine, who was more interested in snapping at flies than the humans who had the audacity to ignore his presence. Catching one—a fly, not a human—he smacked his lips before moving on to the next.

Disgusted, I stomped into the house. "Never mind, I wasn't really that hungry anyway."

* * *

I offered Ramirez a beer but he declined, an indication the recent call had not only brought bad news, it had placed him back on duty. It also meant the longer he lingered around babysitting me, the more time it gave Clark to plot his evil deeds, so I gestured for him to begin.

Ramirez scruffed the back of his head, a gesture that suggested he was revisiting the information he'd received, if not editing it for my benefit. "Details are sketchy at best, though I'm sure they're trying to keep things close to the vest while they investigate. Initial rumblings point to an inside job."

"Ya think?" My tone might have come out a bit snottier than I'd intended but it mirrored my emotions.

Ramirez ignored it and continued, "In the meantime, they are supplying pertinent information to the appropriate agencies, but warning them to keep it under wraps from the media to prevent the public from panicking. Or impeding their ability to track his movements."

I grunted, unimpressed by the sparse details the Feds had collected to this point. It had been nearly three weeks since they'd misplaced Clark. Given all the state, local, foreign and probably extraterrestrial resources they had at their disposal, I would have expected something more promising than he was probably somewhere in the state of Arizona.

Granted, it was a fairly large state but a fifty-mile radius would have been nice. I'm pretty sure my roommate, best friend and news hound extraordinaire, Leah Campbell, would have nailed down his geo-coordinates in a quarter of the time...unless... I looked at Ramirez and tried to gauge his BS meter. When his face revealed nothing, I should have remembered he was a skilled poker player.

"So they've got nothing. Clark could be on my doorstep in

two weeks, two days...or two minutes." Ramirez's silence provided my answer. Even without the benefit of their fancy technology and vast network of resources, I could have told them one thing was certain.

Clark would come.

* * *

Ramirez and I had nothing more to discuss, so I thanked him for the well-intentioned afternoon and saw him on his not-so-merry way before placing two quick calls. The first was to Leah, my partner-in-crime, urging her to come home when she could and the other to an acquaintance the two of us had met months earlier while trying to identify my twin sister Victoria's killer.

A former bureau chief with the *Chicago Tribune* twenty-plus years earlier, Mort Daniels had made more than a pet project of the field of genetic engineering. Specifically, projects related to the top two research facilities at the time: Alcore and GenTech. Alison Anders, a research assistant at Alcore, had been our biological mother and Martin Singer, a geneticist for Alcore's primary competitor, GenTech, our father. *Had* being the operative word in both cases.

Martin had also worked with another scientist, Theodore Winslow, on a human cloning project GenTech had tagged as Gemini, until they'd had a falling out. Quite literally. The result of that fallout had cost my biological parents their lives. But despite their deaths, Theodore held onto his grudge, ingraining his own share of entitlement—and revenge—into his son.

Though Leah and I hadn't known at the time, Mort Daniels' history lesson would soon place us on a collision course with that son, who had changed his name to Winslow Clark. The play on his father's name was intentional, as was murdering my sister and leaving her body in a dumpster behind my house at his father's behest. Now Clark was making his second run at doing the same to me. I intended to thwart his attempt, but needed to locate him first. Even though Mort had retired from the newspaper several years earlier—choosing to spend his days tending to his yard in Ahwatukee—Leah and I agreed, if anyone could get a line on Clark, Mort was our guy.

The elderly gentleman answered his phone after two rings and once we exchanged pleasantries, I dove into the purpose of my call. Once finished, my leg bounced in anticipation as I awaited his response.

"Clark didn't just walk out of a maximum security facility, pat the guard on the arm, thank him for an enchanting visit and disappear off into the sunset—in this case, the Valley of the Sun—he had help. Powerful help."

"The Feds think there was an inside connection. By 'powerful help' are we talking about prison staff...or the warden? Clark's shrink? Both?"

"Maybe." The way he drew it out told me he wasn't convinced. "I'd like to check on a few things. Mind if I get back to you in the morning?"

Despite my disappointment, I managed a courteous and even gracious response before ending the connection. As I stared at the cell phone in my hand, I contemplated the probability his efforts would yield the results I needed in time.

Clark was like a tsunami, a horrific monster that thrived on obliterating the unsuspecting innocents in its path. But unlike those who fell victim to its unforgiving, callous devastation, I had the benefit of anticipation. And knowledge. And while that advantage would mean looking into the monster's eyes as he mowed me down and choked out my final breath, I also had the benefit of something more. I was no victim. Nor was I innocent.

When I went down, I was taking the monster straight to Hell with me.

CHAPTER THREE

Not even the sight of Leah's spiky blonde locks bobbing from side to side improved my mood as I watched her jamming to the tunes filtering through her headphones while she belted out her own rendition of "Crazy Train." Fitting, I mused.

"Whaassup buttercup?" she drawled, taking in my bemused expression.

"Besides the fact you're butchering a classic, you mean? Perhaps you should consider lip-synching. Silently."

My best friend slowly removed the headphones and put her hands up in surrender. "Whoa. What's the matter with you? Someone replace your Lucky Charms with Shredded Wheat? Wait—Nicoh didn't eat all my Nutty Bars again, did he? If that furball so much as—"

"No, wisecracker. Two words: Winslow. Clark."

She nodded, letting out a low whistle as she plopped onto a kitchen stool. "I take it Mort couldn't help, then?"

"He said he wanted to look into a few things. In the meantime, I'm biding my time…festering. Clark could be anywhere right now, meaning he could strike at any moment. And we both know what he's capable of."

Leah pressed her eyes shut and shuddered, recalling the time she'd spent as Clark's captive—a ploy to elicit my attention and my compliance—though in the end his intention had been to kill us both.

"Hey—" I started to comfort my friend but she quickly waved me off.

"Let's not do this again, AJ." After everything that had gone down the past year—including the number of times we'd gotten ourselves into trouble or nearly killed—she was ready for the dramafest to stop. Period.

I couldn't disagree. It would be refreshing to go back to our normal lives, the ones that had been regularly scheduled and already in progress. Not that those lives had always been filled with puppies or an endless supply of gummy bears and margaritas but they'd been *our* lives.

A look passed between us—we both knew good and well—even if Clark was no longer a threat and there was no danger on the horizon, our lives would never be normal again. Somehow, I was okay with that, and given the calmness that washed over my usually impish, energetic friend, I knew, she too, had made peace with it. Her comment had not been one of pleading or evolved from a place of fear—it was a resolution.

We would not grant Clark another free pass.

* * *

Mort called shortly before 9 a.m. the following morning, as I was collecting my camera equipment for my first client and almost immediately, I noticed his tone was unusually curt.

"I was able to gather some information but I'd rather not discuss it over the phone. Can you meet?"

"Okay...I have a photo shoot at the Desert Botanical Garden

that will take the bulk of the morning but I can drop by your house after—"

"No, no..." Mort interjected, his voice sharp and impatient, borderline hostile, "that won't work. The Andean bear exhibit at the Phoenix Zoo—do you know it?"

I was surprised by his choice of location, which was just a quick shot up Galvin Parkway from the botanical garden.

"Yes, I know where that particular exhibit is located but—"

"Be there. 1 p.m."

I stared at my phone and had it not been for our previous interactions, would have called him out for his rude behavior. Now, he just had me worried.

"Alright... Is everything okay, Mort? I mean—"

"Not now, Arianna." The way he enunciated every word made it sound like he did so through gritted teeth. "Just be there at 1 p.m. And make sure you come alone."

The connection ended, leaving me confused and more than a little concerned for the retired newspaperman. The rumbling in my belly wasn't helping matters, though it could have just been the peanut M&Ms I'd had for breakfast, colliding like balls on a pool table.

Typically a warm, gentle man, Mort had been uncommonly harsh and commanding. Whatever he'd learned, it couldn't have been good. I called Leah, knowing she would be disappointed about his insistence I come alone, which also prevented Nicoh from accompanying me—definitely a curious curiosity.

"And here I thought old Mort liked me best." I pictured Leah pulling on the ends of her hair as the corners of her mouth turned down.

"Um, no...sorry. I think he actually likes Nicoh best."

My attempt at lightening the mood fell flat on its big fat face as Leah snorted into my ear. "Whatever, AJ, it certainly doesn't seem to be the case anymore, considering he's left his favorite out of the fun."

"Yeah, what do you make of that?"

"Who knows. You said he sounded irritable. Maybe he had to call in a few favors to get your information? I know I'd be pretty crabby if I had to call in *another* one for you," she grumbled. "In fact, if I had to count the number of unsavory things I've had to do to get your skinny hiney—"

"Is that right?" I was incensed she was taking Mort's request out on me by bringing up old dirt. "Well, I think we'll all benefit from finding out where Clark is, don't you?" Her silence told me she'd conceded the point—a rare occurrence. "So, if I'm going to tackle this meeting without the benefit of your expertise—how do you suggest I proceed?"

"Well..." she spoke slowly as her mind switched into reporter-mode, "if Mort wants to meet with you away from his home, alone, it means he's worried. Perhaps he believes he's given whomever he contacted reason to keep tabs on him, which would explain the need to meet at a public location."

"Okay, so he's being cautious."

"Or completely paranoid."

"Maybe...I think we need to operate under the assumption he has good reason to be concerned and take it at face value."

"Um...hello? What did you do with my best friend? Geez, AJ, when did you become such a cynic?"

"When Winslow Clark decided to claw his way out of Hell and set up shop in my backyard, that's when." As she scoffed in my ear, I added, "So that's all the sage advice you've got stored in your bag of tricks?"

"As if," she huffed, "just try to get him to tell you as many details as you can—who gave him the info, what and how they said it, how they know it, blah, blah, blah. And as a final tip—

record it all. Whatever *it* is, my gut's telling me something hinky is about to go down."

Hinky or not, I didn't need Leah's gastric intuitions to tell me the crazy train was on a collision course with yours truly.

* * *

I was glad to have my work to keep me occupied for the next several hours. I certainly couldn't afford to have my impending meeting with Mort distract me from my professional duties, or the payday it promised. I was fortunate to have had early success with my freelance photography business, which by no coincidence I'd named Mischievous Malamute—a result of a few awkward predicaments Nicoh had put me in at the beginning of my career. In hindsight, perhaps I should have reconsidered allowing him to accompany me to my shoots but after a few near-misses, snafus and a great many apologies, I'd continued to tote him with me from location to location. Or maybe it was vice-versa.

Needless to say, Nicoh was less than thrilled about being left behind and verbalized as much as I hauled my equipment from the house to the Mini. Of course, the howling and moaning increased two-fold as I backed out of the driveway. I cringed, thinking of the poor neighbors, who were likely hustling to their fallout shelters. One of these days, I'd probably receive a lovely note on my front door, compliments of the city, informing me of the various code violations I was infringing upon. Violating the strict noise ordinance and harboring wild animals without a permit would likely be the starters. Yup, Nicoh was gonna make me pay. Today, he'd probably howl until he was no longer able to hear the rumble of my tiny engine before heading into the back-yard to leave a special treat for my homecoming.

On a brighter note, my client was an absolute peach and things ran smoothly throughout the shoot, leaving me with time to spare. I grabbed a caffeinated beverage and reorganized my tote so that my cell phone would be in a prime recording position, as Leah had instructed. It would probably turn out to be overkill but considering we'd both gotten those gut feelings, a girl couldn't be too careful.

I gave the application a quick test to ensure the quality was good and that it wouldn't fall to the bottom of the bag when jostled. Sure, I could have just as easily put the darn thing in my back pocket but after a recent butt-dialing incident at my friend Charlie's penthouse, I was hesitant to place the phone on my person. There was no sense validating my cellularly challenged reputation. I grimaced at the recollection but as I paid the zoo's admission and proceeded to the Andean bear exhibit, my discomfort quickly evaporated as I recounted the childhood moments spent at this exhibit, hoping to catch a glimpse of the spectacled bears—aptly nicknamed for their unique facial markings.

As I reached the enclosure Mort had indicated, I wondered why—of all the exhibits the zoo had to offer—he had selected this exhibit? My stomach formed a volleyball-sized knot, sending signals to the rest of my body, along with an unnerving tingling sensation in the remainder of my extremities. I cursed, wishing I'd not encouraged the barista to be so liberal with the extra shots of espresso. I blew out a long breath and proceeded.

Mort's back was to me as I approached. The ground crunched under the weight of my shoes, causing him to turn. I squinted, taking in the man's features. My mind flashed to a photograph I'd seen while searching for clues related to my sister's murder. He had aged a few decades, given the crinkles at the corners of his dark eyes and slight loosening of skin across his angular jawline but he was a mirror image of one of the men in that photo—still retaining his ruggedly handsome looks and mop of hair, now laced with silver.

A man who was most definitely…not Mort Daniels.

"Hello, Arianna. My name is—"

"Martin."

Surprised by my acknowledgment, he rubbed his hands together, contemplating how to proceed now the cat was out of the bag. A long moment passed before he raised his head and looked me straight in the eye.

"Yes, Arianna. My name is Martin Singer. I am your father."

CHAPTER FOUR

Once I had absorbed the initial shock that Martin Singer was even alive, the hair on the back of my neck bristled at his brazen announcement.

"My *biological* father," I clarified. If the distinction bothered him, he gave no indication. "Yes, I've known about our…connection for a few months now, since the death of my twin sister—your other daughter—surely you heard about her murder?"

Martin bowed his head and said nothing but kept his eyes focused on me. I had the benefit of sunglasses and utilized them to their full advantage to observe him as well. The family resemblance was uncanny, especially around the mouth and nose and the way his eyebrows rose and fell when surprised.

"You look so much like her," he whispered. I nodded, knowing he was referencing Alison Anders, the woman who had given me life; then died a few short hours later. "I assume Ella favored her, too?"

I nodded at his reference to the name Victoria had been given at birth. "From the pictures I've seen of her, yes, very much so." Martin tilted his head and squinted in confusion—another gesture we had in common. My voice came out raspy, "I never knew

Victoria, Ella, when she was alive. I only became aware of her existence after she was murdered." I blew out a breath. "I was the one who found her." Martin's eyes widened at the revelation and when he started to respond, I waved off his sympathy.

"Why are you here, Martin?"

The empathy surrounding him rippled and faded at the harshness of my voice and he realized now was not the time for a family reunion. Though his eyes never left mine, he was silent for so long, I was compelled to fill the uncomfortable void.

"How do you know Mort Daniels? More importantly, why did he contact you, much less know *how* to contact you?" Martin smiled but this time, there was no warmth behind it and something clicked. "You were Mort's contact when he worked at the *Chicago Tribune*, back when he was doing research on Alcore and GenTech. *You* were his inside track." His expression revealed nothing but the shift in the energy surrounding us suggested I had nicked something. "Has he known you were alive this whole time? I personally would like to know how that transpired, by the way, in addition to finding out where you've been the past twenty-odd years? Winslow Clark said his dad pushed you off the Skyway Bridge in an attempt to make it look like suicide. And yet, decades later…here you are. Why? Why now?" As the questions poured out, my skin grew hot as my heartbeat doubled. I attempted another barrage but Martin put his hands up in surrender and chuckled in amusement.

"So much like Alison—so inquisitive, so darned smart…" his voice trailed off as he appeared to revel in some long lost memory. Finally, he shook his head, as though pushing away cobwebs. "But no, I wasn't Daniels' 'inside track' nor am I aware who that person is, or was." I wasn't buying his answer but waved my hand, urging him to continue. "Daniels made contact through a mutual acquaintance. I was notified once the urgency of your phone call had been assessed. He doesn't know I'm alive or that I was the person sent to meet you. He only knew you would be meeting with a resource that could assist you with your current…situation."

I thought about my conversation with Mort—how uncommonly abrupt he'd been—and wondered why he'd felt obligated to set me up for this meeting with an unknown and possibly dangerous stranger.

As though he'd been reading my mind, Martin nodded. "Our acquaintance is very well connected. I assure you, we mean you no harm. My deepest apologies for causing you distress but Mort had sworn to not reveal his source and was also assured your safety would be our primary concern." His explanation seemed dubious but I let it slide. "As for Winslow Clark, the story he told you was true. His father, Theodore Winslow, plotted my demise and lured me to the bridge but his execution—no pun intended—was severely lacking. He didn't stick around to verify the results. Thankfully, he was as sloppy with attempted murder as he was in his work, otherwise I wouldn't be standing here today. But that, my dear Arianna, is a story for another day. Today…today we must focus on the matter at hand: Winslow Clark. That answers the 'why' portion of your query. As for the 'why now'? Because it's time to destroy the monster I've created. Permanently."

* * *

I clucked my tongue at his confidence.

"I know you have many questions, Arianna. I have many of my own. Too many," his voice wavered and I caught a hint of moisture glistening in his eyes. Fortunately my emotions were masked behind sunglasses. "I do hope someday soon you will oblige me but today we do not have the benefit of time on our side. Winslow Clark is here, preparing to strike. For the time being, he must be the primary focus of our attentions. Having said that, I have a favor to ask." I nodded for him to proceed. "The only way I can ensure your safety and the safety of the ones you love is if you agree to leave town."

Oh, heck no. I told Martin as much and after unleashing the sailor on him, I wouldn't have been the least bit surprised if he'd whipped a bar of soap from his pocket. Instead, he offered a bemused expression. Exasperated, I released another round of expletives before slamming my fists onto my hips while tapping my foot.

This time, my efforts were rewarded with a small chuckle. "Forgive me, the similarities to your mother—to Alison—continue to amaze me."

"If I'm half as stubborn as you say she was, then you should know I have no intention of leaving town—leaving my loved ones behind—while I'm off taking a vaca, waiting for the freak show of a monsoon known as El Clark to pass through town. My town. Ain't gonna happen, Pops."

This time, Martin winced and I immediately felt a flush of regret for my callousness before remembering the man had conveniently elected to go missing for the majority of my life. When he said nothing, I added, "Besides, that would kind of defeat the purpose. I mean, Clark came to Phoenix to eliminate me. What purpose would leaving serve anyone?" I shrugged and waved my hands to emphasize the point. Apparently Martin was not one for dramatic flourishes and looked bored, if not a bit impatient. "He'd come looking for me, regardless of where I went, so there's no sense having him tear up the whole country in the process. Let's face it, he's not going to back down or crawl back into whatever hole he clawed his miserable way out of—not empty-handed, anyway."

"He will if he's offered something better."

I had to refrain from bursting out in laughter. "Something better? Like what? A front row seat on the maiden voyage of

Richard Branson's Virgin Galactic spacecraft?" This time I laughed but there was no humor in it and given the look on Martin's face, he clearly didn't appreciate my brand of sarcasm. "I seriously doubt Clark's willing to hang out with the gila monsters and javelinas here in the desert for that long."

Martin shook his head, still not amused. I wondered if Alison had bristled his fur to such an extent. Given the way I was feeling about the man at the present, I hoped her talents in that arena superseded mine. He squinted, regarding me and when he finally spoke, his expression was flat.

"He won't have to wait. He'll have me."

Score one for Martin—that certainly earned my attention.

"You? No offense, Martin but how do you interpret that as 'something better'? To my knowledge, Clark doesn't even know you're alive, much less would believe you were who you claim to be."

Though neither of us was feeling jovial, Martin offered a cryptic smile. "Oh, I believe I can make a pretty convincing argument."

Knowing Clark as I did, I snorted at Martin's bravado. "Okay...say he's got his DNA decoder ring handy and it confirms you're...you...why would he be satisfied with that exchange? And what's to say he won't take us both out anyway?"

"Because I have something he wants, Arianna. And when I present it to him, in all its glory, he'll want it so badly he'll do anything to finally have it in his possession."

"Err...not sure if you're familiar with Clark but unless you've got an in with Versace and Ferrari...with maybe a little Charlie Manson thrown in, I doubt he'll bite."

"Oh, I suspect he'll do a lot more than bite when he learns what I have to offer," Martin gave me a knowing look, "especially since it involves Gemini."

* * *

Martin could only be referring to one thing: the formulas to the human cloning project both Clark and his father had not only coveted, but killed for. Putting those babies in either of their hands, along with the scientist who'd created them was a dangerous, if not monstrous business.

Though strained, my voice found its way past my urge to vomit. "I'll admit, I don't know you very well, Martin, but you certainly don't strike me as crazy." Absently, I rechecked my math—perhaps my initial calculations were off? Was he crazy? There was only one way to find out. "Why would you suggest such a thing knowing what happened...the consequences...last time?"

"I promise you, it won't come to that."

"How can you make a promise like that?"

"Because I'm going to destroy them before it gets that far."

CHAPTER FIVE

I wasn't sure if he'd meant destroying the formulas—or the father and son killing team—but he didn't appear above entertaining both options.

Regardless, I didn't trust him and right now, placing some distance from the situation was starting to sound less hair-brained than when I had initially dredged it up, even if it had only been a few minutes earlier. Yeah, I realized time was a hot commodity where Clark was concerned but that nagging voice inside my skull told me it was worth the risk.

I had just learned my biological father was still alive, which was a lot to contend with and considering he hadn't made his presence known until now, I wasn't convinced he had done so merely out of concern for his daughter. It was far more plausible his reasons were self-serving, which made me question anything he'd said.

Adding another chestnut to that fire, Martin had asked me to keep our meeting private before we parted ways. I understood why he wouldn't want the masses knowing his current status—being presumed dead made one funny that way—but he caught me off-guard when he attempted to swear me to secrecy from everyone, including Leah. In the end, I might have made a few grunting noises that sounded like agreement but I wasn't going to let pseudo-Dad dictate anything to me. We'd only just met and in my book, blood neither earned nor guaranteed him that right.

* * *

I was so busy replaying my conversation with Martin, it took me a moment to register my neighbor Susie was walking a dog as I breezed on past with a distracted half-wave. It took me another moment to realize she didn't own a dog.

She was walking *my* dog.

I threw the Mini in reverse and cursed as she squealed in protest—the car's tires, not Susie.

Susie leaned in as I rolled down the window. "I'd keep the day job if I were you. You'd make a questionable valet and an even worse race car driver. Typically, the goal is to proceed that way." She thumbed in the opposite direction. "By the way, was just returning Nicoh to his yard."

"He thought he'd partake in another adventure, did he?" Content with his current handler, the canine ignored me—part of my payback for that morning.

In addition to the occasional passive-aggressive streak, Nicoh had become adept at creating escape routes now that his gal pal Pandora had moved to Dallas with her dad. I would find him sitting in her backyard, patiently awaiting her return. He would typically become belligerent when forced to return home, where he would give me the stink eye until mealtime rolled around.

Susie gave me a perplexed look. "No, your friend Clark— good looking boy, that one—said you were at a photo shoot that was running late and had asked him to run Nicoh home. It wasn't until he got here he realized you'd forgotten to give him your keys, so he came over to ask if I could watch Nicoh until you returned. I told him I had my own set and could do him one better. He was most appreciative and seemed like he was in a hurry to get back to the shoot." She waved a finger at me. "Say, you didn't tell me you'd expanded your business—hiring assistants and all— nice to hear you've been doing so well."

Though her story nearly made me barf on my shoes and throw various expletives out into the universe, I didn't want to alarm my neighbor. I doubted she'd take kindly to the revelation she'd spent face time with a cold-blooded killer. "Um yeah, business has been good. Clark's been a real lifesaver, though I wish he'd ease up on wearing the designer suits to work. I don't need my clients thinking I'm making so much bank I can afford to pay my associates that well, meaning I can also afford to give them some slack where my rates are concerned."

Susie laughed. "You know, I did wonder. Armani, wasn't it? Boy's a sharp dresser and a definite keeper." She wiggled her eyebrows at me suggestively.

"Err...yeah...sort of already taken but I'll let Clark know you appreciated his wardrobe when I see him again."

Susie giggled and after thanking her for watching Nicoh, coaxed the surly beast into the Mini and continued to the house. "So...Buster, what have you been up to in my absence, besides consorting with the enemy?"

Nicoh was uncharacteristically subdued. At first I figured he was still mopey about being left behind but when I looked into his eyes and watched his laborious gait, I noticed he was acting a bit punchy, like he'd been drugged. This time I allowed the expletives to fly as I checked him over. How else would Clark have gotten Nicoh's compliance, especially after he'd knocked Clark on his arse the last time we'd crossed paths?

I immediately called the vet and was relieved to learn he was on his house call rotation. After providing him with a truncated version of my suspicions, he agreed to swing by once he'd finished with his last patient.

I moved Nicoh into the house, where he collapsed into the corner of the living room. Moments after tucking himself into a tight circle, snores rumbled from the center of the mass.

My impatience got the better of me while waiting for the vet, so I searched for clues indicating how and where Clark had breached my homestead. At first glance, nothing seemed out of place in any of the rooms but when I walked the perimeter of the yard, I found an empty meat wrapper near the back gate. Bingo. I carefully collected it and placed it into a plastic baggie and was about to resume my search when I heard a vehicle pull into the drive. I trotted to the front of the house to find my vet pulling supplies from his van.

Ushering him into the living room, I offered what little I knew about Nicoh's afternoon and produced the baggie. The vet listened with interest as he checked Nicoh's vitals and asked about any vomiting or other side-effects. I indicated there had been none, other than Nicoh's extreme moodiness and unusual physical imbalance. After extracting a few blood samples, he provided follow-up instructions, took the baggie and assured me he would call once he had the results.

I walked him to his vehicle and nibbled on a fingernail while calling Leah. I wasn't prepared to deal with Ramirez or his reaction to Clark's invasion of my privacy and honestly, still had yet to decide what to do about mentioning Martin's sudden appearance. Leah would take whatever news I could throw at her and have advice to spare. Besides, I needed to ensure Clark hadn't paid her a little visit as well.

I suddenly realized I could hear her cell phone, only the

ringing wasn't isolated to my ear. It appeared to coming from somewhere…in the house. I quickly tracked the sound, taking a mental account as I went. Her SUV hadn't been in the driveway and there was no trail of keys, tote bag, laptop, etc. that typically followed her arrival. I squinted, revisiting anything that seemed out of order while searching for evidence Clark had been present. I shook my head in repulsion at the thought of him touching my things or rifling through my undie drawer, noting my fingers had started to go numb from gripping the phone. Impatient, I called again and when the ringing turned to voicemail, I honed in on the sound, throwing the door open to the room where it had led me.

My room.

I had given it a quick once-over when I arrived home and had seen nothing blatantly obvious but now I searched from a fresh perspective and found Leah's phone under my comforter. Thoroughly expecting a Sigourney Weaver *Copycat* moment—complete with ants and a bloody, severed finger—I squeezed my eyes closed and threw the bedding to the side with the force of an arm wrestler gunning toward victory. Sweat threatened to escape my brow as I opened one eye a slit to look at the offending —phone.

Just a phone.

I exhaled deeply and a bead of sweat trickled into my eyes, forcing me to blink rapidly while I attempted to confirm my discovery. Still, it was just a phone. I thumbed through the missed calls and noticed several since early that morning. Surely she hadn't left it behind or placed it under the covers of my bed. I ventured a guess as to who had done the honors, the list not particularly long.

Clark was really getting on my nerves. After breaking into my home, drugging my dog and hauling him around the neighborhood, he had managed to commandeer my best friend's phone. I quickly panned through her text messages to see if they might offer any explanation as to her whereabouts. My eyes settled on one in all caps from an unknown sender—addressed to me.

ARIANNA—IF I CAN GET THIS CLOSE—HOW LONG DO YOU THINK YOU HAVE?

My heart thudded against my chest as I bit my lip in an attempt to rein in the emotion that raged through me. Suddenly, I realized I was no longer alone in the room. I swiveled on one heel, prepared to throw my fists, arms, legs, phone…whatever, to ward off the unwelcome visitor…stopping short of my crazed onslaught as I took in the startled, wide-eyed expression of my roommate.

"Whoa! What's going on? And, hey…where'd you find my phone?"

I couldn't decide whether to flog my roomie, or shriek because she'd startled me, so I grabbed her and hugged her fiercely, until she mouthed, "Oww…" Relief washed over me as I released her and tears spilled down my cheeks.

"Hey, hey…are you okay?" She stuttered, surprised by the downpour, though perhaps it was the side-effects of having the oxygen squeezed out of her.

I stifled a last, small sob and wiped mascara-stained tears on the back of my hand before plopping on the bed. Leah followed suit and glanced at her phone, still clutched in my grasp and threatening to crack until the pressure. She reached for it but I shook my head.

"We need to talk."

She retracted her hand as though a jolt of electricity had shocked her and clamped her mouth into a thin line before nodding for me to proceed. After a few cleansing breaths, I quickly told her about my visit with Mort—who turned out to be Martin—and about finding Nicoh with Susie. I finished with Clark's intrusion.

"Have you contacted Ramirez?"

I shook my head. "I called you first. That's how I found your phone."

"Huh. I had it with me this morning but after my first interview, I noticed it was gone." I tilted my head, curious about what would separate my best friend from her favorite piece of technology. She caught the gesture and chuckled. "Part of my current research involves interviewing the head honchos at a local server farm, including the VPs of Data Center Operations and Infrastructure. Considering how tight their security is—you should see the crap I had to offer up just to get inside—I locked my cell phone and laptop in the trunk." I shrugged. She'd lost me at 'server farm.'

"Anyway, I didn't think about them again until I was at my second interview on the other side of town. I opened the trunk and bam…my laptop was there but my phone was missing. I figured I'd just gotten confused about having it on me before the first meeting—it was only a four shot espresso day, after all." I rolled my eyes, though I knew Leah didn't operate on all cylinders until she'd had twice that much. "Long story short, this was the first chance I had to come back to look for it. You mentioned Clark sent a text to my phone, addressed to you?" I nodded and handed her the phone. She scrolled through the messages and read—and reread—Clark's text.

"Kind of weird he didn't just send it to your phone. Huh, and it was sent at the same time I was in my first interview." It was also the same time I was meeting with Martin at the zoo. So knowing—and loathing Clark as I did—no, I did not think it was weird. Not. One. Bit. I told her as much.

"Sounds like someone's been keeping pretty close tabs on us," she replied.

"Well, except for the phone in the bed and drugging my dog, I guess we should be happy he's keeping a safe distance." Like sarcasm would help me keep my sanity.

Leah nodded and momentarily shifted the subject. "So Martin asked you to keep your meeting a secret—he obviously doesn't know you very well. He's just lucky Clark's not onto him."

I didn't believe in luck and neither did she. Martin had been adamant that Clark didn't know of his existence but it certainly seemed as though Clark was ahead of the game. Whatever game that was, was anybody's guess. With Clark, all bets were off. The bigger question was, was Clark the puppet master—as he liked to fancy himself—or a puppet doing his master's bidding?

My cell phone distracted me from that line of thought, so I put a mental bookmark in its place for later consideration. The number of the incoming call told me it was Nicoh's vet. I immediately put him on speakerphone, hoping he had the results of my slumbering beast's blood work, along with a positive prognosis.

"Looks to be nothing more than a light sedative typically used during outpatient surgery, though based upon Nicoh's reaction, he was administered enough for two dogs his size, which is amazing, considering he was still upright when you found him."

Though Clark's audacity made me livid, I managed to hold my temper. The good doctor need not be apprised of *all* the circumstances surrounding Nicoh's drugging. "Apparently, your pup has an iron will," he added.

"More like an iron gut," Leah retorted, causing the vet to chuckle, "much like his owner." More laughter erupted from the opposite end of the connection. I gave her the evil eye and followed it up with a solid punch to the arm.

"Would these sedatives have made Nicoh more…compliant? Perhaps more likely to venture out of his territory, or go with someone he didn't know?" Go with someone he didn't trust was more like it but again, I didn't need to alert the vet to an already complicated situation.

"Absolutely, and unless the person who drugged the meat was an expert in administering meds, he could have easily ended up with a different outcome on his hands," the vet replied, meaning Clark might have killed Nicoh.

I nearly growled out loud. Perhaps that had been his intention? I quickly thanked him and signed off before he could press me for additional details. I wondered if he would be obligated to report it to the authorities. I needed to keep Ramirez off my back for as long as possible and wondered how long I had if the vet did report it.

As it was, it would only be a matter of time before I had to fill Ramirez in on…everything but right now I needed time—without his coply intuition—to figure things out on my own. Leah seemed to be thinking the same thing and was tugging on the ends of her shorn locks.

"Other than the obvious drama, what's going on with you?"

She avoided my eyes. "I was supposed to meet Vargas tonight."

Jeremiah "Jere" Vargas was a homicide detective for the city of Tempe. He was also the ex-boyfriend of Erica Stone, the editor that had made Leah's life hell at her former place of employment and ultimately initiated her decision to leave her post. Erica was also the primary reason Leah's relationship with the cop never seemed to evolve past friendship. The publishing world was small and though Leah was both talented and successful, there was no need to give a jealous ex ammo for monkeying up the works.

At my raised brow, she quickly added, "For drinks."

I looked at her skeptically but saw her point. If the vet reported the incident with Nicoh, Vargas would certainly catch word of it, considering the veterinary hospital was located within his jurisdiction. And if Vargas knew, it wouldn't be long before his Tuesday night poker buddy Ramirez was alerted. After a few cocktails, he'd drill Leah for specifics and she'd end up spilling the beans about Clark. Worst case scenario, she'd also bring up Martin. Not good. Not good, at all.

"I should cancel. Our time will be better spent doing some recon around this place while keeping an eye on Nicoh."

"Aren't those typically one in the same?" She gave me a small smile. Apparently, my attempt at humor was not completely lost on her, despite her grim expression as she glanced around the room, as though Clark might pop out from beneath the bed. "Anyway, it's really up to you but I won't complain if you decide to stay. I can definitely see why you'd want to avoid having that conversation with Vargas. I'm having the same anxiety about Ramirez." Talk about tall, dark and imposing—especially when agitated; then times that by two—it wasn't pretty. "I know we'll have to deal with both of them sooner or later."

"Alex, I'll take the latter for two hundred." My friend replied dryly while dialing the detective's number. "Fortunately, he's in a team meeting, so I'll be able to leave him a message without getting into too many details." She crafted quite the tale—I would have settled on a headache-themed excuse—and after disconnecting, smugly shoved the phone into her pocket.

"Wow, you are way too good at making up excuses. Anyone ever tell you that?"

"Tricks of the trade, my sweet, tricks of the trade."

I gave her a sideways glance. "And just what trade might that be, sweet?" She scrunched her nose and stuck out her tongue, forcing me to chuckle. "Just saying, Leah. Perhaps you're taking these freelance assignments with the Stanton brothers a bit too literally. They did have you interviewing a few pros while tracking down the leader of that prostitution ring. Maybe you've picked up a few other things you'd like to share?"

She blushed at the mention of Abe and Elijah Stanton. She'd been doing research for them off and on since leaving the newspaper, after they had helped me uncover Clark's involvement in my sister's death. I had always believed that, like Vargas, Abe had a crush on her and that the feeling was mutual, despite her emphatic denials. It was one situation where she just wasn't quite as convincing. I suspected I knew the reason. She attempted to ignore me and though she made a show of straightening my comforter, the pink tips of her ears betrayed her.

"So, are we going to de-Clark this place, or what?" she asked.

I released a long, slow breath and nodded. I was more than ready to let the de-Clarking, disinfecting and exorcising begin.

* * *

Our first order of business was to check on Nicoh. He was sleeping so soundly Leah actually placed her smartphone under his nose for confirmation of life. Of course, she snatched it away after being rewarded with a dollop of doggie drool on her Swarovski-encrusted case. I could barely contain my laughter until we made it outside to perform our search for potential points of entry.

We quickly learned, given the density and prickliness of the oleanders, it didn't seem possible one could, much less would even want to attempt that feat, with or without a canine in tow. Sure, Clark could have tossed the tainted meat over the ten-foot hedge but scaling it or plunging through it didn't seem feasible. Still, we continued to work our way, foot by foot, along the perimeter and as we approached the trailer gate, found what appeared to be Clark's entry point.

I would have missed it entirely had it not be for the bolt that snagged my running pants. As I cursed my clumsiness, I noticed it appeared to be less tarnished than its counterparts and extended nearly an inch farther. But while the bolt was somewhat unusual, the wood panel it held in place revealed our gold nugget. After retrieving a wrench, I unscrewed each nut and bolt and once the board had been removed from the gate, Leah easily slipped between the wrought iron bars. I followed suit, considering I was more of a size match to Clark. Like my friend, I had room to spare, which meant Clark would have been able to pass through and coax a drugged Alaskan Malamute of Nicoh's girth between the bars.

After placing a quick call to a handyman I used from time to time, Leah and I attempted to secure the gate the best we could until he could install a more permanent solution. Less than satisfied with our efforts, we surveyed the yard again before retreating indoors, securing all windows, doors and doggie exits and setting the alarm. Of course, if Clark was still inside—say, lurking in the attic—we were hosed. Neither of us had the energy to venture up there to make that discovery, though it was tempting to fry up a smelly batch of liver and onions or sauerkraut to smoke him out. Unfortunately, we had neither on hand and elected to barricade ourselves in instead, meaning Clark would just have to stay put and suffer as we dusted off the karaoke machine.

Exhausted, we passed on croaking out our favorite 1980s tunes and opted for a movie night. After checking on Nicoh, we settled into the living room, popped in *To Catch A Thief* and pretended it kept our attention. It turned out to be a futile exercise, considering Leah obsessively checked her text messages while I chewed on an unwitting nail.

Leah almost cried out in relief when her phone rang but her expression went from one of excitement to another of puzzlement when she looked at the incoming number. She gasped as the caller spoke and her eyes widened in alarm. After a few murmured responses, she hung up, wringing the phone between clenched hands.

"Leah?" I shook her arm gently when she didn't respond. "What is it?"

It took her several seconds to reply as she struggled to find the words. "That was the managing editor from the newspaper. Erica was found dead in her home…murdered."

"Oh my!"

She shook her head. "That's not even the worst part. They think Vargas did it."

<hr>

CHAPTER SIX

<hr>

"What do you mean 'they think Vargas did it'? Isn't he at some cop-type meeting? You did just text him, right?"

"That was a while ago and he never responded." She shrugged but the hollowness of her voice was a dead giveaway. "Besides, they've initiated a statewide manhunt for him since then."

"Don't tell me you believe this foolishness?" When she said nothing, realization washed over me. "You actually think he might have murdered that woman." It was not a question and again, my friend failed to respond. "Leah Campbell, we *know* Vargas, he's our friend. And a good cop."

She whispered, as if saying the words betrayed their friendship, "But the police have evidence—skin under her nails and blood that isn't hers." She shuddered but waved me off when I went to comfort her. "She fought hard, AJ. Erica didn't want to die...like that." She wrapped her arms around herself. "And then the killer just left her there. Ran away like a coward and didn't even attempt to cover his crime."

I was surprised by her resignation. Leah? Distraught...yes. But throwing in the towel? I didn't think so. I took her by the shoulders and gave her a good shake until she met my eyes.

"The police have got it wrong, Leah. They have to. What you've just described sounds nothing like Vargas. He's a decent, hardworking cop, a loyal friend to not just you and me, but to Ramirez and a whole lotta other people out there."

Her mouthed turned downward. "Even the good guys have a breaking point."

All but exasperated, I replied through gritted teeth, "Not Vargas. Not like this. Blowing off steam...sure. But nothing...and no one would drive him to murder."

"Erica could." As her coloring grew paler and her expression more haunted, it became clear my friend had not finished relaying her horrifying tale. "There was also an altercation at the police station. Erica showed up, made a scene and heaved some gnarly threats at Vargas. Said she'd expose him for the dirty, lying cop he was and by the time she finished with him, she'd not only end his career but the careers of every cop in the department, all the way up to the Chief of Police. After that, things got kind of physical and it took four guys to keep Vargas under control, but not before he issued his own threat. In a matter of speaking, he vowed to rip her throat out for lying."

I shuddered. It was pretty graphic, even for Vargas. "It's just an expression, Leah, said in the heat of the moment. No one would fault him. Not after that."

She looked at me evenly. I had never seen my friend so flat, so devoid of emotion. Suddenly, a chill passed through my bones, like someone walking over my grave.

"You don't understand," her voice was nothing but a husky whisper, "Erica's throat had been sliced so savagely her trachea was severed. The killer also removed her tongue."

* * *

Before she could venture any farther, the doorbell forced us both to jump.

"What now?" I growled as I stalked to the front door and threw it wide. *No sense standing on civilities at this point in the game*, I muttered to myself.

Ramirez filled the doorway. Tension rolled from him in waves, only adding to state of unrest permeating my home.

"You've heard about Vargas." He offered no question, only a statement of fact as he absorbed my friend's grim demeanor. "How much do you know?"

"Leah had just gotten the call from her former editor. We've heard Vargas is your primary suspect but he's magically disappeared, and now there's a bounty on his head."

Ramirez snorted in disgust. "Not *my* primary suspect. And, check your facts. They don't put a bounty on heads in this century. It's considered barbaric—no matter who the murderer is."

I raised my hands in mock surrender. "So, other than to add another burr to our saddles, what brings you by, Detective?"

Ramirez ignored my sarcasm and directed his steely gaze at Leah. "I wanted to see if he's contacted you."

Not appreciating his attitude or the insinuation, she leapt from the couch and stomped until she was within centimeters of him. "What exactly is that supposed to mean? Are you implying that I helped Vargas escape? Or that I know his current whereabouts?" Ramirez said nothing, still eying her speculatively. "I see. Well, if that's the way you're going to play it, Detective, I need to know: are you asking as Vargas' friend? Or as a cop? And be careful how you answer that, because contrary to what you might think, they are not one in the same. And the wrong answer might just get your invite revoked until you've got the proper documentation to compel me to provide commentary for those questions."

Ramirez gave her a hard stare before responding, "Vargas and I have been friends longer than the two of you have been doing whatever it is you've been doing all these months. So I resent *your* implication that I would supersede the boundaries of jurisprudence by using my badge to elicit information against that friend." He shook his head and turned away from her. From us. I thought he was going to leave and moved to stop him when he spoke, his voice so low I had to lean forward to hear him. "I have to find him. Before they do."

I reached out and touched his arm but he wouldn't face us as he continued, "Jeremiah Vargas grew up in a broken home, watched his mother get beaten to death by her boyfriend and by the time he was nine, lived on the streets after being used as a meal ticket by not one, but three foster homes. Even after all he'd endured he never claimed to be a victim, or a product of his environment. He went into the military—served in Desert Storm—then came home and became a cop. All because he wanted to serve and protect those who couldn't fend for themselves. He would gladly put his life on the line to save another. So no, he wouldn't commit cold-blooded murder much less butcher anyone that way."

Leah spoke softly, not wanting to fracture an already unsteady balance of energy swirling throughout the room: anger, fear, remorse, sadness. "But after the incident at the station, surely you could see how they could have come to that conclusion. And then, there's the evidence—"

Ramirez swirled. "Wait, what 'incident'?"

Leah flinched at the sharpness of his tone but quickly filled him in on the scene that had occurred between Erica and Vargas and the unfortunate comments that followed. I moved closer to Ramirez, grasping his arm more firmly though I wasn't sure why. Nor did I understand how he had not been apprised of the confrontation when Leah's editor had already been privy to it. Once she'd finished, I said as much.

Looking a little gray around the gills, Leah looked at each of us before responding, "My editor didn't divulge that little tidbit. I was there when it happened."

* * *

Ramirez started to interject but Leah put up a hand, "I was there in an official capacity—doing some background for the Stantons—and Erica happened to be there, too, though I doubt she ever saw me. When she arrived, she was clearly on a mission. And while Vargas did snap at the end, no one would have blamed him. Erica was totally off-base and out of control—I'm sure every other person in the room was thinking the same thing."

"Only Vargas *said* it," I added.

"Yeah, and now this." Leah vigorously rubbed her hands through her hair and pressed her eyes shut. "I just can't believe…"

Ramirez squinted as he mulled over Leah's latest bombshell. "Leah's right—this is going to go from bad to worse if we don't find Vargas before they—the police do. I had hoped they'd find the evidence circumstantial—possibly planted by the real killer—but that combined with this very public altercation…and the fact Vargas is nowhere to be found…" He shook his head, still not able to fathom his friend and fellow officer could have facilitated such an atrocity. "I can't get any more involved than I already am, especially not when what I'm proposing is contrary to what the department is implementing. We do, however, have a short list of friends who can."

Leah and I both nodded, drawing on his conclusion—the Stanton brothers could do what Ramirez couldn't—reach beyond the boundaries of the towering wall of blue.

"If we could get them on board, focus their energy on tracking Vargas down—preferably before my guys got to him—that would allow me to focus on the evidence," Ramirez commented to himself.

"What exactly was this evidence?" I asked but Leah shook her head in a manner that indicated I didn't really want to know.

Ramirez didn't catch the gesture and commented absently, "His blood from the struggle—she put up quite a fight—and his hunting knife."

Finally, he glanced up to see my horrified expression. "Sorry, I thought Leah had probably already filled you in."

I shook my head. "So…the knife…it was the one used to…uh…"

"Carve out Erica's tongue," Leah finished, belatedly noting her choice of words had caused me to wince. "Where did they find it, anyway?"

"In her apartment." I couldn't help but notice the brevity of Ramirez's response.

"How original. And so like a cop," Leah replied dryly. Apparently, Ramirez's arrival had put the spit back into her fire. "What, did the killer wrap it in plastic and put it in the freezer for safekeeping?"

Ramirez leveled a stony glare before deflating her sarcasm balloon. "Nope. They found it in her dog's stomach."

CHAPTER SEVEN

I barely managed to keep myself from upchucking on Ramirez's boots—though I noted he had moved a few steps away from both of us after divulging that fun factoid—and changed the subject.

"So, you'll see about getting the Stantons involved?" Both of us nodded, though I assumed he thought Leah would be making the call. "By the way, where's Nicoh?" Ramirez looked around, used to his pal venturing onto the scene when he arrived.

"Err...I'll be making that call now." Leah raised her phone and made an animated show of dialing while escaping to her room. Ramirez's eyes narrowed and I felt them zero in, expectantly awaiting a response.

"Um, yeah, about that..." I found myself wringing my hands as I led him to the corner where Nicoh was sprawled on his side, snoring softly as drool glazed the floor. "We had a bit of excitement earlier." I told him about Clark's visit and how he'd lured Nicoh out of the yard and left him with Susie under the ruse of bringing him home early from a photo shoot at my request. When I reached the vet's diagnosis, I looked up to find him with arms crossed. It also appeared the heels of his boots were making nice divots in the hard wood floor, as he worked to contain his anger.

"Just when were you planning on telling me, Ajax?" Uh oh, out came the nickname, spoken through gritted teeth—never a good sign.

"Well—"

Ramirez put a hand up to stop me. "Let me guess, you avoided calling me about Clark's break-in, but calling the police in general was never a consideration, was it?" I felt like a chastised five-year-old who about to be banished to the corner for snagging cookies out the jar without asking.

I didn't have a chance to plead my case—as thin as it was—because Leah bounded into the room, sporting a satisfied look. "The Stanton boys are on board. They'll drive over from L.A. tomorrow morning. In the meantime, they'll put the word out about Vargas and start some intel. Discreetly, of course."

"Good. I'd appreciate it if you—or they—kept me in the loop." I noticed Ramirez addressed her, refusing to acknowledge my presence now that he'd finished chewing me out. Leah nodded, sensing the tension in the room and started to say something when his cell phone buzzed. Ramirez looked at it and frowned. "Gotta run, duty calls. We'll finish this later."

He briefly directed his gaze at me and I saw disappointment, mixed with frustration. Before I could speak, he strode out of the house without looking back.

"Probably a good thing you failed to mention this." Leah wiggled her phone at me, referencing the text message from Clark.

"Listening in, were we? I figured he already had enough on his plate." I glanced at the space Ramirez once filled. "Besides, even if you hadn't managed to trounce your way into our conversation, I probably wouldn't have made it that far. You saw the look on his face."

She nodded and tapped her chin. "Yeah, funny how you seem to have that effect on the men in your life."

I sniffed. "Not all men, just the homicide detectives." She shivered at the thought of Vargas and I immediately regretted the words no matter how innocent they had been. "We'll find him, Leah, and bring him home." Again, she nodded but there was no conviction behind it. Her mind had returned to the dark place where our friend was considered a dangerous fugitive. A savage killer. "In the meantime, there's a call I need to make and someone I need to see." Leah looked at me with curiosity. "I need to see a guy who knows a guy," I replied in my best gangster accent.

"I have absolutely no idea what that means."

"Neither do I." I shrugged, causing her to laugh. It was a small concession, given the circumstances. I gave her a quick hug before she headed for her room then reached for my phone.

The fact was…I did know what it meant.

And I was betting Martin did too.

* * *

The following morning, I found him sitting alone on a worn bench near the duck pond at the park a few blocks from my house. As I approached, my gaze shifted to the movement that had captured his attention. It was a young couple, perhaps in their early twenties, coaxing a toddler to venture to the edge of the pond's bank, where several baby ducks were happily playing while the mama duck looked on. The tiny girl clutched a piece of bread that easily filled the span of her hand, despite her daddy's insistence that it was okay to release it to the duckling's care. The mama duck posed no threat but given their similarities in size, it was easy to see the child was more fearful of the repercussions from her than she was of feeding the babies.

Finally, she opened her fingers just enough to prompt the ducklings to waddle over to retrieve her offering. One nudged her toe for an additional morsel, making the toddler giggle and clap with delight. I looked at Martin and found a smile eclipsing his face. Though his eyes crinkled at the corners, the simple gesture made him seem youthful, giving me a glimpse into the man he had once been.

Not wanting to spoil the moment, I put my head down to avoid his eyes and approached. He stood and when I finally raised my head, saw his smile was still present.

"Lovely, isn't it?"

"The park? The city takes pride in maintaining it. Fortunately, this is just one of many it has to offer." His smile slipped when he thought I hadn't captured his meaning.

"Yes, that too." He looked longingly at the family, still laughing as the little girl gently patted the top of her new friend's heads under the mama duck's watchful eye.

I looked at the family, a happy memory forming as I thought of my own parents. I had been that child once, long ago. Martin hadn't had the benefit of such a memory, with me or my sister, Victoria. I wondered what he saw when looked at the child. Did he see me…us…and long for what might have been with Alison? Of the years—and people—he'd lost? Or was it something deeper? A lifetime of loneliness and heartbreak? Whatever had brought him to me now couldn't be resurrected in a lifetime of those moments.

And still, here he was.

"Why did you come, Martin?"

"Why did I come? Because you asked me to, Arianna—"

I shook my head. "No, Martin, I mean, why did you come out of hiding after all these years? Why now?"

He appraised me, pressing his lips together as he struggled to find words for the questions he wasn't prepared to answer.

"You're asking why I didn't come when I could have done something to save your sister," he murmured.

"Maybe, though I guess we'll never know," I replied.

He sighed. "I've spent a lifetime hiding. Sometimes even fooling myself into thinking it's been because of Clark, or his father but truthfully, I've been running. Running from myself. Running from choices I made. And perhaps, others I didn't or wouldn't make. I guess after I found out about Victoria, I could no longer allow my mistakes to become my children's—my remaining child's—burdens."

"Mistakes?"

"Gemini, Theodore Winslow, my association with Alison..." He trailed off, his eyes wandering to the small family.

His choice of words struck me as odd. "You didn't love her?"

"Alison? Of course I loved her. But if I hadn't been so adamant about my work, the project, perhaps she'd still..." Despite the years that had passed, finishing the thought was still too raw for him.

"You know what they say about hindsight, Martin."

"I guess the same could be said about saving Victoria," he replied somberly.

"True. But you still haven't answered my question."

"No, I suppose I haven't."

"Are you looking for absolution?"

He laughed and shook his head, amused by my forthrightness. "No, nothing as simple as that—nor would I ask it of you, daughter."

I ignored the familial reference. "That remains to be seen. In the meantime, I came here to discuss another matter." I told him of Clark's visit to my home and his abduction and poisoning of Nicoh.

When I finished Martin quietly uttered, "I'm assuming you still won't entertain my request to leave town for the duration?"

I leveled a glance that effectively closed the book on that

question before responding, "No, I actually have something more urgent to contend with."

He frowned. "Something more important than Clark?"

"One of my friends is in trouble. Serious trouble. Missing, actually."

"Is it the Tempe Homicide Detective…Vargas, I believe is his name?"

I nodded. "I don't have many friends but yes, he's one of the good guys…and I'm really hoping we'll find him soon."

"I understand. And I hope everything works out," he replied.

"Are you talking about me, or yourself?"

He regarded me for a moment but did not break my gaze. "Do what you need to help your friend. I'll reach out to my network to find a solution for dealing with Clark."

Normally, I would have snickered at his mention of a "solution"—ever the scientist he was—as though Clark was a mere puzzle that could be solved by concocting an elaborate formula in his lab. Now his second comment about having outside help piqued my interest.

"Your network?" I asked.

This time, Martin's eyes failed to reach mine. "For now, the less you know the better."

"Better for me? Or for you?"

He chuckled, shaking his head. "Point taken. You're more like your mother—like Alison—than I could have imagined."

"Yeah, well, from what I hear about Victoria, we would have made quite the trio."

Martin nodded solemnly. "I don't doubt that for a minute. Alison would have been proud, you know."

I dismissed his comment. I only had Martin's word for it and while he was probably onto something, we'd never know for sure.

"Ever thought about having your own?" Martin tipped his head in the direction of the family.

"Oh sure, that's what I have Nicoh and Leah for," I replied dryly.

Martin laughed. It was a hearty, joyous sound, tainted by a hint of sadness. "While I'm sure both your canine and best friend can be a handful at times, it's not exactly what I meant."

I shrugged. I didn't know Martin well enough to get all chatty about personal details, though it did make me reflect on the fact that my attempts at wrangling a stubborn, demanding Alaskan Malamute often exceeded the bounds of my maternal instincts.

After wrapping up the conversation, I left him sitting on the bench, where he resumed his quiet observation of the small family. Perhaps he was pondering what life might have brought him, had he selected another path. I wondered if he would he ever find the answers he sought.

As I turned away, I realized he'd never fully provided me with the reason behind his sudden appearance. Then again, perhaps the answer to that question was just as much of a mystery to him as the answers to his own.

* * *

Regardless of the life or moral crises Martin was facing—or my feelings toward him at moment—I had no choice other than to leave the proper care and handling of the Clark situation in his hands. Clark, after all, wasn't a gently simmering pot you placed on the back burner while you went about your business. He was more like the kettle that had been overfilled and now was vomiting scalding water over everything within its reach.

Presently, I had a bigger kettle to boil—finding my friend Vargas and bringing him home. Hopefully, unscalded and in one piece. I pursed my lips at the thought, until I realized there was a figure leaning against my Mini Cooper.

"Is there something you've been meaning to tell me, Ajax?"

CHAPTER EIGHT

"It's apparent that you followed me, Ramirez. The question is why?"

"What's apparent is that my spidey senses, as you like to call them, weren't far off the mark when I got the impression you were holding out on me. I'll ask you again, is there something you forgot to tell me?"

"Are you asking me as a cop? Or as my boyfriend?"

"Depends. Who's your friend?" Ramirez nodded in the direction of the bench, forcing my heart to thud against my chest. He didn't know who Martin was and I needed to keep it that way.

"Jealous, Ramirez? He's a prospective *client*." I held up a hand to keep him from interjecting, though he'd made no motion to do so. Okay, I was crap for ad-libbing. Oh heck, where was Leah when I needed her?

"Being a *professional* photographer, don't you usually meet the client at his place of business?"

"Not that it's any of your business but he's from out of town." Not a lie.

"Okay then, what about a portfolio? I'd assume he'd want to

see your work before he hired you? And, I didn't see you taking any notes."

"That's why I have a *professional* website, Detective—so that prospective clients can browse through my previous projects, see the companies I've worked with and their testimonials—and hey, I even have client list so that they can make direct inquires. Geesh, this is starting to sound like an interrogation!" I threw my hands up and exhaled a long, frustrated breath. Ramirez didn't appear to buy my sudden flair for the dramatic. "As for the 'notes,' that's why we professionals carry these." I sarcastically wiggled my smartphone under his nose. "It's called technology, Detective. You might try coming out of the cave once in a while and sniffing around before clobbering a gal over the head."

Ramirez uttered something he should have had his mouth washed out for before adding, "If you're trying to tell me I need to evolve, AJ, you're going about it in a very snarly manner."

I huffed out a harsh laugh. "*I'm* being snarly?"

"You know, I can tell I'm not getting anywhere with you. It appears your roommate's tendencies to circumvent the truth are wearing off on you."

"Seriously? First you have the audacity to follow me, accuse me of doing something unsavory and then call Leah, my best friend of twenty-plus years, a liar? To my face? You have some nerve, buddy. And you're certainly not winning any Eagle badges, or whatever it is you neo-man types aspire to…" I turned on my heel and marched as quickly as my thirty-six inch legs would allow, hoping he would not follow.

He didn't, though his retort was more damaging, "You're actions are simply proving my point, Ajax. I can tell you're dodging me."

I marched on, muttering under my breath. "Yeah, well maybe someone's got his panties twisted because his detection and interrogation skills are on the fritz and he's got the relationship acumen of a baboon."

Behind me, I heard Ramirez blow out an exasperated sigh.

Then again, maybe I'd erroneously said that last bit a little too loud.

* * *

By the time I got home, a black Ferrari—in all its luxurious and shimmering glory—filled my driveway—an indication the Stanton brothers had arrived. Early. I sighed as I got out and patted my Mini on her top.

"No worries, old girl, I'm not replacing you today, though you're welcome to make nice with the pretty pony." I hoped my reassurance would keep her jealousy under control and ensure she started for me on my next go-around. She was fairly feisty that way and prone to fits when she observed me salivating over other chassis.

Unfortunately, a temperamental chariot was the least of my concerns, as was overanalyzing my squabble with Ramirez. I had enough on my plate with Clark's reappearance, Nicoh's poisoning, Vargas' issues, Erica's murder…and of course, Martin. I bit my lip to hold back tears before entering. Muffled voices came from the kitchen and as I rounded the corner, found Leah, Abe and Elijah hunched over what appeared to be a kitchen-turned-command-post. Maps, diagrams and paperwork were taped or strewn across every surface. Cupboards bore colorful topographic maps, flip charts and several official-looking documents. Had I really been gone that long?

I watched them from the doorway, talking in hushed voices, pointing at various points on the map. Leah absently twirled a red pen in her hair and nodded as the brothers took turns explaining the various highlighted portions of the geography, until something wet nudged my hand, nearly making me shriek.

Nicoh's soft brown eyes gleamed as his tail beat in a slow, leisurely wag. I smiled and kneeled to nuzzle my face into his warm neck, thankful he had come back to me. Though he still seemed to be recovering from the effects of the poisoning, as he leaned his sturdy frame into me, his heartbeat was strong and his demeanor was...Nicoh-like. I scratched him gently behind the ears and was rewarded with a low whoo-woo of approval, before he nudged me again.

"Hey, stranger," the older brother, Abe, drawled.

Hugs were forthcoming as I gave the Stantons a quick once-over. Neither had changed a bit since I had last seen them and both were still just as easy on the eyes. At six feet three inches, both towered over Leah—their angular features and tanned skin striking in a masculine, rugged way. Abe's hair was masterful as ever, with artfully gelled spikes jutting in every direction, a perfect complement to his all black ensemble. Elijah, the younger of the two, let his sun-bleached waves carelessly brush his shoulders while the front fell into his eyes. His casual appearance ended with the preppy, buttoned-down shirt he'd paired with expensive jeans and Italian loafers.

"How's Anna doing?" Their right hand gal, Anna Goodwin, had become a close friend since she and the Stantons first worked on my sister's case. A looker in her own right, she had brains and a fierce kick to boot. Needless to say, she kept those boys on track. And in line.

"Good, good...working on wedding plans while keeping the business running. Girl's definitely a multi-tasker." Anna had recently gotten engaged to a rising L.A. film producer and earned her own private investigator's license.

"Well, you tell her we're happy to come over and help out whenever she needs us."

"Yeah, right. Just what we need—all three of you casing the streets of L.A.," Elijah teased.

"Oh, we're not going to case the streets, silly, we're simply going to borrow the company credit card and go shopping on Rodeo, in your car," Leah retorted, not bothering to hide her smugness. "And, of course, that will be followed by the most outrageous bachelorette party you've ever seen."

I nodded. "You know what they say…what happens in…"

Abe threw up his hands, "Okay, okay! Enough already! I can't handle the torture." Everyone laughed until one of the charts came loose from the cupboard and collapsed onto the floor—a grim reminder of the task that had reunited us.

"We set up shop. Hope you don't mind?" Elijah's voice was pensive as he retrieved the fallen chart.

"No, not at all," I replied. "Our kitchen is yours to use. Not much cooking goes on in here, anyway."

Abe scratched his head. "Err…well, we might have strayed. We're just mapping things out in here. That's the evidence collection area." He pointed toward the living room.

"Oh?" My curiosity got the better of me and before he had a chance to issue a warning, I ran smack-dab into a massive white board filled with crime scene photos. And Erica. Dead. "Oh my!"

"AJ, I am so sorry!" Abe stammered.

I diverted my gaze from the colorful images but one imprinted on my mind. Even in death, Erica's eyes were wide with shock. Combined with the gaping hole that had once been her mouth, it bore an eerie resemblance to Munch's *The Scream*. Abe rushed to pull the photo down but I shook my head.

"It's okay, guys. It just caught me off-guard. She…she was alive when that…happened to her?" It came out in a squeak.

"Afraid so," Elijah replied, eying me skeptically. "Are you sure you don't want us to pull these down or cover them, at a minimum?"

I shook my head. "I'm okay, really. How did you get them so quickly?"

Elijah looked at me, clearly confused. "Ramirez didn't tell you he'd gotten them to us?"

Now I was confused. "You've spoken to him, already? Leah and I just talked to him ourselves, when he asked us to get you involved."

Both crinkled their brows and Abe responded, "Um, no, Ramirez actually contacted us before Leah did. Right after they found Erica. We thought you knew."

I glanced at Leah. It certainly seemed as though we weren't the only ones holding back information. If that wasn't the pot calling the kettle—Abe cleared his throat, interrupting my thoughts.

"I did just see Ramirez a few minutes ago but it was on another…matter," I grumbled.

Leah's eyes went wide as she realized Ramirez had seen me at my meeting with Martin. "AJ, would you mind taking a look at my eye—in the other room—where the light is brighter? There's something in it."

Smooth, Leah, real smooth.

"I thought you girls only went to fix your faces in groups when you were in public?" Abe teased.

"Who said anything about needing to fix our faces, Stanton? We're simply going elsewhere so that we can talk about the two of you behind your backs," Leah retorted. "In the meantime, why don't you continue getting organized—we've got a lot of work ahead of us." She ushered me into her room with Nicoh in close pursuit. I was surprised by the latter until I realized she had two candy bars sticking out of her back pocket.

"Saving a snack for later, are we?"

She absently checked her pocket. "Oh, shoot, I wondered where I had put these. Those boys tend to overfeed the d-o-g."

"Why are we spelling?" I asked.

"He's been particularly alert since he's come back around and now that we have guests, he seems to be more persuasive than usual."

I sniffed. "You're overestimating his abilities, Leah."

"Whatever, the d-o-g's eaten like a p-i-g ever since those two have arrived." She waved a hand. "Anywhoo, what gives?"

I quickly filled her in on my meeting with Martin and the events that transpired with Ramirez immediately following.

She gasped in surprise. "So he doesn't know about Martin? Didn't he recognize him?"

"How could he, Leah? We're the only ones who've ever seen the pictures, much less know he's still among the land of the living."

"And, Martin? I forgot to ask earlier but he looks…well, does he look like you?" She slapped herself upside the head. "Of course he looks like you. Does he look good? And, I don't mean that in a creepy I-want-to-know-if-your-dad-is-a-hottie sort of way."

"No, you just want to know in a guy-whose-been-dead-for-over-two-decades sort of way."

"Exactly."

I shrugged. "I guess. I wasn't really there to bond."

"Well, of course not. You hardly know the guy," she huffed.

"I don't know him at all, Leah. And right now, I don't know that I want to."

"Whatever. At least he's taking care of Clark while we work on this other…issue."

"He's got to find him first," I countered.

"Sounds like a familiar dilemma." Meaning Vargas. "You think Martin will come through?"

I shrugged. "Don't know. At least it will allow us to focus on

Vargas. Of course, we'll still have to watch our backs in the meantime."

"Err…about that…"

I swiveled my head to look at her. "What…about that?"

"Ramirez asked Abe and Elijah to keep an eye on us."

"Big surprise there. He obviously doesn't think we can manage to stay of out trouble. Then again, they'll be off looking for Vargas, so they can't be here watching us day and night," I replied.

"Uh, that's exactly what he instructed them to do." I raised an eyebrow. "They're moving in with us."

CHAPTER NINE

Before I could formulate a G-rated response, Abe knocked on the door and poked his head in. "Everything okay in there?" We nodded and moved back into the kitchen. "I take it Leah told you about Ramirez's suggestion?"

"Sounds more like a directive than a suggestion," I replied.

"If you're not cool with it, we can certainly stay out in the car," Elijah offered, sounding mildly amused.

"Oh sure, and fill that lovely machine with boy stink?" Leah scrunched up her nose.

"Boy stink?" Abe asked.

"Don't even get me started—"

I waved my hands, indicating a cease fire. "It's fine, guys. No problem. I'm sure we can make it work. It might even be to our advantage." When Leah wiggled her eyebrows, I quickly added, "I meant having the evidence, maps and all of us in one place could be beneficial for brainstorming and in coordinating our efforts."

"So, we're ready to proceed, then?" Once everyone had given Abe a single nod, he clapped his brother on the back. "Let's do it. Time is wasting away and Vargas certainly needs friends out there looking for him and clearing his name. Speaking of which, Leah, I meant to ask you, did you happen to work with Grace Turner?"

"Erica's assistant? Sure. Grace was at the paper before I started. Why?"

"Would you be willing to have a chat with her—see if she has a short list of people who had it in for Erica?"

Leah snorted. "Not to be disrespectful but that list ain't going to be short."

"That's what we've been hearing," Abe replied, looking less than pleased.

"And you thought she might be more willing to share the goods with a person she's already familiar with," I added.

"Yeah, and she might have a better idea of how to narrow that list down." Elijah looked at Leah. "What do you think?"

"Certainly worth a try. Of course, you do realize"—Leah tapped her chin—"Grace's probably already earned her place at the very top of that list."

* * *

Leah filled me in on our way to the girl's apartment in downtown Phoenix. We'd left Abe and Elijah with Nicoh so they could continue reviewing the documents Ramirez had provided. Hopefully, they'd also be able to identify acquaintances to shed more light on Vargas' possible whereabouts, as well as the situation with his ex. Given Leah's pursed lips, it wasn't something she was ready to tackle on her own.

I interrupted whatever negative thoughts she was chewing on, "So Grace worked for Erica before you joined the paper?"

"Grace was actually an associate editor before Erica was hired and would have been a shoe-in for the lead editorial position had Erica not used her assets to work her way into it. And I don't mean the brainy type."

"You're saying she blackmailed her way into the editor's seat?" I asked.

"Pretty much what happens when you have evidence placing your boss in some compromising situations, including ones that you're personally privy to," she replied dryly.

"Yuck, sounds like Erica was a piece of work. Didn't even think that sort of thing flew these days with all the human resource policies."

Leah laughed. "Oh, you'd be surprised. It happens more than people think. People like Erica have just gotten more creative about it. And the Internet, social media and smartphone apps make it a lot easier to capture and disseminate incriminating information. So yeah, Erica not only got the brass ring, she skipped all the other rings to get it."

"And bypassed Grace and others along the way? That *is* going to be a long list."

"You've got that right, my friend. There certainly won't be any love lost there," Leah replied.

I shook my head. "It's not the love part I'm worried about."

* * *

Grace lived in a modest apartment complex in a recently revitalized section of the downtown area. It took her a few moments to register the visitor was a former co-worker when she opened the door but after the initial surprise passed, she pulled Leah into a quick hug. As she ushered us in, I noted Grace was pretty in a natural way. Her sun-kissed hair was cut into an angled bob that was longer in the front and ended at her chin. Her eyes were a luminous hazel and despite being puffy and red from crying, were warm and inviting. She was thin but athletically muscular. Leah mentioned she had been a former long distance track runner in college and hiked either Camelback or Papago Mountains on her days off.

She motioned toward the small living room that was just off the kitchenette and the two of us sat on a tan microfiber loveseat while she chose its matching chair.

"Sorry, I don't have anything but water to offer you but I can make a mean glass with ice?" We both indicated we were fine. "I guess you've probably heard about Erica?" If there had been any resentment between them, it certainly wasn't apparent. Grace appeared more miserable than elated.

Leah nodded. "We came by to make sure you were doing okay and see if there was anything we could do for you."

"You were always so sweet, Leah. Even now, despite the fact we no longer work together, you are the only one who ever consistently remembers my birthday." She turned to me. "Leah brings me African Violets every year. And somehow manages to find Peanut Butter Frangos. Both are my absolute favorite, though I'll never know how you learned that."

Leah wiggled a finger. "Not telling, my friend. Trade secrets." She used her thumb and forefinger to fabricate a locking movement across her lips and then tossed it over her shoulder.

Grace chuckled easily but the laughter was gone just as quickly. "I think there were a lot more secrets being tucked away than anyone ever imagined."

"You're referring to Erica." I let Leah take the lead. Though I'd seen Grace on occasion when visiting Leah at her former workplace, we were no more than passing acquaintances.

Grace nodded. "Despite her overtures to move up the ladder, she kept stuff pretty close to the vest and had irons in every fire. Everyone else's fire." She smiled but it wasn't one that emitted a great deal of fond memories of her boss.

"Sounds like the Erica I knew and loathed." Leah scrunched

up her nose, thinking about her own interactions with the editor. "Anyone top your list of suspects?"

Grace snickered. "I see your mind still works like an investigative reporter's. Unfortunately, I think people would be scratching, clawing and outright clamoring over one another to be at the front of that list. It's like they say, it would be simpler and quicker to identify who *wouldn't* be on it. The police department, media, etc. tend to like her ex, Jeremiah Vargas, though I have doubts where he is concerned. Then again, the timing of his disappearance doesn't make any sense." She shook her head, as baffled as we were. "Of course, Detective Ramirez, Vargas' poker-playing buddy, is currently spinning his own theory."

"So…who does Ramirez like for it?" I asked, causing Leah to roll her eyes. Apparently, I hadn't come off quite as nonchalant as I'd anticipated.

"Ramirez has his fan favorite, all right." Grace was less than pleased, given the downward turn of her mouth and the sour undertone. "Me."

"What?" both Leah and I exclaimed, loud enough to rattle the glasses in her cupboard.

Leah offered a quick apology before continuing, "Why the heck would he think that?"

"I don't have a credible alibi. I was here alone and no one tends to see me come or go. Of course, there are other reasons: Erica was promoted to a job I had actually worked for, her treatment of me, the book deal—"

"Whoa…whoa…whoa…hold up the truck. What book deal?" It was definitely news to Leah.

Grace snapped her fingers. "Oh, right. I forgot you weren't around by the time that opportunity popped into her lap. Actually, if memory serves, it was shortly after you resigned. But no matter, like most of Erica's side projects, she kept the important details buttoned up, even from me. She'd wave me off when I pressed her, convinced she was the only one capable of getting the real story—she even bragged she could make it a bestseller."

"Huh. I take it this wasn't Erica's usual fictionalized take on reality, spun as the truth?" Leah asked.

Grace laughed harshly. "She did have a unique...flair for wordsmithing when it came to sensationalizing an ordinary, run-of-the-mill situation, didn't she?" Grace turned to me. "Erica could...and would...make your average ninety-year-old grand-mother look like a lying, scheming, adultering con artist."

"Nice chick," I replied dryly.

"That she was." Grace shook her head.

"So, getting back to this book, what was it about?" Leah asked.

Grace smiled. "Ah, it was an oldie but goodie and something right out of a science fiction novel. Remember when scientists cloned that sheep named Dolly back in the late 1990s?"

Leah looked at me and suddenly my stomach felt like it was doing backflips. "Um, yeah, we're not much for science—fiction or otherwise—but we're both familiar with the story." I nodded, unable to offer more without launching my latte.

"Anyway, it turns out there was another group of scientists who had been working on a similar project years earlier. Only, they weren't interested in cloning farm animals."

I knew how this story went. Leah slid me a warning glance. We needed to get as much out of Grace as we could without adding our own distractions into the mix. Fortunately, Grace was so wrapped up in telling the story she was oblivious to my attempts at preventing the latte, now shaken, from making an appearance.

"They were cloning humans," she concluded.

"Wow," was all we could manage.

"Yeah, there's even proof the experiments were successful. To this day, there are probably a handful of cloned humans out there somewhere." She inhaled a deep breath. "We could walk by one every day and not even realize it. Isn't that something?"

"Err…yeah. And you're saying this guy was willing to give information like that to Erica? Don't you find that a bit strange? I mean, if she was supposed to dig up details to run an article, or even a series of articles, that's one thing. But trusting her to write a *book*? Why?" Leah was breathless and a little more than exasperated. I couldn't say I blamed her.

Grace shrugged. "Strange? Yes and no. Yes, considering he knew of Erica's body of work he'd still choose her. But they knew one another from the days she worked for him as a copywriter back east. He needed an unbiased source to put a stamp on the book, so he agreed to supply her with the necessary resources, evidence…whatever she needed to make it happen."

"Meaning if Erica had made it public—"

"She would have been worth a few bucks. It would have also put her in the kind of spotlight she'd always wanted," Grace responded.

"Front and center of the entire world." Grace nodded. Clearly, she and Leah had known and understood Erica for who and what she was. "And her death…"

"Would have been construed as…timely, to certain individuals," Grace finished Leah's thought, pressing her lips together in a tight line.

"You mentioned Ramirez liked you for her murder?" Leah asked.

"Because I would have been a likely shoe-in for her position," Grace replied.

Leah nodded. "And as her assistant, you'd also be a suitable replacement for writing the book."

"Given I did much of her research, yes. Erica was just a vessel to put it out into the universe—one that could be replaced." She scrunched her face. "Sorry, that was really insensitive. I meant her death wouldn't have prevented it from being written."

"So the editorial position combined with the possibility of becoming the author of a bestselling novel…"

"Only compounded my lack of an alibi and put me right at the top of Detective Ramirez's list of suspects," Grace replied, her expression tight. "Funny thing is, on any other night, I would have been at the office or at Erica's pulling an all-nighter."

"Why was that night different?" I asked.

"She said she had an important meeting with her contact on the book and sent me home."

"Did you ever know who this contact was?" Leah prodded.

Grace shook her head. "Oh yeah, he was her former bureau chief when she worked at the *Chicago Tribune*."

I gogged while Leah managed to stutter, "Erica worked at the *Chicago Tribune*?"

"Back in the early days, yeah. She claims she'd made quite an impression on him but we all know what that meant in Erica's world. Anyway, word has it he helped her get on the staff there but retired shortly after. In fact, he lives here in Arizona now…in Ahwatukee."

This time, I groaned out loud, making Grace pause. Fortunately, Leah, always the quick thinker, jumped in, "She had some bad sushi earlier." I nodded, while trying my best not to kick her. Like I said, she was a quick thinker. I didn't say she was tactful.

My heart thudded as my stomach threatened to stage a protest. "So…this contact, does he have a name?"

Grace looked at me curiously, perhaps wondering why I was so interested. Still she offered me the benefit of a response.

"Sure, his name is Mort Daniels."

CHAPTER TEN

"Well, that was interesting," Leah commented after we'd said our goodbyes to Grace with the agreement we'd be in touch.

"Yah, think?" I replied, feeling no less nauseous, though the latte seemed to be temporarily taking a siesta. "I mean, what are the odds?"

"The bigger question is why now? And did it have any correlation whatsoever to Erica's death?"

"At this point I have no idea."

"Mort didn't mention anything to you?" Leah asked.

"You mean between Clark's B&E, poisoning my dog, Vargas being accused of murder and oh yeah, the surprise visit by Bio Pop?"

Leah chuckled. "Is that like a Blow-Pop?"

"Might as well be. It's leaving a nasty taste in my mouth."

"So, I take that as a 'no' on Mort?"

"Honey, I doubt I gave Mort the time to divulge that bit of information—though it would have been nice to know my life as a science fiction guinea pig was about to be exposed to the world." I groaned; then jabbed a finger at my best friend. "But don't you dare mention it. Next thing you know, *I'll* be at the top of Ramirez's crap list."

"I thought you already were." Point taken.

"Anyway…" I gritted my teeth. "No, I've only talked to Mort briefly—on the phone—after that we were supposed to meet at the zoo."

"Only Bio Pop shows up instead."

"Exactly."

"Then perhaps we need to pay our friend Mort a little visit," Leah suggested.

"I'm down with that. Let's do it before someone else does."

"Given our history, I doubt we'd get that lucky." If she only knew how true that would turn out being.

* * *

We were silent on the trip to Ahwatukee as we mulled over the information Grace had provided. I found myself wondering just how much she had known about her boss' new project. While it was clear Erica had been very bright and more than capable of handling her own research and writing, she'd delegate whatever would allow her to pursue other more fruitful activities. She was definitely greedy and power hungry, which by no means suggested she'd deserved to be murdered, though it might have explained why she had been mutilated in the manner she had. Had her tongue been extracted to shut her up? To serve as a warning to others? Or both?

We parked in front of Mort's home, which in my book was more of an estate. He had planted annuals around the perimeter since our last visit, along with a combination of succulents and blooming varietals, which added a pop of color to the desert surroundings.

The driveway was empty, though his car could have easily

been tucked in the garage. After ringing the doorbell several times and walking around the side to take a peek—without success—it was clear he was elsewhere. We cursed the fact we had not thought to call ahead. He typically welcomed our visits and would not have expected us to breach the subject of Erica or the book.

Perhaps I was naive but I hadn't thought he would have considered such a move and until I heard it straight from the horse's mouth, I was giving him the benefit of the doubt. It could have simply been a collaboration on a fictionalized version of the project. Erica could have concocted the tell-all aspect to suit her own interests.

Unfortunately, the Sour Patch kid doing the trampoline in my stomach was telling me this collaboration was much more than a work of fiction and the truth would be far more profitable.

For someone.

I was letting the hamster run the wheel in my head when I heard a thump, followed by a squeak. Realizing it wasn't Mr. Hamster taking a dive, I looked over my shoulder to find Leah sprawled across one of Mort's newly planted flower beds.

"Leah! What the heck?"

"A little hand here? I just trashed my new Kate Spade boots."

I reached over and yanked her up with both hands. Moist dirt and a few stray petals covered her knees and the tips of her boots, but other than a bruised ego, she didn't look any worse for the wear. "That's what you get for tromping through Mort's landscaping. See those flagstones there? That's called a pathway. Perhaps you should try using it."

"Alright, Ms. Smart Alec. I really appreciate your concern. Do you know how long I had to save up to buy these boots?"

"You got them on eBay."

"Yeah, well, I was forced to give my keyboard and my manicure a workout on that auction. I'm still convinced there were ringers bidding."

"Whatever. Can we get on with it? We're bordering on trespassing here."

Leah sniffed. "It's not my fault he put that viney crap there. It practically reached out and grabbed me."

I pointed at the cell phone peering from beneath the fleshy succulents. "I don't suppose that could have anything to do with your face plant?"

My friend's cheeks flushed. "I was not texting! And even if I had been, I am perfectly capable of walking and chewing gum at the same time."

"My point exactly," I replied evenly, receiving an exasperated huff in return.

"I'm just saying Mort shouldn't be putting those things so close to the walkway. They don't go with the whole cactus theme anyway." She kicked at the mud, frowning as it landed on her boots.

"You should probably leave the landscaping to Mort," I replied as I bent down to retrieve her phone. She was correct, though. The plants, whatever they were, seemed an odd choice with the other mix of foliage and plant life.

Then again, given my black thumb, I probably needed to take my own advice.

* * *

Abe took one look at us as we entered the Stanton's command station. "Playing in the mud, were we?"

"You can shut up now, Stanton. I need to go wash up," Leah retorted, flipping her non-existent locks over her shoulder as she spun on her heel and marched away.

"Maybe you should put a little elbow grease into cleaning up that attitude," he called after her, his voice playful.

Leah huffed in annoyance. "You could use your own spit

shine, buddy."

He watched her stomp down the hall and slam the bathroom door. "I do like a little spit-fire."

I glanced at Elijah and we both snickered. Grumpy boots or not, Abe had it bad for my best friend. When not flicking mud off her pride, she had been a bit flirty with him, too, despite her on and off thing with Vargas. Thinking of the missing detective wiped the smile off my face.

Elijah took note and quickly changed the subject. "So, we did a bit of recon while you were gone. Took inventory of your alarm system, beefed up the motion sensors, added a couple more cameras…"

"Please tell me there aren't any trip wires?"

"No trip wires but we surrounded the back of the property with about fifteen feet of barbed wire."

"You didn't."

Elijah shook his head and chuckled. "Why don't Abe and I run you through the new mods and show you how to use the updated alarm system."

"Err…you probably should mention the minor construction, too," Elijah added.

I groaned. "What 'minor construction'?"

Elijah shook his head at his older brother. Clearly, they hadn't managed to craft a plan for springing this delightful news on me. "Well, before we could add the new equipment, we had to make a few modifications to your office to allow for the monitoring console—"

"Monitoring console? What do you think this is—the Pentagon?"

"Come on, is that all you think we can manage? We're more on the level of an octagon." Abe flashed a knowing smile at his brother, who offered me a cheesy grin and a double thumbs-up.

"Maybe you'd better just show me," I grumbled.

"You want to wait for Leah?" Elijah asked. "We don't need her tripping things up."

That was an understatement. "Perhaps we'd better make sure she's not wearing those darn boots. I don't need the swat team swarming my compound."

"I do like those boots," Abe teased; then added, "besides, it would probably just be the bomb squad."

I continued to grumble until Leah emerged from the bathroom, mud-free, though one look at her pursed lips indicated her demeanor was still favoring the prickly side. Our new security setup was going to be a real hit.

I quickly filled her in before the boys led us outside for a summary of their enhancements. For the most part, everything was strategically placed and hidden from view. It was a bit surreal to think my home, which had once been my parent's little slice of paradise, needed such an elaborate system. But thanks to the return of Clark, it was best to be on the safe side. And besides, I trusted the Stantons, so who better to secure my home and our livelihood?

It wasn't until I saw the new monitoring console that I began to worry about the bill.

I took a deep breath as we entered what had once been my father's office. Except for a few additions here and there, including a new computer and some camera equipment, it was exactly as he had left it just over two years earlier—the day he and my mother never returned home. I was pleased to see the Stantons had taken this into consideration and at first glance, didn't notice the difference.

Abe noticed my confusion and nodded toward the walk-in closet, where my father had kept a few file cabinets and a small safe. Both Leah and I gasped when he opened the door. One wall had been replaced with state-of-the-art monitors and a tablet. Views of the house's exterior and interior could be seen from every angle and though they'd been careful not to invade the more private spaces of the home, it would be hard not to make a move without having the camera's eye on us.

"Cool, huh?" Elijah asked, looking fairly pleased with himself.

"Kind of…overwhelming." Concerned filled the Stanton's faces as they misread my astonishment for disapproval. I quickly dispelled their worry. "Oh, yes! It's cool! There's just so…much."

"We can certainly taper it back. It's all customizable to your preferences." Elijah picked up the tablet and outlined the system's features.

"And we can set various alarms from here, too?" Leah looked on, equally amazed by the complexity of the system.

"Yes, and we can also install apps on your cell phones, so you can make adjustments from there, set the alarm, check status and even monitor activity," Elijah replied.

"Hmm, this could help clear up those missing cookies." I nodded at Nicoh, who was the prime suspect in a rash of late-night cookie-nappings. Realizing all eyes were on him, he let out a low rumble and sauntered out of the room. Apparently we had insulted his sensibilities.

Leah laughed and pointed at one of the monitors. "I swear he just checked the kitchen counter when he went by."

Sure enough, Nicoh perched his head on the "cookie counter," inhaled a deep sniff, grumbled and moved to his pet bed, where he positioned himself with his back to the camera.

"I guess we got his goat." I offered a bleating sound, causing laughter to fill the room.

After a few more instructions, we moved on to more pressing matters, filling Abe and Elijah in on our chat with Grace and our strikeout at Mort's.

When we finished, they glanced at one another before Abe replied, "Your friend Grace is being less than honest about her involvement in the book project. At the very least, she's downplaying it."

"Spill, Stanton. At this point, I'm more concerned about finding Vargas and clearing his name than protecting Grace." Leah could be pretty direct when she wanted.

Abe nodded and continued, "With Anna's help we asked around, made a few inquiries…essentially, Grace's been sharing—though gloating may be a better word for it—details about the book deal." He blew out a long breath before proceeding, "A couple of weeks ago, she was out celebrating, had a few too many martinis during reverse happy hour and ended up chatting up the bartender at this joint downtown."

Leah rolled her eyes, clearly not convinced Grace was doing anything underhanded, and certainly not at some 'joint.'

Elijah raised a hand and picked up for his brother, "The bartender indicated Grace's boss had pissed her off about something. Whatever it was, she never told him. Anyway, it must have been quite a brewhaha because the bartender said Grace bragged about contacting Mort directly to schedule a meeting—sans Erica—where she divulged her involvement in writing and researching the book. She even went as far as supplying him with proof. In a nutshell, Grace wanted Erica thrown to the curb and demanded whatever concessions Erica had been promised. We're still trying to find out how far it had gotten but according to Grace's rants to the bartender, it was just a matter of time before it was a done deal and Erica got the boot." Leah winced at the reference, the emotional wounds from her damaged Kate Spade's still fresh.

"Wow, pretty ballsy for such a little thing," I murmured. It was hard to imagine Grace undercutting someone so callously, but the bartender certainly couldn't have had that knowledge if at least part of it weren't true.

Leah nodded. "Knowing Erica, who could blame Grace? I wonder what her tipping point was?"

Abe shook his head. "We're still trying to figure that one out, though it must have been something pretty drastic. From what the bartender said, she was going after Erica's editorial position next."

"Certainly an interesting turn of events," Leah replied, "but it also shows someone other than Vargas had the means and motive to kill Erica."

"But if Grace was going to get the brass ring in the end, why murder Erica?" I countered. "Wouldn't she want Erica to witness her own downfall? And why would she bother with secret meetings if she already had proof to back up her claims?"

"Getting her ducks in a row? Or using it as a diversion? Trying to make it appear as though she had no reason to kill Erica?" Leah threw her hands in the air. "I don't know, maybe the deal fell through or Erica caught wind of it and intervened."

"Gosh, and here I thought you liked Grace," I replied sarcastically.

"I do, but if she's up to her neck in this and framed Vargas for it, then all bets are off."

I nodded. "We've got a ton of blanks to fill in before with can even connect Point A with Point B, though. What about the presence of Vargas' knife at the scene?"

Leah waved her hand. "Bah, the knife could have been circumstantial, placed there after the fact to make Vargas look guilty."

"By Grace?" I asked, my tone incredulous.

"Whoever, all I'm saying is that the *possibility* is there."

Abe interjected our volley, "Little problem with that theory. You didn't give us a chance to tell you that Ramirez called. Vargas' blood was all over the crime scene. And given the quantity identified as being distinctly his and not Erica's, it's clear he didn't get away unscathed." He released a long breath before continuing, "In fact, he could be mortally wounded."

CHAPTER ELEVEN

"Mortally wounded…as in dying?" I gasped, while Leah looked mortified.

"According to the evidence at the scene and span of the blood, Erica didn't go down easily. She probably fought her attacker for several minutes before she was subdued."

"Don't you mean killed?" I asked.

Elijah shook his head, looking me straight in the eye. "She was still alive when her tongue was removed. Her throat was slit after the fact, almost to the point of beheading."

As horrific and vicious as the last moments of Erica's life had been, of one thing I was certain: there was no way Jeremiah Vargas was capable of cold-blooded murder.

For once, I was thankful Martin was tracking Clark so I could focus my attention on Vargas. I would have to check in with Bio Pop sooner or later, but thanks to the Stanton's quick work, I would hopefully prevent Clark from getting into my home or hurting my dog again.

At least Nicoh had recovered, though it shouldn't have happened in the first place—much like having to lie to Ramirez about Martin. Ugh, Ramirez—I bristled, realizing I hadn't spoken to him since I'd walked away at the park. Just one more thing I would have to deal with sooner or later.

I snapped out of my reverie to find Abe, Elijah and Leah in the midst of formulating our plan of attack. Abe and Elijah would follow up on Anna's conversation with the bartender and hopefully once in person, attempt to elicit a few more details than he'd elaborated on over the phone. It was too bad they couldn't have sent Anna in person—she would have had the guy eating out her hand the moment she crossed the bar's threshold.

They would also see if Ramirez had any updates on the investigation; then reach out to their network for possible leads on Vargas or friends inclined to assist him.

Leah and I would place another visit to Grace and then continue on to the newspaper to chat up Leah's former co-workers. Hopefully they would be able to shed more light on the contentious relationship between Erica and Grace and offer additional insights surrounding the book deal.

We'd also try to reconnect with Mort—surely the elderly gentleman would have returned home by now? If we knew anything about him, he was dedicated to his landscaping endeavors. One couldn't fault him for that. At least it kept him occupied during his retirement. I wondered what would keep us moving through ours. Then again, it would be nice to believe we would even make it that far.

If the last couple of years were any indication, we were in big trouble.

* * *

Upon receiving Grace's voicemail, we continued on to the newspaper. After checking in at the front desk for visitor's badges, we were escorted to Leah's old floor by a very large, imposing security guard. Vibrant chatter filled the open workspace. Cubicles had long been replaced by half walls to encourage collaboration. Staffers scurried about like mice in a maze—their cheese being a deadline met and the editor's approval. Disapproval meant a return trip through the maze for a rewrite, humiliation or possibly starvation. No cheese would often mean no job. It was a tough business but once again, technology had changed the way publishers did business and ultimately, the way the news was crafted and disseminated. It was a hard road, often walked barefoot on broken glass. Without the benefit of one's cheese.

Several hugs, high fives and cheers abounded as Leah quickly made the rounds. We didn't have much time, so we had to zone in on a few key people to get the details we wanted, stopping when we reached a desk whose occupant—a freakishly tall, pencil-thin man with John Lennon-style glasses and a mop of red hair—raised a finger to indicate he would be with us once he'd concluded his phone call.

He was rather cute in an I-want-to-take-the-puppy-home kind of way and had it not been for his direct and forthright manner in dealing with the individual on the other end of the connection, I would have taken him for someone who endured getting his cheeks pinched and hair mussed on a regular basis.

From his side of the conversation, it was clear what topic he was fielding. "As I've already told you, Phillip, we're fully cooperating with the authorities on the matter, as is our policy. Having said that, it is also within that policy to refrain from divulging details that could be pertinent to the ongoing investigation or that may inhibit or prevent the future arrest and prosecution of the individual or individuals—" A squawk emitted from the receiver before the man responded by slamming the phone back onto its base. "It's one thing to report the news…quite…something else… to be part of it."

"Tough day, Darrell?" Leah asked as the man bounced up and hugged her. He was twice her height, so I withheld a giggle as she spoke to his belly button. Catching me mid-snicker, Leah backed out of the hug and introduced us, "Darrell Petrie, this is my best friend, Arianna Jackson. Darrell's an associate editor on the crime beat. We go way back…" She waved her hand.

"Ah, the elusive AJ." He gave me a knowing smile and squeezed my arm. I had no idea what stories he'd heard about me and noticed my friend did not have the good graces to look even remotely embarrassed.

I decided to give her a break and played along. "One and the same but don't let my looks fool you. I can kick some serious boo-teh when I need to."

"Oh…*I know*." I inadvertently gasped when I realized Darrell might have been a bit smitten, given his goofy, lopsided smile and quick wink.

Of course, Leah couldn't help but snicker, before adding, "Yes, your notoriety precedes you, Ajax. Anywhoo…Darrell, we came to pick your brain, so get your eyeballs off my BFF's assets. At least until we're done interrogating you. After that, I'll let AJ decide what she wants to do with you."

"Mmm hmm, I like that." He plopped into his chair and gestured toward two spares in the next workspace.

Once we pulled them around and huddled in his tight quarters, Leah proceeded. "So, I know you told *Phillip* you were required to keep your lip buttoned but I'm here now…so spill your guts, Big D. What's your take on Erica's murder?"

"You know, I miss your directness, LeeLee." *LeeLee?* I snorted and was rewarded with a sharp pinch on my thigh. I refused to look down, hoping that it had come from LeeLee and not Big D. "Are you sure you don't want to come back now that the witch has melted?"

"Pretty harsh, even for you, D. And no, I'm still not inter-ested, even if that broomstick has been laid to rest. I've moved on to greener pastures."

He clucked his tongue. "It does appear our boss has moved on to a…toastier climate. Couldn't have happened to a nicer…witch. Anyway, not to be disrespectful the dead—or Erica—but she probably crossed one too many lines and it finally bit her in the behind. You know what they say about karma."

Leah nodded. "Indeed I do, Big D, indeed I do. But, *who*, D? I need names."

He laughed. "You don't ask for much, do you?" She gave him a bored look. "Oh…gosh…just the same ones you've probably got rattling around in your melon. If you take the ex-boyfriend off the table—none of us have our money on him." When Leah raised her eyebrow, he waved his hand at her. "Come on, I know you two have a thing going and I'm not shining you on to get on your good side, but seriously? I don't think killing her would have made it onto his radar, no matter what the cops think or the evidence they have. Sure, it looks a little hinky that he skipped out—a lot hinky, actually—but let's put that on hold for a second and look at the real facts.

"After Vargas dumped Erica, he got as far away from her as a man can muster without a restraining order. He'd moved on. Besides, she was more interested in accumulating things than chasing them: money, power, men, prominence…whatever. The chase had to be worth the effort. Even if that hadn't been the case, there is no way Vargas would have inserted himself back into that drama, much less have risked his career and livelihood on her."

Leah waved her hands. "Okay, okay! You're preaching to the choir. Enough about Vargas—any other fan favorites?"

Darrell nodded. "Sure. Like I said before, my list probably jives with yours. And, as I'm sure you're aware, the possibilities are endless. Other editors, associate editors, reporters, staff, politicians, law enforcement, the grocery store clerk, her laundromat owner, her tanning salon owner, her stylist—"

"Dude, I get the picture," Leah interjected. "Anyone and everyone and everyone's dog had a motive. What about Grace?"

Darrell frowned. "What about her?"

"Anything about her working relationship with Erica change in the past few weeks or months? Anything that would indicate it was *her* line Erica crossed?"

His eyes widened. "Gracie? Our girl's no saint but she'd put up with so much for so long. If the bough hadn't broken yet, it wasn't ever going to."

Leah twirled her hair in an attempt to appear nonchalant. "So there were no rumblings about Grace wanting Erica's job? Or about any new projects?"

Darrell threw his head back and snorted out a harsh laugh. "Everyone wanted Erica's job at one point or another. Present company included. As for new projects—not that I'm aware of…" He squinted at her. "Why? What is it you've heard?"

"Nuh uh…buddy, don't try to out-maneuver the pro. I'm merely here on a fact-finding mission—posing a few routine questions."

He wasn't convinced. "Riiight, but nope, still no idea. However, if you believe there's something to it, why don't you ask her yourself?" He gestured over his shoulder, toward one of the offices that bordered the main workspace.

"Grace's *here*?"

Darrell shrugged. "Yeah, she's in Erica's office." When Leah looked at him questioningly, he added, "She's been temporarily assigned as Erica's replacement. Looks like she's the one moving on to greener pastures."

* * *

I'm not sure what I expected but Erica's office was something… else. The twenty-foot by twenty-foot space was garishly decorated, making it look like someone had barfed on top of a splatter paint machine—you know, the ones you sometimes see street vendors use to attract small crowds to their spun art? One would think they would eventually go the way of the Pet Rock, but I digress.

The office was a shrine dedicated to its owner, complete with a Warhol-style Marilyn Monroe—of Erica. Trophies loaded the shelves but I doubted Erica had been the one who had earned them, regardless of the name etched on the base. Another large photo of Erica sat on the armoire behind the desk, so anyone seated facing her would be staring at two of her. It was a bit unnerving, if not disturbing. Even in death, Erica appeared to have her beady little eyes on everyone and everything.

I certainly didn't think we'd find Grace doing a victory dance or handing out glasses of celebratory champagne but as we gently knocked on the door and peered in, I was surprised to find her so frazzled. We watched in silence while she desperately scribbled on various papers and checked them against several computer monitors. Traces of sweat were visible through her thin tunic as she muttered to herself.

Leah spoke quietly to avoid startling her, "Grace?"

It took her a moment to look up and when she did, another to register who we were. "Hey. Twice in one day. I'm not sure if I should be flattered. Or paranoid."

Leah played it off. "Oh, we came by to say hi to Darrell—long time no see and all. We're surprised to see you here, though. Are you sure you're up to it?"

Grace slumped in her chair. "Honestly? No, not really, but the world keeps moving no matter who dies, which means the news does too. The editor in chief called me after you left and begged me to come in using excuses like 'we're short-handed' and 'crap's really hitting the fan'… yada yada…"

"Because of Erica?"

She shrugged. "Partially. We've got people all over the place —including Darrell—fielding calls about her death but as the publisher preaches, 'We still have news to deliver, deadlines to meet and competitors to beat.' "

"Darrell mentioned you were assigned her post?" Leah asked.

She waved a hand. "Temporarily. They probably felt sorry for me and tossed a coin. I doubt it will last very long before a permanent replacement is assigned."

"You don't want the position, then?"

"Doesn't really matter what I want. Sure, it would be nice. But it's not very realistic. There are others already in line equally deserving and probably more suited for it."

"Huh. Well, if I can put in a good word, let me know," Leah replied.

"Don't trouble yourself. Like I said, it was more of a sympathy play on the publisher's part."

My friend chuckled. "I doubt that, Grace. You're good at what you do. And given the opportunity—the right opportunity, without all the drama attached—you'd make a fine editor."

"It's nice of you to say. If that time comes, be prepared. I'll be coaxing you back." We all laughed, despite the cloud that permeated the room. "So, what else is on your mind?"

Leah looked at her curiously and Grace laughed harder. "Oh, come on, Leah, you've got that look. I worked with you long enough to recognize when you're on the warpath. I'm not buying the whole 'visiting Darrell' bit. You haven't come to our office once since you left. Suddenly it occurs to you to come to my home for a visit and now you're here. And before you try to convince me otherwise, it doesn't bum me out in the least that you have an agenda. I was aware of it the first time you stopped by— so let's have it." She gestured for us to sit.

We did and Leah, as per usual Leah, took the direct approach.

"We've come across an individual who claims you were writing Erica's book."

Grace frowned. "What individual?"

Leah snorted. "Does it really matter? Is it true, Grace? Were you ghostwriting Erica's book for her?"

Grace's scowl deepened as she stared at Leah. After a moment, she got up and closed the door.

"This doesn't leave the room." She pointed a warning finger at each of us.

Leah shrugged. "Nothing's going to come from me but it will come out, Grace. In fact, part of it is already out there."

Grace crossed her arms. "So I guess I should prepare for additional interrogations, then? And what do you consider this, my prep run?"

Leah put her hands up in surrender. "Whoa, we didn't come here to put you on notice. We're simply trying to find our friend and clear his name. So if that means asking tough questions along the way and you're on the receiving end? Well, I'm sorry for it. But if I've already gathered this information, the cops will eventually do the same. Either way, Erica's real killer will be exposed."

Grace scoffed. "And you think I'm a likely candidate because someone told you I was writing her book for her?"

Leah shook her head. "Didn't say that. But if I drew that conclusion then the cops might, too."

"And I suppose if I don't give you the answers you want, you'll go to them and tell them about this 'information' you've stumbled across?"

"Again, didn't say that. And no. Even though it would help remove some pressure from Vargas, we wouldn't do that to you. Not unless the crumbs lead directly from the cookie jar to you." Grace shot Leah a look that insinuated she was less than amused.

"So, enlighten us. We're probably the only ones in the position—and with the inclination—to help you."

"You've got a real way about you, Leah." Grace shook her head, looking more amused than angry. "I just never thought I'd be on this side of it. Okay, here's the deal. Yes, I was collaborating—Erica's word, not mine—with her on the book, even though she was more than capable of doing the work herself." Leah pursed her lips, apparently doubtful but Grace shook her head. "She was quite a talented writer and researcher when she wasn't obsessed with delegating. She'd just gotten lazy and wasn't willing to do the legwork." This time her laugh was filled with disgust and years of frustration. "And why should she, when she had me? Let's just say it got old. Fast."

"If you didn't want to collaborate, why'd you do it?" Leah asked.

Grace looked at my friend, her expression incredulous. "Hello, you met Erica, right? I needed to keep my job."

Leah shrugged. "But this wasn't part of the job."

"No, but as you are well aware, Erica got whatever she wanted. She could have made things difficult for me. Don't tell me you weren't affected by her manipulations, Leah. I know you left because of those crappy and usually dangerous assignments she forced you to work. You had other options. I do not. I have other responsibilities and can't afford to lose my job or branch out on my own, as you've done."

"What responsibilities?" Leah pressed.

"They are none of your concern, so drop it." Grace gritted her teeth and flashed Leah a look of warning.

Leah shook her head. "Sorry, Grace, like I mentioned before, if I was able to get this information, it's only a matter of time before the police do, too. And while you may not go to the head of their list of suspects, they'll dig so deep you'll start preferring daily root canals to the havoc they'll wreak on whatever 'responsibilities' you think you have."

Waves of contempt rolled from Grace as she shot to her feet. "You're a real—"

"Pill? Yeah, I hear that a lot. Just ask AJ." She thumbed in my direction. "But we're in a better position to *help* you if you *tell* us what's going on. The whole story. The whole enchilada. The whole rotten tomato—"

"All right, all right. Got it! Geesh!" Grace collapsed back into her chair and threw her hands up. "My responsibilities are not as self-serving as you're thinking. I'm doing this for my daughter."

We both blinked. I didn't know Grace well but certainly hadn't seen any evidence of a child in her tiny apartment.

"Your daughter?" Leah asked.

"When I was sixteen, I was a handful. Partying, a few recreational drugs…you know…the usual rebellious teen crap. I also had a penchant for bad boys. I hooked up with one, got myself knocked up and found myself kicked out of the house. I roomed with a friend, cleaned up for a short while, had the baby and life was good. I had a plan…you know? I had finished high school, gotten really good grades and even had a scholarship to the University of Arizona all lined up.

"Enter hottie bad boy baby daddy. I went off the rails again, went back to my old tricks…partying, clubbing. Still thought I was being a pretty good mom, though. Always found a babysitter. Made sure she was clean, fed and loved.

"But then, one night, my old habits kicked me in the butt. Woke up screaming in a hospital room with IVs hanging out of my arms and a whole lotta people I didn't know poking and prodding me. From what they told me, I gave myself a nice case of alcohol poisoning after drinking an entire bottle of Jack and chasing it with about twelve Red Bulls and at least three Jager Bombers. Somehow,

I managed to top that off with a nice display of theatrics, followed by an award-winning face plant. Anyway, half the club either saw me, or captured my fine moment on their cell phones. Next thing I knew, I was out of the hospital, out of a place to live and minus a child. Child Protective Services came and collected her from the babysitter while I was still unconscious in the hospital. The father's parents found out—he was a lawyer and she was a nurse—and they took me to court and were awarded temporary custody.

"I went to rehab, got sober and still lost custody of my daughter. That was nine years ago. Sure, I catch glimpses of her but she doesn't even remember me, much less know I exist. I've been sober ever since, even went back to college, earned both bachelor's and master's degrees in journalism and really tried to put my life back together.

"Then, shortly after Erica got the book deal, I found out my ex's parents were moving to Florida. Both have retired and are planning on making a permanent home there. If that happens, I'll never get to see her. I've saved my pennies and put away enough to give my daughter a good life but I'm not rich. Not like they are, anyway. I needed a way to quickly make more." Grace absently shook her head.

"So you thought you'd approach Mort, show him proof you'd done the work and secure a cushy deal for yourself?" Leah asked.

Grace grimaced at my friend's bluntness but still offered a response, "Erica had boasted the story was worth six figures easily…seven if it really took off."

"But if you couldn't afford to lose your job, why would you even take the risk? If your plan backfired…" Leah drew a line across her throat, wincing only after she took in our horrified expressions. "Ooof…sorry, a little too close to the collar?"

"Geesh, Leah, try to contain yourself—a woman is dead," I growled.

She started to respond but Grace interjected, "I was desperate but I wasn't greedy. I didn't expect to take the deal away from Erica. I simply wanted what was fair—a share of the deal. I was the one doing the work, after all."

"Regardless, Erica would have viewed it as the ultimate betrayal," Leah replied.

"Again, it was worth the risk at the time. Only Mort Daniels knew about it."

Leah snorted. "Yeah, and everyone at that joint you frequent. Let's talk risky…"

Grace looked at her in confusion. "I didn't—"

"Come on, Grace. You were seen tossing back martinis, spouting all the juicy details. Gloating. The bartender confirmed it."

From the look on her face, she'd taken the comment as though we'd passed judgment on her.

Maybe we had.

"I wasn't drinking. I wasn't gloating. And I certainly wasn't blabbing my business. But yes, I did tell one person—one person—in that bar." Grace got up, threw the door open and glared at us over her shoulder. Before storming out, she heaved a last piece of venom. "For the record…that lousy bartender? He happens to be the father of my child."

CHAPTER TWELVE

"That went smoothly. Good going, Leah. Anyone else's heart you want to rip out today?"

I should have known better than to ask.

"Nah, I leave the organ-ripping to the killer. Is the tongue even an organ?" she replied, causing me to blanch and fake-wretch. "Whatever, AJ. My tactics got us the information we came for, didn't they?"

"Not sure where they got us—other than they confirmed she wrote the book and probably didn't kill Erica. Point being, I hope it was worth losing a friend over."

"Grace? She'll be okay, I'll—"

"What? Buy her African Violets and Peanut Butter Frangos with a 'Sorry I was a giant boob' card attached?" I interjected.

"No, wisecracker, Grace will be fine. She has a temper like a redhead but she'll cool down soon. I'll talk to her tomorrow. For now, let's say goodbye to the other redhead and blow this popsicle stand."

"Don't you mean looney bin?"

"Like I said."

After the fun-filled conversation with Grace, we made the

rounds and chatted up a few other people but didn't get any more out of that exercise than we'd already known. No one liked Erica. No one was surprised she was dead. And frankly, except for the fact it added fodder to the newsreel, no one cared.

* * *

As we ventured to Mort's Ahwatukee neighborhood, Leah appeared to be mulling over the mysteries of the world, given the way she tortured the ends of her hair.

"Penny for your thoughts?" I asked.

"No, but I'd kill for a frappuccino."

"Extra whip?" I teased.

"Heck, I'd lick someone else's Starbuck's cup just to taste the remnants," she huffed.

I shot her a sideways glance. "After we get through this, we really need to have a little chat about that. In the meantime, let's see where we can get with Mort and then I'm buying."

"Promise?" Her face brightened at the thought.

I rolled my eyes. We might need to have that chat sooner than later. For the time-being, it would have to wait.

"Hey, you're driving, I'm buying."

"I like your style."

"I'll remind you of that when we get done with Mort." It came out more of a grumble than I'd intended.

"Troubling, isn't it?" she asked.

"Oh what, the fact he's putting my life story on display?" I replied, feeling the hairs on the back of my neck bristling.

"Yeah, and the fact he never seemed eager to put the story out into the universe before."

I nodded. "Maybe he needed the money. Or maybe he felt he had a moral obligation. Either way, I would have appreciated the courtesy of a heads-up."

She sighed. "One would have thought. Then again, he did ask Erica to write his book."

"It sure seems like it would have been more trouble than it was worth," I replied.

"No doubt, it certainly seems hinky to me."

"Which part?" I asked, though I agreed with her assessment.

"How the offer to write his book just sort of fell into her lap."

I nodded. "I'm curious to find out about that, too. I'm not convinced he was as impressed by her skill set as Grace had implied."

"We'll certainly find out when we finally track Mort down."

"*If* we finally track Mort down," I replied somberly.

"Way to keep your chin up, Ajax."

"Whatever, Leah, just saying."

She nodded and neither of us spoke again until we exited the freeway and wove our way through the various streets leading to Mort's neighborhood.

"Huh." Leah tilted her head, as though finally realizing calculus wasn't her strong suit. "It just occurred to me—this is not only Mort's neighborhood—it's Erica's, too."

"No way, really?" I swiveled my head, taking in the surroundings. I'd known Erica had done well for herself, but was surprised to learn it extended to living in such an exclusive area.

"Yeah, I'd totally forgotten she lived over here. You don't mind if I take a little detour, do you?"

"Be my guest. Now you've got me curious. Aren't you surprised she could afford this neighborhood?"

She shot me a look. "We're talking Erica, AJ. Anything is possible." She slowed as we approached a modest ranch house, tucked among the generous estates and custom-built homes. "Who the heck do you think that is?"

I squinted in the direction she was pointing. In front of Erica's house was a dark blue suburban with heavily tinted windows.

"No idea. Are those even legal?"

Leah snorted, "I doubt it, but then neither is that license plate." She was right—the plate was conveniently obscured by a cover.

"Suspicious." And way too coincidental. "You thinking what I'm thinking?" I nodded toward the suburban as it eased away from the curb.

"Oh, did you want me to take pursuit?" Leah wiggled her brows at me.

"Hurry, before they get away!" I growled, waving at the suburban, which had disappeared around the corner.

Leah rolled her eyes in an "as if" gesture before stomping on gas, surging us forward. I'd give her credit for knowing how to make that tennis shoe-sized vehicle fly, even if it meant we weren't always on all four wheels. Unfortunately, this time around, it appeared the extra ooomph hadn't helped. The suburban was nowhere in sight.

At least not in front of us.

We both craned our necks at the sound of the massive engine barreling down on Leah's tail end.

"Where the heck did he come from? Punch it, Scottie—the Clingons are in hot pursuit!" I shouted as the suburban continued to close the gap.

I hoped the "objects are larger than they appear" sticker on the side mirror was wrong, otherwise the loaded missile had already locked in and was prepared to strike in less than a millisecond.

"I'm doing my best, Captain! Any faster and she's gonna blow!" I prepared for impact as Leah screeched, "Son of a—"

She turned the wheel hard, causing us to skid as we hit the sandy shoulder. Panicking, she over-corrected, sending us into a spin that finally ended in an abrupt halt, just inches from landing us in a drainage ditch. As we performed a quick sanity check, the suburban whisked past, disappearing around the next corner.

Leah shot me a look that said we weren't to speak of the incident again.

I nodded and patted her on the arm. "Way to save the ship. And crew, Mr. Scott."

"Aye, Captain, all in a day's work."

* * *

If coming inches from ending up face down in a stinky sewage ditch wasn't punishment enough, it turned out Mort was still MIA. We returned home, exhausted and empty-handed, only to find Ramirez's police cruiser parked next to the Ferrari.

"Oh joy, this should be fun," Leah muttered under her breath.

"I am so not prepared to deal with this." I placed my forehead against the dashboard, which was surprisingly cool despite the workout the SUV had just been given. I contemplated staying in that position. Indefinitely.

"Then don't deal with him."

"What do you propose I do, stay out here all day?" She raised an eyebrow. I did sound a bit too hopeful.

Leah shrugged. "Ignore him, I do."

"You do not."

"Yup. I've developed a knack for pretending to be interested in what he's saying, especially when he gets that lecturing tone."

"I know the one you mean," I replied.

"Anyway, I like to pretend his is mouth moving but no words are coming out." She made a flapping gesture with her fingers.

"He doesn't even sound like Charlie Brown's teacher?"

"Nope, in my head, he's the strong, silent type." She quickly added, "He doesn't need to know any of that.

"No, I suppose not," I replied.

"I suggest you give it a try."

"Maybe I should."

I had finally summoned the nerve to get out of the SUV when Ramirez emerged from the house. I sucked in a deep breath as his eyes pierced mine. He stood that way for a long moment before thrusting his sunglasses on; then turned his back, got into the cruiser and pulled away.

"Um, that seemed a bit...abrupt." Leah released a breath, which made me realize I had been holding my own.

"I guess. Maybe it's foreshadowing," I replied.

She looked at the dust Ramirez had left as he departed. "A sign of things to come?"

"Or the beginning of the end."

Thankfully, Abe and Elijah were more sociable than Ramirez had been and if they had sensed any discontent on anyone's part—including Ramirez's—they certainly didn't acknowledge it. Instead, both seemed eager to share their news but encouraged us to divulge our recent findings first—being ladies and all. Ha, did we have those boys snowed or what? Then again, perhaps their mama had brought them up right. Personally, my bet was on the latter.

We proceeded to give them a play-by-play of our outing, starting with our visit to the newspaper, which resulted in our second meeting with Grace. Neither seemed surprised to learn she had been ghostwriting Erica's book. It was Grace's relationship with the bartender that got their investigative juices flowing.

"So, the bartender, Darian Hopkins, is Grace's ex-boyfriend?" Abe asked.

"Well, not so much boyfriend. It was more of an unfortunate hookup situation," Leah replied.

"Friends with benefits, then," Elijah clarified.

"Friends with benefits...with child," I added.

"So that gives us a common denominator." Abe appeared to be contemplating this new thread.

"That about sums it up," I confirmed. "Grace has no contact with the child due to some legal mumbo-jumbo, which she was trying to appeal. And now the grandparents are moving out of the state."

"Out of Grace's reach?" Abe asked.

I nodded. "It would be a difficult reach. Florida."

"So, the grandparents are retiring. Downsizing. Whatever." Abe thought aloud, "And they're taking the child with them." He turned to us. "Did you get the impression they were doing so on purpose? Perhaps they were aware Grace was planning to take them to court and decided to make a preemptive strike before she had a chance to do so?"

"Hard to say," I replied. "Grace didn't mention any preemptive maneuvering on the grandparent's part. Besides, she'd made her intentions pretty clear years ago, once she'd gotten her life back on track. Killing Erica would only derail those plans."

"What did Bartender Darian have to say?" Leah asked.

"Nothing, he didn't show up for work today and didn't call in either. His boss was steamed. In fact, when we identified ourselves as private investigators, he offered to pay us to track him down." Abe chuckled. "Of course, we declined but he was still agitated enough to share Darian's address without being asked for it." He referenced a piece of paper from his pocket. "It's an apartment on Pecos Road in Chandler."

"And when you got to the address?" My voice sounded more hopeful than I felt.

"Gone, according to the next door neighbor," Abe replied.

"Let me guess, this was right after he had his little phone chat with Anna?" Leah confirmed. When Abe nodded, she shook her own head in frustration. "Kind of a coincidence, don't you think?" I shot my friend a look—there were no such things as coincidences.

"It now appears we have three individuals who are MIA." I held up my fingers and counted. "One: Vargas. Two: Darian. Three: Mort."

"Mort Daniels is missing?" Abe and Elijah both asked at once.

I held up my hand and offered clarification, "Not so much missing," I shot a look at Leah and she shrugged, "as evasive."

We took turns filling them in on our failure to locate Mort and the attempted tail on the suspicious-looking suburban at Erica's. Of course, we left out the part where we nearly wrecked. No need to make ourselves look like amateurs, right?

"Did you get the suburban's license plate?" Abe asked when we finished.

I gave him a scribbled list of possibilities, explaining how the license plate cover had impeded our view.

"How about the state?" Elijah prompted. After Leah and I both shrugged, he added, "Even a front license plate might help narrow things down."

I replied, thinking about my glances in the rearview mirror, "Arizona doesn't require one but even if there had been one, it could have been obscured by a cover, too."

"And you didn't see the occupants because the window were tinted," Elijah confirmed, frowning after Leah and I shook our heads.

"Don't tell me this entire day has been a bust," Leah growled at no one in particular.

It was Abe who replied, "We did manage to track down several of Vargas' friends, family and co-workers, and while none of them have heard a peep, we were able to come up with a pretty extensive list of places he might go if he was in trouble. None of them expected him to reach out, so wherever he's gone, he's gone there alone."

"Probably didn't want to drag anyone into this mess with him," Leah murmured, just loud enough for me—and no one else—to hear. I gave her hand a quick squeeze and she nodded somberly.

Elijah continued, "Anyway, we have no reason to believe anyone was lying. In fact, all offered assistance if more bodies were needed to search the various locations."

"Err…Elijah…can we refrain from talking about bodies?" I asked quietly.

"Oh geez, just a turn of phrase…warm bodies, of course." We shook our heads, indicating that it wasn't much of an improvement. "Sorry. Resources. Helping hands."

Leah was eager to change the subject. "So, you'll let us know when you start looking into these locations? We'd like to take our fair share of the list."

Abe nodded. "We were planning to start when Ramirez stopped by. He basically confirmed what we'd already learned: Vargas hasn't made any contact to date, nor has he used his credit cards, cell phone or returned home since the incident."

Elijah continued, "They were, however, able to identify another source of blood at the crime scene. While Ramirez indicated they were still waiting on results to see if it matched anyone in the system, he did confirm the individual had lost more blood than Vargas, but less than Erica before she expired."

Leah's hand flew to her mouth. "But if Vargas could be mortally wounded, then this person…"

"Is in really bad shape," Abe replied, his tone dark.

"Have they been able to recreate the scene to determine the order of events as they transpired or identify who did what to whom?" I asked.

"Ramirez said they're working on it day and night. It doesn't help that Erica's dog spent an entire day in the apartment with her. Crime scene is pretty…contaminated," Elijah replied, causing me to shudder as I glanced at the white boards.

Abe continued, picking up several documents, "Ramirez did manage to obtain a copy of Erica's cell phone records. Guess who the last call was from, just an hour before they believe she was attacked?"

"No idea…Elvis?" Leah offered, her mind still reeling.

"Close…Mort Daniels. He called her via his cell phone, talked to her for about eight and a half minutes—"

"Wait a minute—Mort doesn't have a cell phone," I interjected.

"I'm just telling you what Ramirez said the investigating team found. They retrieved Erica's cell phone records, came across the last incoming call and pulled those records, which turned out to be one of the numbers associated with his wireless account," Abe replied.

"Mort has multiple cell phones?" I asked, still perplexed by the fact he had one.

Abe shrugged. "According to these printouts Ramirez shared —on the sly—he's got one…two….six?"

"Six cell phone numbers? Leah doesn't even have that many." My comment was rewarded with an indignant scoff.

Elijah squinted at the printouts his brother was holding. "Didn't you mention both Erica and Mort lived in the same area?"

"Yeah, both live in the Ahwatukee Foothills," Leah replied.

"And despite the proximity of their homes, their signals are transmitted from different towers?" Elijah asked.

I snorted. "Uh, have you seen the metro area? There are towers everywhere—buildings, mountains, churches, dog houses."

"Thanks AJ, I get the picture," Elijah replied, still focused on the printouts. "On the night of Erica's murder, Mort was not only the last person to talk to her when she was alive. He was also within the vicinity of her house."

Silence filled the room. It could mean something. Or it could mean nothing.

One thing was certain. Until the police could get their hands on evidence proving someone other than Vargas had murdered and mutilated Erica, he would continue to be the primary focus of their investigation. Given his injuries, every day we were unable to locate him could mean minutes sheared off his life. Unless we caught a break, time was the ultimate enemy.

I hoped, for Vargas' sake, the sand hadn't already sifted through the hourglass.

CHAPTER THIRTEEN

Now that we had Mort's list of cell phone numbers, we had to decide if we should use any of them. After much discussion, the consensus was no. While it might have yielded us faster results, in the long run we still didn't know exactly how involved he was. I was having a hard time convincing myself that the sweet, grandfatherly man could have been connected to such a heinous crime. Given his age and physical stature, he certainly could not have done so alone. Still, he'd never suggested an interest in turning the Gemini project into a book. I wondered how Martin would take that news.

Martin!

I was mentally chastising myself for not checking in with him sooner when I heard Leah's banter with Abe.

"By the way, you never said—how is Mort even remotely close to Elvis?" Leah had taken his bait. Hook. Line. And sinker.

"Well, just like Elvis, according to the two of you, it appears Mort has 'left the building.' "

If Leah wasn't sorry she asked I knew I was.

In the end, we decided to call Mort before venturing to his home again. I wasn't surprised to receive his voicemail and after a bit of coaching from Abe, Elijah and Leah, did my best to craft a message that would elicit a return call. Let's just say, I didn't share my whole package of mint Oreos but I left enough crumbs to leave him wanting his own cookie.

We proceeded to review the list of locations Vargas' friends and family had supplied, grouping them by location so they could be searched quickly by the assigned team. The four of us would tackle the locations in the metro Phoenix area, allowing us to maintain proximity to the home base. Law enforcement already had the borders covered, so Vargas' friends would take the rest of the state, breaking them into quadrants. It was still a lot of ground to cover, considering a resourceful man like Vargas could safely remain under the radar for an extended period. The question was…if he was innocent, why would he need to?

I hoped we'd have answers before it was too late.

We were all busy collecting whatever we needed to make our necessary rounds when Abe pulled me to the side.

"Say AJ, when Ramirez was here, Elijah and I got the sense there was some tension between the two of you. He didn't mention anything and normally I wouldn't pry but if it's because we're staying here—at your house—we could certainly make alternative arrangements."

I flushed at his mention of Ramirez. Tension? Oh yeah. But not for the reason Abe was thinking. I couldn't easily explain Martin's sudden arrival, much less my meeting with him or what I had asked him to do while I concentrated on Vargas. I had already told Leah—against Martin's wishes—and hoped I wouldn't live to regret it. Her life was already in grave danger due to her association with me and her previous encounters with Clark. This time around, he may try to rectify his earlier misstep, when he had failed to kill us both. Strike that—at some point, he would make an attempt. Unfortunately, he was good at biding his time—

exceptional really—and there was no way of knowing when he would pounce.

Enter Martin. I hoped my request would yield an outcome worthy of the price I would have to pay when it came to my fractured relationships. I assigned a plural because I was convinced that by the time all was said and done and the truth came out, like Ramirez, the Stantons would harbor resentment and disappointment for my failure to confide in them.

Abe peered at me intently, awaiting an answer. I cleared my throat but the lump that was Ramirez remained, making my voice gravely. "Not to worry, Abe. It's an entirely separate matter we'll address once this is finished. I do appreciate your concern, though." I chuckled. "Besides, he's the one who suggested you keep an eye on me. He wouldn't have expected you to do any less." I gave him a quick hug and though he nodded, he didn't look convinced. I quickly added, "And believe me, you guys are more like a buffer between what he's facing with Vargas and my ordeal with Clark."

"Crap, AJ, I hope you don't feel as though we'd forgotten about Clark—"

I put a hand up to stop him. "In this whole crappy scenario, we can be certain of one thing and one thing alone—Clark *is* out there. And yeah, sooner or later he'll pop his head out and we'll let the mongoose bite it off. In the meantime, I can't spend my life worrying about what he may or may not do to me. We need to focus on finding Vargas. Preferably alive."

I realized Leah and Elijah had joined us and much like his brother, Elijah didn't appear convinced Clark could be taken down quickly or that my issues with Ramirez would be resolved easily. Both looked at Leah for confirmation but thankfully, she did a fabulous job of making it appear as though she was none the wiser.

Abe surveyed me for a moment before responding, "Okay

then. We could always make the security room into an extended panic room and lock the three of you in. That would certainly take a load off Ramirez's mind, knowing you were all safely tucked in and out of danger."

"Rather than out causing it," Elijah added.

I laughed and punched him on the arm. "Nice try but I think not. Though, now that you mention it, a panic room may come in handy—with the caveat the locks are on the inside—to keep all you bad boys out."

Both laughed. "Sure, sure, we'll get right on that," Abe replied.

"We may just hold you to that, Stanton," Leah added.

"I'm counting on it." He wiggled his eyebrows at her, causing her to blush before she took her turn at punching his arm. He feigned injury and limped out of the room.

When they were safely out of earshot, outside packing up their car, she whispered, "You really need to get Martin on the horn, touch base and make sure that he doesn't blow us out of the water. All this covert stuff is making me itchy."

I cast a doubtful look in her direction. "I thought you lived for this stuff. Isn't it part of the standard reporter repertoire?"

She threw a hand to her chest, pretending to be offended. "I'm anything but standard. And, my problem isn't with actual spy stuff—it's remembering who knows what."

"So basically, remembering when to keep your mouth shut." She smirked and stuck her tongue out at me. "But yes, I was thinking the same thing. Though I doubt he'll be making a spectacle of himself, or us, for that matter. His goal is to fly under the radar, not *be* the radar."

"More and more that seems to be our job," Leah sighed.

"Tell me about it."

* * *

We waited until the rumble of the Ferrari faded to call Martin, placing it on speaker with the strict directive Leah was to remain on her best behavior—meaning not seen, nor heard. Anything above a peep would result in a month-long ban on junk food *and* margaritas, even though she protested at first, claiming the agreement was damaging to her physical, psychological and emotional well-being.

Martin picked up on the first ring. "Arianna, this is a surprise."

"Uh, I wanted to touch base. Also to let you know there have been some other…developments."

"I see…" His voice was low, as if he was somewhere he did not wish to be overheard. "Are you alone?"

"Yes." I winced when there was a pause. Apparently, I was pretty bad at this lying stuff.

"I'd prefer not to talk over the phone. Can you meet me at the same place we met last time?" he asked.

"Yes, I'll come now. But I'll need to be brief. There are other…matters I need to attend to."

"I understand. It won't take long," Martin replied. I started to hang up when he added, "And you might as well bring your friend Leah along."

Before I could respond, he disconnected.

Leah's eyes were wide. "I swear I didn't make a sound!" When she misconstrued my head-shaking, she threw her head back in agony and wailed, "I shouldn't be punished for this. It's not right. How could he have known? Don't tell me he's got people watching us too!"

Maybe I was paranoid but given the way our lives had changed over the last several months, anything was possible, if not probable.

* * *

There was no little family at the park to entertain us this time around as Leah, Nicoh and I made our way to the bench in the park. Once again, Martin was already waiting, only this time he stood as we approached. I made brief introductions and after Martin gave Nicoh a few scratches on the head, he gestured for us to walk with him.

"You said there have been some developments since we last talked?" he asked.

Given the frown that formed when I relayed the details surrounding Mort's book deal with Erica, he had not been aware nor was pleased by the news. At the same time, he didn't appear terribly surprised, either.

I said as much.

"It wasn't going to remain a secret forever, Arianna. At some point, the public was going to find out, whether it was Mort or someone else associated with the project. What's troubling is the proximity in timing of the book deal, Clark's arrival and now, this girl's death."

"You think Clark is involved?" The thought had crossed my mind but I'd set it aside, thinking I was simply grasping for the longest straw.

He shook his head. "I don't know. It might actually work to his and Theodore's benefit if the details surrounding the project were to come out."

"How so?" I asked.

"Clark and his father might try to use the project to cast blame elsewhere, to use it as a distraction for their own crimes."

Leah's coughed out a laugh. "Seriously? Kind of like those kids who kill and then claim they were products of their environment?"

"Not exactly but as long as the details surrounding Gemini are kept under wraps, the original benefactors can continue to fly safely under the radar. If, however, Clark and his father use what they know to save their own hides, well…" he opened his hands, inviting us to draw our own conclusions.

"That's kinda sick thinking, Marty." Leah looked as though she'd eaten sauerkraut.

I attempted to get a handle on Martin's logic. "You're saying Clark is seen as a liability to these benefactors? That he basically already has a target—one that has nothing to do with law enforcement—on his back?"

"Knowledge is power, Arianna."

"So, if the information were to come out, say in a book and not from Clark or his father…"

Martin finished my thought, "Then the people who brought Gemini to fruition would be at a greater risk of being exposed, given the source would likely be considered more credible and unbiased. Ultimately, the same people could also be held responsible for letting the project get out of control."

"It would have also placed Mort and Erica in extreme danger," I added. "One thing I don't get—surely you're not insinuating Clark and his father would use this little revelation as a means of getting away with the crimes they've committed over the last twenty-plus years?" I thought of my parents, my sister, my birth mother and countless others. Leah looked equally mortified.

Martin put a hand on my arm, a calming gesture a father might make. "I wouldn't go quite that far. If that were the case, why wouldn't they have shown their hands already—divulged what they knew once they were captured?"

Leah was having none of it. "Who knows half the reasons Clark and his father do the things they do—perhaps they were biding their time. Getting the most bang for their bucket list. I don't know, Marty. But what I'm saying is that it's within the realm of possibility. Clark and his father could use what they know to get away with murder." These were all things Martin could not possibly know for certain much less guarantee.

Still, he remained calm, shaking his head as she continued her animated pontifications. "To people like Clark and Theodore, it's more about vindication. Justice has no hand in their game."

"Spoken like a man who knows," Leah muttered. If Martin had heard her, he ignored her comment.

"What about you, Martin?" I asked.

He was taken aback by my question, or perhaps my forthrightness. "What about me?"

I looked him straight in the eye. "What do you get out of this?"

He thought for a long moment, his gaze never leaving mine. "Either way, I will get closure."

Leah wasn't buying either. "So for now, you're hedging your bets. Surely, you have a preference, if the scale could be tipped?"

He broke my gaze to meet hers. "My preference would be to keep the information under wraps until it can be evaluated by the appropriate and responsible parties. Without boundaries and parameters, the information is a time bomb waiting to be detonated. If it were to find its way into the wrong hands…"

Leah didn't appear to be impressed by his answer. If anything, she thought he was grandstanding for my benefit. "Huh. Are you shooting this from the hip, Marty? Or do you have a bloodhound with his nose to the ground?"

He seemed amused by her directness, his mouth quirking at the corner, yet his tone was serious. "My opinions are mine and mine alone. They are not based on certain knowledge but more from inference, based on decades of analysis, introspection and reasoned conclusions." I looked at Leah and shrugged. Spoken like a true scientist. As he looked at us, realization dawned and disappointment filled his eyes, "You're thinking it also gives me a motive to kill the deal, so to speak?"

"If you've drawn that conclusion, then others likely will, too," I replied.

"Except others are not aware I exist."

"Not yet, anyway."

It wasn't a threat but like Martin, we had drawn our own conclusions. The opinions were ours and there was someone out there, other than the two of us, who could reveal his identity and confirm his existence in the land of the living. Martin may have gone off the bridge that day but today he was very much in front of us, in living color. And we weren't the only two with the benefit of this knowledge. Others also knew—Grant wasn't buried in Grant's tomb.

If we'd jarred him, it didn't make its way to his face, or his body language. "For now my focus is keeping you safe." He nodded at Leah and Nicoh. "I don't want you losing any more than you already have."

I nodded. "I appreciate that, Martin."

He looked at his shoes and kicked at a clump of dirt in the grass. "It's the least I can do, after all these years."

I changed the subject, uncomfortable with this daddy and daughter moment. Apparently, it was none too soon for Leah either, who looked as though she'd spent some time in the rhubarb patch. "So, has there been any movement on Clark's part?"

"We haven't pinpointed him to an exact location but we have identified places he's been over the past several days, so the team is looking at patterns. As I'm sure you're painfully aware, Clark doesn't do anything without a reason."

"So we've got patterns to look forward to, huh? Sounds really promising, Marty," Leah's tone implied she still hadn't gotten the rhubarb out of her mouth.

Martin looked grim. Apparently, he thought his news on Clark would ease our minds, if not elicit a more positive response.

"Unfortunately, right now, I can't tell you any more than that without jeopardizing the team working on this."

Leah snorted, crossing her arms, "'Jeopardizing the team'? We can somewhat appreciate that but geez, Marty, keeping us in the dark isn't exactly making us any safer. Or preparing us for when Clark strikes."

I nodded, the optimum word being 'when.'

"My associates will not allow him to get that close. Not again, anyway."

"But how—wait a minute, do your 'associates' have us under surveillance? Are you following us?" I gritted my teeth.

"Yeah, Marty, been driving any oversized SUVs lately? Driving us off the road? Is that your definition of safety?" Leah added.

Martin squinted, confused by her questions but still offered a reply, "Things are being monitored from a safe distance. You won't even be aware of their presence—no matter where they are." I looked at Leah. Like that cleared things up.

"Great, guess I'd better stop that nude sunbathing," Leah retorted. "So, do you have anything else for us?"

By this point, Martin looked completely exasperated. Clearly he wasn't skilled in the art of dealing with sassy twenty-somethings.

He shook his head. "Nothing as concrete as a smoking gun—"

"Who cares about the smoking gun, Marty?" Leah interrupted. "We'd rather have Clark delivered with an apple in his mouth."

"I will be in contact when we have him in our sights." Before Martin disappeared into the night, he turned, an ominous expression crossing his face. "Just for future reference, Ms. Campbell, once we have Clark, would you prefer him skewered or sautéed?"

CHAPTER FOURTEEN

"It's not that I don't like him, Leah, I just don't know him. And I certainly don't trust him." We had returned to Leah's SUV and were perusing our list of locations to scout for Vargas.

"That makes two of us, sister."

"No, I'm pretty sure you just don't like him."

Leah absently chewed her thumbnail. "Probably true. Guy doesn't give off a warm and fuzzy vibe."

"He's not a puppy, Leah."

"Not even close. He's too shifty for puppydom." I motioned for her to continue, having drawn a similar conclusion. "His body language is closed off—crossed arms, the way he positioned himself when he talked to us and his intermittent use of eye contact."

"At least he made eye contact," I commented.

"Yeah, but only when he wanted to get his point across, when he wanted to make sure we believed him."

"You're saying he was selling us a line of bullpucky?" I asked.

She shrugged. "Half-truths at a minimum. I'm sure parts were true."

"Yeah, like the parts that would lend credibility to the other not-so-true parts."

"You picked up on it too, I take?" My friend surveyed me. "No, I can definitely see that you don't trust him. I had to wonder…"

"Wonder…what?" I asked.

"If you were just saying it to convince yourself you shouldn't trust him."

"Are you suggesting I am reverse-psychologizing myself?"

"Maybe. You're a good person, AJ. You give people the benefit of the doubt. You think they are good and decent, until they prove otherwise. And even then, you believe they have a few redeeming qualities."

"You make me sound like a sap. Do you think I'm being naive?"

She shook her head. "You just see the world from a more positive perspective. Less jaded. With Martin, you are being more cautious than usual but it troubles you doing so. Perhaps you feel you owe him some sort of concessions?"

"Concessions? For what? Being my biological father?"

"That's part of it," she replied, her tone softening and her voice quiet. "I think you feel sorry for him."

"Feel sorry…for Martin?"

She nodded. "For the life you think he's given up."

I frowned. Perhaps Leah was right. Maybe I felt badly for the things he had lost: his work, the woman he said he loved, his children and ultimately, his identity. For nearly thirty years, Martin Singer did not exist, except for the name shared on a lonely, forgotten grave.

There I went again, falling into my old trap, letting my guard down. I thought about what Leah had said and decided to put myself first for a change. This time, I reflected on what *I* had lost:

my parents, my twin sister and the opportunity to have a relationship with her.

I would have liked to include my biological mother, Alison
Anders and perhaps once, Martin, too, but you can never really lose
something you didn't have to begin with. When it came to Alison, I
never would. Perhaps in time, I would get to know and understand
Martin, but when I thought about the time he'd spent hiding, never
revealing himself, I had to wonder why. Perhaps I was fooling
myself into believing it had been a form of sacrifice? Perhaps, in
reality, it had been a choice—much like choosing to make an
appearance in my life now—and there was more to his agenda.

Something struck me. "You said I feel sorry for the life I *think*
he's given up?"

"Like I said, you're being particularly cautious. Something
deep down beyond your gut, deep in your soul knows he's not
being entirely truthful, that he didn't just suddenly show up out of
the blue to have some precious daddy-daughter time or to swoop
in on his white horse to save the day."

She was right about the gnawing feeling of discontent I had
when it came to Martin. He hadn't returned solely for the benefit
of a reunion or even to intercept Clark. What if the reason he had
come out of hiding was much simpler? Had I been over-thinking
it all along? What if the real reason Martin rose from the grave
was to beat Clark to the punchline? What if Martin had come out
of hiding…for me?

Leah interrupted my thoughts. "By the way, Ajax, you still
owe me junk food and margaritas."

* * *

Eight hours, six iced caramel sauce lattes, four bags of gummy
bears and three sets of tired paws later, we trudged back into the

house, our list of potential Vargas sightings a bust. Not even a stray morsel indicated he had even been there, much less had been seen in the vicinity since the time of the murder.

"Do you think it's odd that we haven't heard anything from Clark since his initial handiwork? Not even a vague text message with an extremely poor use of punctuation and grammar?" Leah asked as she plopped onto the sofa.

I collapsed into a nearby chair and tugged the scrunchy holding my ponytail, which had been giving me a headache since noon. "Funny…no. Strange…yes. Does make me feel a bit itchy, though. It's like you never know when the other shoe's gonna drop with him." Leah dropped hers onto the floor, resulting in a resounding thump.

"Honestly, I wouldn't mind adding him to the missing list," she replied.

I nodded. "Only if we could exchange that sicko for one of the others we're not able to currently locate."

"Agreed. My vote would be for Vargas. I am really worried we won't find him in time, especially given his injuries…whatever they are." I knew it had been hard for her to admit that out loud. Neither of us had wanted to think about Vargas…alone…hurt… possibly dying. It was much easier focusing on finding him. Alive.

We heard more than one vehicle rumble into the driveway and Abe and Elijah entered shortly after, with Ramirez in tow. Given their wrinkled shirts, the sleep-deprived shadows under their eyes and their grumpy dispositions, whatever news they had to offer didn't appear to be promising.

Abe was the first to confirm our suspicions, as he and his brother plunked on either side of Leah. "We got nada, please tell me you two gals came up with something better?"

Leah repositioned herself, jockeying for more room between the two brothers. "Does zilch trump nada?"

"It does not." Elijah frowned, his tone revealing the depth of his weariness. "You've got to be kidding me. We've been all over this city. How does one man bury himself that far underground without leaving any breadcrumbs?"

I directed the conversation to Ramirez, who had remained standing since his arrival. "How about you, Detective, you got any news for us?" Though I hadn't more than glanced in his direction, I could feel his eyes on me. Disconcerting to say the least.

"It would be a wasted effort, supplying anything of value to you two delinquents." His eyes flashed and I swore under my breath as the temperature of the room spiraled.

Leah glared at Ramirez. "Just who are you calling 'delinquents,' Detective? I thought we were all on the same side?"

Ramirez's penetrating gaze finally moved to her as he replied. "We are. It's the way you two—three, if you count Nicoh—go about things I'm questioning."

"Our way works just fine, thank you very much." Leah crossed her arms in defiance.

A smirk danced across the corner of his mouth. "Oh? And just what juicy tidbits have you managed to drum up since I last saw you?"

"Like I told Abe here…zilch. Nothing. Nada," she replied.

"Thanks for making my point for me," he replied.

Leah started to argue. "No, Detective your *point* would be made if we'd actually found something. Not finding anything doesn't count."

Ramirez shook his head, only slightly more amused. "That's some messed up logic. So what's your point?"

Leah threw her hands up. "Hey don't look at me! You're the one who's counting points here."

This nonsensical banter—no matter whose point I saw—was

getting us nowhere, so I changed the subject. "Did anyone manage to find the owner of the suburban?"

Ramirez eyes narrowed. "What suburban?"

Leah waved her hands, annoyed. "The navy one parked outside Erica's. We couldn't get a license plate because it was covered by one of those thingies."

"Thingies?" Ramirez asked, frowning.

"Here at the Jackson household, we like to think of them as license plate covers," I clarified.

"Why is this the first time I'm hearing about it?" He took turns glowering at us while grinding his teeth.

"Right after it happened, you were too busy peeling out of our driveway." I referenced his visit—or lack thereof—earlier in the day.

"I wasn't peeling out of anything. I was on the clock and had to get back to work," he snapped as he turned to Abe and Elijah. "Why didn't you tell me about it?" When Elijah started to respond, Ramirez impatiently waved him off and addressed me. "Getting back to this suburban…what have you got?"

I shrugged. "It was just your typical navy suburban. Except for the license plate cover which blocked most of the number, there wasn't anything out of the ordinary, though the windows were tinted pretty heavily, too." Ramirez nodded in a way that meant he was confirming something he already knew. "Why so curious about it?"

His eyes met mine, their intensity unnerving. "Because a vehicle exactly like the one you just described went missing from the Tempe Police Department's impound lot."

"Went missing?" Leah asked.

Ramirez nodded. "Shortly after the altercation in the police station."

"The one between Erica and Vargas," I confirmed.

"That's the only altercation I'm aware of," Ramirez's voice

was challenging. This time, I didn't check to see where his glare had landed, but one could venture a guess.

I didn't appreciate his tone but let it slide. "Okay, connect the dots, Detective, I'm not a mind reader. Certainly you guys have video surveillance at your impound lots?"

"We do. And we've reviewed it and the person who last checked it out was clearly visible."

"Err...I hate to break it to you, Ramirez, but if you already know who checked it out, then it's technically not missing." My response came out a bit snappier than I had intended.

Ramirez shook his head. "The person who checked it out also went missing shortly after."

Vargas.

Dots A and B connected, he proceeded, "The vehicle was confiscated as part of a drug bust and placed in the impound lot with others that resembled the suburban you saw at Erica's. Vargas doesn't work narcotics so the vehicle would have had no prior association to him. Anyway, the theory is that he researched the vehicles impounded, picked the most vanilla, checked it out under false pretenses—for a stakeout, whatever—then used it to facilitate not only the crime but his getaway."

"So the vehicle was seen at Erica's around the time of her murder?" Abe had been so quiet I had forgotten he was still there. Perhaps once a cop, always a cop. I tended to forget that. Like Ramirez, law enforcement had been part of his past.

Ramirez nodded. "By a neighbor of Erica's. Of course, some would like to believe Vargas' acquisition of the vehicle shows premeditation—that he needed something other than his own ride to commit the crime and allow enough time for a clean getaway." I bit my lip. I had already provoked Ramirez enough, but if the vehicle would eventually be traced back to the impound lot—and to Vargas—why would he have taken the risk? It was not a detail a seasoned detective would overlook.

I elected not to poke the angry bear. "What do you believe, Detective?"

"Honestly, I think he intended to use the vehicle for a case he was working on. I can't divulge the details of an open investigation, other than to say it merited some discrete surveillance a vehicle like the one he checked out would have offered. Unfortunately, it doesn't matter what I, or anyone else, chooses to believe. It comes down to what we can prove. Right now, the best proof is Vargas himself," he replied and for the first time, I saw the beginning of a crack in his armor and the uncertainty that overwhelmed him.

"I'm not sure I agree," I commented and immediately felt the intensity of six pairs of eyes on me. "I mean, we've got to find Vargas before the police do especially considering his wounds, but we don't physically need him to prove anything. At a minimum, we just need to find evidence that contradicts their theory or casts reasonable doubt on it. The next best thing would be evidence proving someone else killed Erica. And the icing on the cake? *That* would be finding Vargas and bringing him home…safely."

"Quite a speech, Ajax," Ramirez replied after a long moment, "but you're absolutely right—perhaps we…I need to change my perspective. Not that we shouldn't continue looking for Vargas, but we should also focus on finding evidence that would help clear him. Maybe then, he'd be able to come out of hiding."

None of us wanted to say it on the heels of my rah rah speech, but the looks that passed throughout the room indicated we were all thinking the same thing: we hoped Vargas still possessed the ability to come out of hiding.

We spent the next several minutes rehashing what we'd learned. While none of us believed Grace killed her boss—now including Ramirez—when the police had learned she'd contacted Mort about the book deal, they were forced to take a closer look at the editor's assistant. If she hadn't murdered Erica directly, she had the means, motive and opportunity to conspire with the person who had. Of course, in their book, that person was still Jere Vargas.

Their newest theory was that Grace—having undergone years of emotional abuse and setbacks in her career and family life—discovered an opportunity to have the last laugh, at Erica's expense. She'd found an ally in Vargas and together they had gotten revenge on the person who had interfered in both their lives one too many times. I didn't know Grace all that well, but from what I had learned about her and what I knew to be true about Vargas and his character—the theory was based more on trying to make fictitious pieces fit a puzzle than meeting any factual certainty.

No one brought up Clark but the topic did venture in the direction of Mort Daniels, whose name had come up in conjunction with the book deal with Erica and again when Grace had made her play. Ramirez quickly assured me the police were not aware of the nature of the book and indicated what few details they did have led them to believe it was a work of fiction. Until they spoke directly to Mort, there was no way to confirm otherwise.

While Abe, Elijah and Leah were busy referencing their notes and updating the white boards, I took the opportunity to clear the air with Ramirez.

"Can we talk?" I gestured to the patio.

An uncomfortable silence filled the air, long after we'd sat on opposing lounge chairs, the distance between us as stifling and unforgiving as his gaze.

I cleared my voice. "I'm sorry." It came out in a raspy whisper.

"Sorry for what?" His eyes never left mine but his tone

conveyed a hint of distrust I would never have dreamed I could have been responsible for creating.

I broke his gaze and stared at my hands, clasped tightly in my lap. "Sorry for all this. For Vargas… For Clark…" I paused, my voice cracking. "For us…"

I didn't dare venture a glance, fearing I would not be able to handle what I saw and was surprised when he moved to my side and pulled my hands into his.

"You don't need to be sorry for Vargas or Clark. Those situations were not your doing and certainly not within your control. We have a good team here and there are still boys in blue who believe in Vargas' innocence. Like you said, if we can put our heads together and focus on the evidence, perhaps we can clear his name and bring him home. As for Clark, we've got people on the streets looking for him, the security system is amped up here and you, Leah and Nicoh have skilled babysitters…" I shot him a look and found a small smile gracing his lips. But even in his teasing, the smile did not reach his eyes. He looked weary. And sad.

"And us?" I prompted.

He shook his head. "I'm not sure, AJ. Every time we seem to make progress, something gets in the way…some sort of barrier. And while I believe you're sorry, I don't think you know what you're really sorry for."

"Are you saying *I'm* the barrier?"

He nodded. "For as trusting as you are of people—the blind faith you put into others—you don't put the same level of trust in yourself. So while you think the best of others, when it comes to you, the opposite is true. You expect to let others down, to the point you not only anticipate but accept it. In the end, you force yourself to ignore anything that could allow you to believe otherwise."

I hadn't ever really thought of myself in that way but as I

reviewed the recent events in my life, I could see his perspective. Perhaps subconsciously, I blamed myself for my parents' death—though I had no control over the way I'd come into this world—my life had led to the ending of theirs. Victoria's, too… had she not come looking for me…to warn me, she would have been spared. These were the things that haunted my dreams at night, the things that gave me sweats and woke me up screaming. The blackened hand that clawed and scratched in an attempt to reach me…perhaps it hadn't been Death? Perhaps it was guilt. My guilt. My hand, scorched by the wrongs I had subconsciously taken credit or accepted responsibility for. Perhaps it was the reason I'd refused to tell Ramirez about Martin, fearing my burdens would become his and ultimately, lead to his demise.

I knew Ramirez would eventually forgive me but until I accepted and addressed it myself, he would not forgive my deception. Meaning, we could not be.

I swallowed, the realization sobering. The inherent problem-solver inside wanted to fix it. But this was not a wound a Band-Aid would heal. It would take time to absolve myself from the guilt; to trust myself. I looked at Ramirez's sad expression as he gently rubbed his rough thumbs over my clasped hands and knew what small step I needed take.

I moved my hands over his and squeezed them gently, until he raised his eyes to mine. "I need to tell you something about the man in the park—" Before I could utter another syllable, his cell phone's shrill ringtone forced us both to jump.

"I need to get this." I nodded and Ramirez stepped out of earshot before answering.

The conversation appeared tense as he listened to the caller, given the way his muscles strained against his shirt. Several minutes passed before he spoke, too low for me to hear. After he ended the call, he stared up at Camelback Mountain. I wondered if he wished he were there, perched on her highest peak, away from the insanity and troubles of the world below.

Finally, I couldn't bear the silence any longer and went to his side. Gently touching his arm, I whispered, "Is everything okay?" Mentally kicking myself—of course it wasn't—I started to add some clever quip when he beat me to the punchline.

He turned to me, his face grim. "They found Mort—"

"What? That's great news—"

Ramirez cut me off with a single shake of his head, gazing back at the mountain in the distance before responding, "Mort Daniels is dead."

CHAPTER FIFTEEN

"No…no…no…that can't be right. I just talked to him." The words came out sounding mechanical as I realized another person in my life—and a potential lead that could have helped Vargas—had slipped away. Accepting the reality that the gentle man I had known was gone was entirely a different matter.

"No, AJ. Not unless you talked to…a dead man," Ramirez replied, his voice so quiet I could barely hear it over the thoughts racing through my head. "Daniels has been dead for a while."

Before Ramirez could continue, I led him back to the living room where Abe, Elijah and Leah looked at us expectantly—perhaps hoping we had worked out our differences—until the detective dashed those hopes as he shared the news of Mort's death.

"His body was found in a remote section of the desert, between Marana and Tucson. You might remember the discovery being mentioned on the news?" Leah and I nodded, still numb with shock. It had been hard to forget.

The local television and radio stations had been buzzing for at least a week, having gotten their hands on some fresh meat or in this case, a not-so-fresh corpse. "Who was this person?" filled the news stream, where members of each outlet took best-guesses and offered conjectures. At the time it was considered big news—until the next story came along. In this case, updates on the body in desert were quickly replaced with the capture of a woman who habitually targeted mall spas, where she received Botox injections and then ditched before paying her tab. Big news, indeed.

According to Ramirez, the degradation of the skeletal remains had made its identification more challenging, so the results had only recently been confirmed. No one had reported Mort Daniels missing, so until now, there would have been no reason to think the body could have been his.

It did raise the question—if the man in the desert had been identified as Mort—who had I spoken to just one day earlier? And then there was Erica, who had known Mort longer than any of us and up until the time of her death, had been working with him on the book. His absence certainly would not have gone unnoticed, nor would his replacement by an impostor.

Even though the police considered Grace a possible suspect, we agreed that she might be able to shed some light on the situation, considering she'd recently been in contact with Mort, too. Leah quickly placed a call to her former colleague. As expected, she was still at the newspaper, toiling away and harried under her new responsibilities. Once Leah managed to smooth things over from our previous meeting—using their mutual shock over Mort's death as an icebreaker—Grace agreed to answer a few additional questions and allowed Leah to place her on speakerphone so the three of us could converse.

"Well, at least it clears up a few things," Grace huffed. We could hear shuffling paper in the background as she attempted to multi-task. Apparently, it wasn't working out too well for her, because a few mumbled curse words managed to escape immediately following a solid thud.

"Err, everything okay, Grace?" Leah raised an eyebrow and I shrugged in response.

Grace cursed again before replying, "Noooo…I just knocked my iPad off the desk. Actually it was on the chair and the notebook fell of the desk, hitting the iPad—" I made a motion to Leah to circle the cattle before Grace wandered completely off the prairie.

"You were saying Mort's death clears up a few things up?" my friend prompted.

"Well, just that I haven't been able to get ahold of him for days." More shuffling ensued from her end, followed by more muttering, followed by more cursing. Obviously, the girl was a little distracted.

"Um, Grace, what exactly do you know about Mort's death?" I asked, looking at Leah. We both assumed that—working at a newspaper—she'd already been privy to more information than we were currently working with.

"Oh, just that he'd been found dead out in the desert. Some of the other editors and reporters were talking about it but I've been so darn busy—between answering questions from cops, fielding phone calls from yahoos, keeping up with the investigation and ongoing manhunt and all Erica's other duties—I haven't had time to breath, much less catch up on it. I assumed he went hiking, got dehydrated, fell. Why? What have you heard?"

We waited for her to actually take that breath before dropping the anvil on her, ACME style.

"Mort's been dead for weeks, Grace," Leah replied, her voice much quieter and calmer than she appeared, given her constant fidgeting.

"Are you trying to convince me I've been communicating with a dead man?" Grace asked after Leah filled her in on the specifics.

"Oh, I am quite sure you were communicating with a living person, it just wasn't Mort Daniels," Leah replied.

Grace snorted. "Are you kidding me? Don't you think Erica, of all people, would have recognized her former bureau chief?"

"Perhaps…" I gave it a moment to sink in. Erica may have been murdered because she *hadn't* recognized the man and could have pegged him for the impostor he was. Eliminate the problem to perpetuate the lie. Who else besides Erica could identify Mort? "When was the last time you remember meeting with Mort?"

It took Grace a moment to respond—we'd hit her with a lot and she was justifiably confused. "What? Met him? I never actually *met* Mort in person. All communications were done by phone and text but email seemed to be his preferred method."

"Surely Erica had met with him? Talked to him on the phone?" Leah asked.

"Oh, yeah, definitely. Especially at the beginning, when they were hammering out the book deal, deciding who would do what—discussing numbers, signing contracts, things of that nature."

"When was that…the beginning?" Leah asked.

"Oh, let's see. It's been several months now, back at the start of the year." We heard her shuffling papers. "Of course, in the weeks before her death, she was furious because he repeatedly missed their meetings, wouldn't return phone calls, barely returned emails or texts." I looked at Leah. That didn't sound like Mort at all. "She finally got so riled up she decided to track him down and have it out with him in person."

"So, how did that turn out for her?" Leah asked.

Grace's voice was barely a whisper when she replied, "It was the same meeting she scheduled with him the night she…was murdered. I guess we'll never know, will we?"

Then again, I think we already did.

CHAPTER SIXTEEN

"So neither Erica nor Grace saw this person posing as Daniels?" Ramirez clarified, once we'd finished our conversation.

Leah shook her head. "Grace said Erica had talked to the real Mort Daniels both in person and on the phone and from the dates she could remember, it would have shortly before his death. After that, Erica couldn't get him to return her calls and was barely communicating with him via email."

"Grace, too," I added, "though she'd never met Mort—either one of them—in person." Something occurred to me. "Didn't she mention she had at least *talked* to him? Which means Mort would have been replaced by the impostor by then."

"You're absolutely right. Of course, maybe it's not surprising this fake Mort—or Mork, as I like to call him—wouldn't want to talk to, much less be seen by someone who could out him for the lying, conniving, faker—"

"Mork?" Ramirez interjected.

"Fake plus Mort equals Mork." Leah waved her hands, impatient with having to explain what she believed to be common sense.

Ramirez shook his head and slid a look at Abe and Elijah that suggested my friend had fallen off her pogo stick and bonked her head one too many times.

"Allriiiight…*Mork* took a risk calling Grace. We'd be lucky if he left a voicemail—risky and stupid—but is it possible she recorded their conversation? And the text messages and emails—any chance she would have saved them? I can get ahold of Erica's—hopefully pre-Mork and post-Mort, but it would be helpful to have Grace's as well," Ramirez replied.

"Oh, I'd bet a good bottle of hair detangler she recorded their conversations." Leah stopped when she noticed the men's confused expressions. "I'm saying I would have recorded them. Old habits die hard with reporters."

I cleared my voice. "What are you thinking, Detective?"

"Patterns," Abe replied for him. "He's looking at patterns and clues surrounding the impostor."

Ramirez nodded. "Abe's right. Mork will slip up and give us something. So, yes, it would be helpful to have the voicemail in case we needed to make a match. You two think she'll cooperate?"

"Does Nicoh like to howl at the power company man?" Leah nodded at me.

"The gas company man, too," I replied.

"Don't forget the phone man," Leah countered.

I laughed. "Oooh, especially when he's up on that pole…like eighty feet up—"

Ramirez voice boomed, "Enough you two! I have no idea what that means and I'm not sure I want to."

"It means if it shifts the focus off Grace and places it onto someone else, then I'm sure she'll be more than willing to give us…give you whatever she's got."

Ramirez sighed. "Sometimes having conversations with the two of you can be challenging and more trouble than it's worth."

"Hey buddy, what's that supposed to mean?" Leah snapped.

"It means, why can't you just say what you mean?" Ramirez replied.

"I think we just did," she huffed.

Ramirez shook his head. "Without the shenanigans, innuendos and secrecy."

This time, my cheeks grew warm—he wasn't talking about whether we could get Grace's cooperation. It wasn't my fault I hadn't been able to finish telling him about Martin. I rocked back and forth on my Chucks, noting the shoelaces could use a good washing, when thankfully, Leah responded.

"We'll make the call, Detective. In the meantime, you said you were going to see what else you could learn about Mort's death? You never did say *how* he died."

"I didn't. Because I didn't know then. And now I do," Ramirez replied.

Leah looked at me. "And he said talking to us was challenging."

Ramirez leveled an icy glare at the group. "His throat was slit, the trachea severed." He refused to look away as he delivered the rest, "And though it was missing, there was evidence his tongue had been forcibly removed."

* * *

Leah and I were uncharacteristically quiet as Ramirez continued. Though the specifics were still being pieced together, Mort had been bludgeoned several times before his throat was slit and tongue extracted. His body had then been dumped, far enough off the beaten path for the desert scavengers to easily feast in solitude and where human foot traffic would not normally have been an issue. Mort's killer hadn't accounted for the possibility that hikers would venture deep into the desert in search of various rocks and other treasures. Mort's remains had not been the type of trophy they had intended to add to their collection, nor had their discovery likely been part of the killer's plan.

I did a mental breakdown. To date we had two dead; one—possibly two—missing, two prime suspects and one unidentified impostor. Erica and Mort had been killed in the same manner and despite the fact they had worked together in the past, the only thing linking them recently was the book. I wondered how many others had been aware of the proposed tell-all, and if Erica and Mort had been eliminated to keep their mouths shut. Or as a warning to others.

This led to Vargas and Grace. While both had motive to kill Erica, Vargas hadn't even known Mort. Grace would have only benefited if Mort were still alive. Why set up two people—who previously had no connection—when they would likely be cleared once Erica's murder was linked to Mort's? What were the killer's motivations? To squash the book deal? If so, why eliminate *both* Erica and Mort? Had one of them seen something? Or posed some other risk?

And then there was the bartender, Darian. It was too soon to tell if he was really missing or simply trying to stay off the cop's radar for a different reason. Grace had made him seem like a bad boy. Perhaps once he'd thrown her under the bus, he belatedly realized his words bore meaning and to ensure their validity, the police would need to look into the background of the man who'd spoken them. Maybe he had a few of his own things to hide. Unfortunately, until we found him, it didn't help us clear Grace or Vargas.

And who was this impostor? Though he had quietly stepped into another man's shoes, it did not seal his fate as the murderer. At the very least, however, he did have knowledge of the circumstances surrounding the life and death of the man he was hired to or had volunteered to portray. I silently vowed to uncover his level of complicity and expose the truth—no matter what that truth revealed.

Processing the parts and pieces made my head hurt and didn't even take the outliers into consideration—the issues that had no bearing on the murder investigation. It wasn't as though I needed a full-blown migraine but Clark had been uncharacteristically quiet after poisoning Nicoh. It made me antsy, knowing he was out there somewhere…waiting…watching. I hoped Martin would deliver some positive news soon.

I winced, thinking about Martin. Of course, Ramirez chose that moment to glance in my direction and once he'd latched onto my guilty expression, I knew there was no way I was sidestepping the conversation a second time.

"Can we talk for a minute?" I asked him quietly but found everyone, including Ramirez, looking at me. "Err…Ramirez. I wanted to talk to Ramirez. Alone."

Leah looked mortified as she realized what I intended to do but I interjected before she could stage a protest. "Not now, Leah." She gave me a look of concern as I took Ramirez's hand and led him to the patio; then scurried to the kitchen so that Abe and Elijah couldn't press her for details.

"What's this all about, AJ?" Ramirez asked after we'd been sitting on the bench near the pool in silence for a short while. "You wanted to talk to me but haven't said a word, or looked at me after insisting we come out here."

"I know there's a lot going on with Vargas, the murder investigation and all—"

"AJ, relax. Just tell me what's going on. Is this about our fight at the park? Because I can assure you, it's the furthest thing from my mind right now."

I waved a hand. "No, it's more than that. I have to get this off my chest. Like now. Wait, did you think that was a fight? 'Cause I didn't really think of it as much of a fight as a difference of opinion—"

"AJ, stop it!" Ramirez's voice was stern but when I looked at him, there was no heat behind the words. Only concern. "Stop babbling and use your words!"

I chuckled at the *Must Love Dogs* reference—a romantic comedy I had recently forced him to watch. And despite that it fell into his chick flick category, as a fellow John Cusack fan, he seemed to enjoy himself and even commented it hadn't been all that bad. Of course, that was after he inadvertently noted Diane Lane looked hot. I couldn't deny him that, as long as I got to be his leading lady.

"It's not about the fight in the park, specifically…" While Ramirez waited patiently, I fidgeted. Sure, I'd committed to telling him about Martin but I'd never really mapped out *how* I would do it. Not that I needed an outline with bullet points but a general plan to keep it in the ballpark probably would have been warranted. I sighed, hindsight was so overrated. I clenched my hands until a couple of fingers went numb; then took a deep breath and prepared for the worst. "It's about the man who I was there to see."

"Your client?" There was skepticism in his voice.

Just let me get through this, I told myself.

"Not my client. It's a personal matter. Between me and this… man." Err, bad choice of words.

"Okay…" This time, Ramirez sounded wary, just enough so that I looked up and saw something I hadn't expected—jealousy.

"Oh…oh…it's nothing like that. Honestly." Ramirez cleared his throat, indicating he was not buying. "Seriously, Ramirez… Jonah. What I'm about to tell you is probably the hardest thing I've ever had to say and even as I'm telling you, I'm not sure I fully believe, much less can comprehend it myself."

"Do you love him?" Ramirez's voice was earnest.

"What? Love him? No, though I suppose I should…" I gritted my teeth, realizing I needed those bullet points more than I'd thought.

"How long has this been going on?" This time, his tone cast a chill over the warm evening.

"How long has *what* been going on?" I slapped the side of my head in frustration. "I'm not cheating on you, Ramirez!"

"If you say so." He shrugged, a failed attempt to dismiss me.

I shot to my feet and placed my face millimeters from his. "I'm not saying anything!"

"Oh, you've said quite a lot without actually saying it, AJ. You have quite a knack for it." He started to rise but I pushed him back down. The gesture surprised him but not as much as the volume of my voice.

"I'm not in love with this man! And I'm certainly not having an affair with him!" I belted out. "He's my father, you bobble-headed baboon!" If I'd been concerned about letting Martin's livelihood out of the bag, the entire neighborhood—including my houseguests—had now been informed.

Ramirez looked incredulous. "Your father, Richard Jackson? That's not only ridiculous, it's impossible."

I shook my head. "Not my adopted dad, my biological one. Martin Singer."

"Now I know you've gone off the deep end, Ajax. He's been dead for nearly as long as you've been alive." Under different circumstances he might have been amused but now he was just plain angry, thinking I had fabricated an atrocious lie to cover up an affair.

I winced. "Not quite. He went missing less than two weeks after my sister and I were born."

"Went missing? If I remember correctly, he took a trip off the Skyway Bridge in Chicago, compliments of Theodore Winslow." His sarcasm was not lost on me, especially when he offered a belligerent snort to further his point—quite unnecessary, in my opinion. "I'm sorry, AJ, but I don't have time for this. I seriously thought you were a different person. A genuine person. But between you and your roommate, you cook up more shenanigans than the Three Stooges, Lucy, Ethyl and Steve-O combined. I just don't have the time or energy for all this drama. Grow up, AJ—or at the very least—try to live in the real world. Because right now, that's where I need to…have to live. My friend is out there… dying…and I just can't…I won't deal with this right now." His verbal purge apparently concluded, he crossed his arms and huffed out a long breath.

"Sufficiently calmed, Mr. Maturity? Done with your discharge of insults?" Though his demeanor didn't change, his pinched expression indicated he hadn't prepared for my redress. And frankly, given our distinctive bull-headed natures, I was glad to have the advantage, no matter how long I was able to hang onto it. Ramirez had crossed a line, no matter how invisible it was. He'd cut deeply enough it could not be buffed out or thrown under the rug. I needed to call him to that carpet. Now. "Let me give *you* a dose of reality, Detective. My reality.

"Two days ago, I called Mort Daniels—or at the time the man I believed was Mort Daniels—to see if he had heard any rumblings about Winslow Clark. At the time, Mort was abrupt, distracted, but said he would get back to me. The next morning he did, and we agreed to meet at the Zoo, near the spectacled bear exhibit. When I got there, Mort was not, but another man was. Though he had aged twenty years, I recognized him from pictures I had acquired from Mort as being my biological father, Martin Singer." I took a moment to catch my breath and collect my thoughts, but did not give Ramirez the concession of even a glance. "He confirmed his identity and though he has not told me how he escaped death, he did indicate he was forced to go into hiding, for the safety of his newborn twins. For Victoria and I. He only came out into the open because he had received word Winslow Clark had escaped from the FBI facility and was on the warpath for me. He came to offer his assistance—"

"'His assistance'? AJ, are you listening to yourself?" Not the reaction I had expected from Ramirez. Cool as tempered steel.

"Perhaps you're the one who should be listening...no... checking...yourself, Mr. Hotshot Hotdog Detective! You don't even know Martin."

"*Martin*? So, you're on a first name basis with a man who claims to be your father, after a couple of *Terms of Endearment*-filled moments?"

"For the record, it was three visits and he doesn't just *claim* to be my biological father, Ramirez. I've seen the pictures. I've seen the proof. He looks a lot like me, down to my sharp little eyes!"

"Huh, I thought you said your favored your mother," he replied smugly.

"Why are you being so difficult?" I managed to grit out. "The man came to help me find Clark and has made some serious progress, which is a lot more than I can say about you and your cop friends!"

"Low blow, Ajax, low blow." Ramirez's eyes narrowed. "You know I've been trying to deal with that, in addition to this murder investigation, which happens to involve one of my best friends."

My laugh came out harsh. "Then you should appreciate the fact that someone else has offered to step in and offer a life jacket so you can focus your attention on finding Vargas and apprehending the real killer!"

"Appreciate what? Vigilante justice? Your father is a scientist...was a scientist, AJ. What is he doing, using a microscope to find Clark? And oh...just how did he find out about Clark in the first place? Oh, that's right! Mort Daniels, the impostor, informed him. Yeah, that makes it all seem okay. One has to wonder how he plays into this? Oh, but you're too busy *appreci-*

ating Martin's efforts." Ramirez ended by emitting a healthy snort.

I chose to ignore it, as well as the comment regarding Mort for the moment because frankly, I wanted to ask Martin the very same thing. The other comments, however, were not getting past my radar.

"Oh my, look who's talking about low blows and maturity levels, Ramirez." I shook a finger. "Shame on you. For your edification…yes, my biological father was *merely* a scientist. And while that may not mean much in the garbanzo-sized brain you're walking around with, others considered him a great scientist for his time. A revered scientific mind—"

Ramirez snort cut me off. "More like a *twisted* mind…"

It was my turn to cut in. "At least he makes good on his promises. Meanwhile, what are you batting?" I formed a goose egg with my thumb and forefinger, spun on my heel and walked away. I flung the slider door open. Before stomping in, I turned to face him and threw my last bit of venom, "And for the record, Detective Ramirez—that twisted mind? It made me."

CHAPTER SEVENTEEN

Ramirez certainly hadn't won any brownie points. As I stormed in the house and slammed the slider shut with a satisfying thud, it was clear everyone in the surrounding counties had heard our volatile exchange. In fact, I was more than a bit surprised Nicoh hadn't begun howling, though it pleased me immensely when Ramirez entered a short time later and my canine companion pressed himself against me, serving as my stoic protector. Ramirez reached out a hand for him to sniff but Nicoh sensed my anger, thrust his head and shoulders higher and ignored the offering.

Meanwhile, Abe, Elijah and Leah attempted to make a show of reviewing various notes, spreadsheets and laptops, though I could feel the heat of their stares on my back.

"We're not finished having this discussion," Ramirez uttered roughly as he passed.

I snorted and muttered my own snarl, "On the contrary. I don't think we ever *started* a discussion. You listened to a few words, drew a conclusion and then passed judgment. Before hearing all the facts. Not very coply of you, Detective."

Ramirez sighed, his voice slightly less tense, "AJ, *please*. I'm merely looking out for you. You don't know a thing about this man. And yet you seem so eager to take everything he says at face value."

I shook my head. "I never said that."

"No, but it's the vibe you give when you talk about him. You defend him at the first sign of resistance. You've met with him on more than one occasion but it's the first time you've bothered to mention him. Yet, I know you've told Leah. Don't bother denying it, I can read her face, too." Ramirez looked exhausted as he opened his hands in resignation. "Why didn't you just tell me that day in the park?"

"He asked me not to, for safety reasons."

He retracted his outstretched hands as he worked to contain his anger. "Uh huh, there you have it, because 'he asked you not to.' " His emphatic use of finger quotes—my gesture—was not appreciated.

I crossed my arms and tapped my Chucks impatiently. "Are you going to parrot everything I say, or do you have a point?"

"The point is—I am a public safety officer, AJ. But more than that—I am your friend—your boyfriend when you allow me to be," he replied through gritted teeth, causing a flutter of paper shuffling behind me. Can you say awkward? Ramirez remained unaffected. "So while this stranger asks you not to talk about him to anyone, you run and tell Leah but don't trust me enough to bother mentioning it, even after I'd asked you point blank?"

I pressed my lips together in defiance. Frankly, I didn't like having to justify my actions under pressure. Still, I offered him the courtesy of a reply. "Honestly? I felt like you were checking up on me. I don't know, Ramirez, sometimes it feels like you're the one who doesn't trust me." More harried paper-shuffling arose from the peanut gallery.

Ramirez ignored them, his tone solemn. "I was worried about

you because Clark was on the loose. No sooner than I told you to stay put—off you ran."

"It actually took me a day to get the meeting with Mort, err… Martin. But people knew where I was." I waved in the direction of Leah and noticed she was trying hard not to appear interested in our conversation.

Ramirez shook his head and again, anger and frustration boiled to the surface. "The point is, Arianna—*I* didn't know. You didn't tell *me*."

"Well, apparently I didn't need to tell you because you knew where I was all along," I replied.

"Argh—you are so frustrating," Ramirez growled. For a moment, I wondered if he considered sending me to my room, or worse, giving me a good spanking. Under different circumstances, I might have enjoyed the latter but given his mood and present company, reserved my comments on that topic for another day.

Instead, I decided Ramirez needed to take a handful of the blame. "Oh, and you're quite the communications champion yourself. You know what, Ramirez? Why can't you just concede that you got jealous over something you thought you saw, mad because I didn't do what you told me and outraged because I told my best friend of twenty years before I even considered telling you? Oh and by the way, I told her because she's not so judgy and when she says she's helping me, she really does."

"She's right, I really do," Leah piped in, despite both Stanton's attempts at shushing her.

"Shut up and mind your own business, Leah," both Ramirez and I snarled.

"Geez…just trying to help a girl out…I'll let you two…get back to it," she murmured.

We ignored her and continued to glare in a silent standoff until Ramirez finally broke it, "You're missing the point, AJ. You're so blinded by the shiny new toy you're not seeing its sharp little edges."

I threw my head back and released a harsh laugh. "The shiny toy being Martin, I presume."

"The man managed to stay in hiding for over twenty years, AJ. *Twenty years*." He enunciated the words to ensure I understood his warning. "He didn't show up to save your sister, so why did he suddenly choose to show up now? If you think it was to help you with your Clark problem, you are not only naive— you're fooling yourself into believing something that isn't real. Rather than asking yourself *how* he's going to save you from Clark, you should be asking *why*."

* * *

Ramirez left without as much as a head nod to anyone. Despite his accusations, he had made a valid point. Or two. The first of which was that Martin had been notified about Clark by the impostor. How did he know where to find Martin? How did they know one another? Had Martin actually known the real Mort Daniels? Before I could wade through the myriad of thoughts forming, a hand was on my arm.

"You okay?" I turned to face my best friend. Her eyes were filled with concern and tiny mouth formed an unhealthy frown as she absently stroked Nicoh's back.

"Okay with what part? The part where I got into it with Ramirez? The part where my biological father is alive and kicking after twenty-plus years? The part where the man we thought was Mort Daniels may or may not have been involved in the real Mort Daniels' death? Or the part where our friend Vargas is mortally wounded, missing and being hunted like an eighteen-point buck during deer season?" Winded and a bit light-headed, I finally took in a deep breath.

Leah looked at me carefully before responding, "I meant the part where Ramirez walked out."

"It seems to be a theme of ours lately." Leah nodded but said nothing. I noticed Abe and Elijah had been purposely quiet, pretending to work on their white boards. "So, what did I miss?"

"Hey, welcome back." Elijah made a feeble attempt at sounding cheerful. Odd comment considering it was my house and I'd just been outside, not on holiday in the south of France. "We've just been reviewing our notes, looking for different angles. While you were out…err, talking to Ramirez, the three of us contacted Grace again to see if we could have access to her email, texts and any phone recordings with Mork and she agreed to collect the emails and send them over." It reminded me Ramirez had said he'd try to get his hands on Erica's and hoped our tiff hadn't changed his mind about sharing his findings with us.

"What about the phone recordings and text messages? At the very least it would be nice to use those recordings to confirm Grace and I had talked to the same individual."

"No go. As Leah had suspected, she did record their conversations but her phone went missing shortly before Erica's death," Abe replied.

I groaned. "Went missing? Don't you mean stolen?" Realization dawned and I groaned again, thrusting my fists in the air in utter frustration. "Which means her text messages are gone, too," I didn't need verbal confirmation. The looks that crossed their faces told me what I had said was true. "Wait! What about her cellular carrier—the backups they keep—surely she could access them that way?"

Elijah dashed my hopes. "Nope. She already tried that and their system sustained some sort of hiccup that wiped her data from the server. All of them."

"Convenient. And let me guess—only Grace's data was affected during this hiccup?"

"They couldn't confirm it, for confidentiality purposes, yada yada," Abe replied, his tone matching the disappointment we all felt.

"Seems like their confidentiality went out the window when their system suffered a glitch," I replied. "Perhaps they could benefit from a little security tune-up, compliments of Stanton Investigations."

Both laughed, though the amusement was short-lived as I recapped what I had just learned, "So, we have a second 'missing' phone in a matter of days, which leaves us without a recording of Mork's voice or text messages. Please tell me the emails contained a glass slipper?"

"Not a chance," Leah replied as she handed me the printouts. "It's all pretty much boilerplate stuff that could have been copied and pasted from anywhere. Guy likes his Caps Lock key though." She scrunched her nose, clearly not a fan of reading her correspondence in all capital letters. I didn't blame her, I loathed it myself. "Grace mentioned his texts were much the same way, in all caps with minimum word usage. She said it gave her the impression he wasn't a fan of electronic messaging." Or perhaps, it was simply a means of preventing anything from being inadvertently divulged about himself? Vernacular or tone in written correspondence can often tell you a lot about a person. Regardless, the missing phone was just icing on the cake, for someone.

Frustration turned to anger as I thought about the heinous, cruel murders and the single thing that tied them together—the book. A book, according to Grace, that outlined every detail of the Gemini project.

But who would resort to murder? Who also possessed the means, method, motive and sadistic predisposition to carry it out?

I could think of one person. A devil in sheep's clothing if one placed eyes on him because like the impostor, his appearance and demeanor outwardly masked the evilness that enveloped his soul like tar and allowed him to suck the life force from unsuspecting victims at will—without remorse or concession.

As I thought about it, the individual I had in mind had the annoying tendency of typing threatening correspondence in all caps. Lately, he had a penchant for stealing cell phones that didn't belong to him to aid in his nefarious activities. This same individual had broken out of prison, threatened my security and harmed my dog. He also lived to torture my psyche, nearly as much as he wanted me dead.

Winslow Clark.

CHAPTER EIGHTEEN

As I wove through the various threads of this revelation—no matter how loosely based in fact they were—I was suddenly very, very worried. Martin suggested Clark and his father could have benefitted from the book. Whether he was mistaken or trying to convince me otherwise remained to be seen but it did raise several questions. Was Clark working with Mork? Had he orchestrated Clark's escape? Was Mork a ruthless killer like Clark and his father or simply a pawn in their game—a minion convinced to aid in their cause? Or was he complicit in the murders of Erica and Mort—an equivocal deliverer of death?

Had Vargas come into contact with them or done something that made him a threat? Or like Grace, simply a means to an end? I shuddered, not wanting to tread that path, which told me that Vargas was also very disposable.

I lifted my head and was met with grim faces as I realized I'd mumbled that last bit out loud. Against my better judgment I shared the director's cut of my thoughts, only to be met with a myriad of expressions—disbelief, skepticism and alarm.

"Okay, let's say Mork has been working with Clark, do you

think he's providing him a hideout—a way to keep off law enforcement's radar?" Elijah asked when I had finished.

"I suppose it's possible," I murmured. It would also explain why Martin and his team had only been able to determine where Clark had been, but just shy of identifying where he was at any given moment. Clark would have had resources to help him elude not only law enforcement, but anyone else on the lookout for the escaped killer. Something else occurred to me. "That blue suburban we saw at Erica's. It could have been Clark. Or Mork. Or both."

Leah nodded. "It would also place both of them at Erica's house on at least one occasion, if not a prior." She shuddered at the possibility Clark had been involved. None of us wanted to think about what that could mean for Vargas.

"Do you think we could get into Mort's house to look around?" I asked of no one in particular.

"I assume the police have already gone over the house with a fine-toothed comb, now that Mort Daniels has been officially identified," Abe replied.

He was probably right but I wasn't prepared to give up—not before I started, anyway. "Maybe they missed something. They weren't looking at the situation from the same perspective." Perhaps we'd see something relevant they wouldn't know was pertinent or even something meant just for me.

"She's got a point." Elijah nodded at his elder brother. "You think we'd be able to get inside, now that they're done?"

"What about a police escort?" Leah offered, giving me an apologetic glance.

Abe nodded. "I'll see what I can do." He excused himself to make the call. If our request was granted, I crossed my fingers Ramirez would send another detective in his place.

My hopes were thwarted as Abe returned, looking mildly amused as he glanced in my direction. "He'll meet us there first thing in the morning." Fabulous. I loved it when a plan came together.

Leah squeezed my arm. "Are you sure you want to do this?" Her eyes were pleading—pleading for me to be honest with her. And with myself. Only Leah could understand the depths of the betrayal I felt in keeping secrets from Ramirez. That secret being Martin.

I shrugged and sighed. "It's not like I have a choice. Besides, it was my idea."

She gave me a quick hug. "Then let's go wrangle up some bad guys."

* * *

The next morning, we convoyed over to Mort's. Nicoh and I tucked into the Mini, Elijah in the Ferrari, followed by Abe and Leah in her SUV. Why we needed three vehicles was beyond me but Leah winked, indicating she wanted to have a little chat with the older Stanton brother. While I didn't think the timing was right for one of her romantic interludes—her other boy toy being our primary concern—I could hardly throw a hissy, considering I'd recently had my own relationship sidebar.

After arriving at Mort's, we walked the perimeter as we waited for Ramirez, Leah grumbling all the while. "Last time I was here, those darn vines reached out and tackled me to the ground!"

"And nearly ruined your Kate Spade boots," I added.

"Those viney rooty things are nasty!" She huffed, still peeved about the incident.

Abe and Elijah looked left and right; then back at us. "What vines? All I see is a bunch of bushes." Elijah made a barrel shape with his hands, as if we needed a lesson in shrubbery at the moment.

"'What vines?' I'll show you what vines." Exasperated, she marched toward the side of the house where the travesty had occurred.

As the troop followed in close pursuit, an indescribable odor filled the air.

"Whew! It really stinks back here!" My eyes started watering from the intensity.

Leah paused, scrunching her nose. "Yeah, what *is* that?"

"How would I know?" I shrugged. "Probably a form of weird plant food or dirt Mort was using."

"Yeah? Well it sure doesn't smell like dirt," Leah muttered.

"Well, the sooner we do this, the sooner we can move away from it," Abe snipped. Apparently, he took no pleasure in the eau de toilette Mort had selected, either. "Where's this vine thing?"

"Duh, dude. It's right here." Leah rooted around with her foot but quickly pulled away, squealing when she found it covered in mucky grime, "Ewwww!"

"That's what you get," Elijah replied dryly.

"What the heck did I do?" Leah growled and was about to take the offending shoe off and toss at his smart mouth when Abe interrupted them both.

"Err…guys? Those aren't vines…or roots." He dropped to his knees and started working the ground with his bare hands. Elijah squinted before quickly joining his brother.

Leah and I looked at one another, unsure if we should follow suit, or call the men with the little white jackets.

"Um…Abe? Elijah? What are you doing?" I whispered, though I doubted I would have interrupted their manic search. That's when I noticed Nicoh had engaged in his own digging frenzy, dirt and grime covering his muzzle and paws as he attacked the earth, looking like a bear going after a tasty snack. Then again, thinking about the peanut butter fudge brownies Leah and I devoured last week, we may have been placed in that category on occasion, too. "Nicoh!"

"Let him be, AJ. He's on the right track," Abe said, his voice filled with excitement. "See here?"

Hands and nails filthy from digging, he pointed to a section of the ground he and Elijah had managed to clear. What Leah had mistaken for a vine was a worn piece of rope, threaded through a series of thick iron hooks. The ground below them wasn't dirt, but a large wooden door.

My mind did a mad dash back in time. I'd seen something similar years ago, when my parents had visited friends on their farm on the eastern side of Washington State. It had been used as an underground storage space—a root cellar, I believed they had called it. I remembered it had taken two of us—children of eight or nine years at the time—to lift the trap-like door from the earth using the roped-handle. Once were able to maintain enough leverage to toss it to one side, it revealed a steep set of uneven stairs.

Undaunted in our youth, we had descended the rickety steps and were rewarded with a cool, dark haven. It had been filled with the garden's bounty as far as the eye could see which served as the family's food surplus. Of course, my imagination ran a little wilder back then but my recollection yielded a treasure-chest filled with burlap bags and wooden crates overflowing with more varieties of potatoes, carrots, onions, squash, beets and other root vegetables than I had ever seen in my young life. Though dry and safe from the elements, the harvest smelled as fresh and earthy as it had the day it was picked.

Setting up forts framed with empty crates and draped in burlap, we had played in our secluded fortress from sun-up to sundown when our parents collected us for supper. We did so hesitantly, rising with the sun the next day to fabricate a new adventure, more elaborate than the one before. It had been a wondrous time to be a child at play, while our parent had looked on in amused silence. Perhaps they had been a bit envious, too, remembering their own carefree days of summers long past.

I let the memory drift. A more sobering task was at hand as I contemplated the uses for a root cellar in an urban neighborhood in the southwest. Suddenly I found myself on the ground. Leah followed and the five of us worked side-by-side, scraping and scratching at the dirt.

Several minutes later, we sat back on our haunches, sweaty, dirty, panting and marveling at our discovery—a pair of four-foot by six-foot doors. Abe's suspicion had been correct—Nicoh had been on the right path. The section he'd cleared had revealed the handles for the double doors, latched together by the same vine-like rope that was threaded through the rest of the iron eye-hooks. But it was not the door that had drawn the canine's attention. It was the vile, noxious stench that enveloped every gasp of fresh air that remained.

My eyes continued watering and I fought the urge to vomit. The others looked equally distressed and Leah's color shifted from pink to a grayish-green as she pressed the back of a filthy hand to her mouth to suppress a gag.

"What died?" she finally managed to choke out.

From the looks we gave one another, we hoped it was a matter of what...and not *who*.

CHAPTER NINETEEN

"Do you think we should call Ramirez?" I asked quietly, surprised by my own suggestion.

"He should be here soon." Abe brushed grime from his watch.

"I think we should look." Leah's voice was shaky.

"I agree." I threw my vote in but it lacked conviction.

"Elijah?" Abe prompted his brother, who gave a single head nod. "All right then, let's do this." He hefted himself from a squatted position before offering us each a hand.

"Any chance we could get him to pull this thing open?" Leah nodded at Nicoh, who sat off to the side of the cellar door, still panting and silently observing the stupid humans contemplating opening the gates to Hell.

"Not on your life," I replied, immediately regretting my choice of words.

"I'll do it," Elijah offered, trying to put on his best game face.

"*We'll* do it," his brother countered.

"Alrighty, then. What can we do?" Leah asked, with faked enthusiasm.

Abe look at each of us skeptically before replying, "Stand back. And be prepared to—"

"Wretch?" Leah offered.

"I was going to say hold your breath," Abe replied.

"I was thinking run," I added.

"That might be good, too." Abe turned to his brother. "On the count of three?"

As the countdown began, I braced myself for the worst but ended up looking like I was posing for the Heisman trophy. Leah wrapped her arms tightly around her core and absently bit her nails until she realized they were thick with the same grime permeating from beneath the wood and iron. The look on her face indicated she would have vomited on her shoes, had she not been so anxious to see beyond the cellar's doors.

The hinges moaned from the stress of being awoken as Abe and Elijah each hefted a panel. Once open, they immediately backed away and covered their faces. The stench slapped me in the face, forcing me hack out a brutal cough. I attempted wiping my mouth on a clean section of shirt but none remained, so I distracted myself from the disgusting taste by rummaging in my pocket for the tiny LED travel light I had remembered to grab from the Mini.

"I know it's not much but maybe it'll help." I waved the two-inch light, trying to sound positive, until I realized its beam only extended to the tip of my shoes.

Unimpressed with my Eddie Bauer point-of-sale impulse splurge, Abe grunted. "I've got a Maglite in the Ferrari."

Leah glanced skeptically in his direction. "Wonder where the heck he manages to keep it in that thing?"

"Says the girl who drives an SUV the size of a tennis shoe from Baby Gap," I replied.

"Huh, this coming from the girl who drives a Mini Coop while carrying ninety-eight pound canine on her lap," she retorted.

"I don't *carry* him on my lap. He sits on the front passenger seat."

She scoffed. "Ha! You've proved my point."

"Ladies, please!" Abe presented not one, but two Maglites. Speechless, Leah could only shrug after he'd handed her one.

We all crept toward the edge of our discovery—noses covered, armed with Maglites and a muddy, less than fresh-smelling canine—and peered into the gaping hole. Blackness filled the void, despite the flashlights. All that was visible from our vantage point was a set of wooden stairs that offered nothing more than a twenty-foot plunge to whatever morbidity awaited us.

"Oh my, that is…awful!" Leah attempted to reposition her hoodie so that it doubled as a mask.

"Awful doesn't even begin to cover it," I managed to choke out from beneath my shirt.

Even Nicoh rethought his curiosity and moved away to observe from a distance. I gave him a look and he returned a guttural whoo-woo. I took it as his final warning.

Abe was the first to attempt the descent. Despite the size of the opening, the stairs were narrow, not more than eighteen inches and lacked any supporting handrail or sidewall. Grasping the edge of the door to brace himself until he could no longer reach, he carefully made his way from one step to the next, checking his footing to ensure they were sturdy while using the Maglite to investigate his surroundings. He hadn't quite reached the bottom when we heard him suck in a deep breath.

"Abe? What is it?" Leah's voice cracked.

Abe continued down the steps, until he was out of view before answering, "Bro, I'll think you'd better call Ramirez. Tell him to bring his team."

"Abe?" Elijah's brow furrowed in concern.

"Just do it!" Abe snapped, causing his brother to recoil as he fumbled in his pockets in search of his phone.

"Here, use mine," I offered.

Elijah gave me a nod of thanks as he took the phone and moved toward the street to make the call. Leah, meanwhile, had perched near the top of the stairs and appeared to be weighing the pros and cons of what she was about to do. Before I could stop her, she skidded down the first half-dozen steps until she lost her balance and slipped, crashing at the bottom with a bone-crunching thud.

"Leah!" Mortified, I chased after her and barely avoided the same fate as I leapt over her and nearly collided with—

"Oh, oh!" I screeched as I came within inches of a faceless mass.

I scrambled backward but the soft dirt made the footing uneven, causing me to stumble as I struggled to keep from pitching forward. Abe caught me but dropped his Maglite in the process. It rolled to a stop at the feet of the body, illuminating the space and casting eerie shadows on our ghastly surroundings. Only the shadows weren't playing tricks.

The deceased was propped against the left-hand corner of the cellar and had it not been the sizable hole where his face had been, one would have assumed he was sleeping. The figure was male in stature, approximately six feet three inches with broad shoulders, thick arms, torso and legs, given the way his shirt and blue jeans stretched against his once taut frame. Dark cropped hair in a military cut covered what remained of his head.

Blood stained the walls, splattering every surface and transforming the clay-like dirt into the murky reddish-brown of a rusted-out car. Only this was not a vehicle, it was a dungeon for this person, whose warden had used him to create a gruesome Jackson Pollock imitation.

I tried hard not to notice the details but they stained every surface and oozed from every crevice, coating even my shoes and hands. I shuddered, all too familiar with the horrors of violence.

Of death. Of the toll it took on the human body. I tried averting my eye, focusing instead on the man's shoes. As I scrutinized the black lace-up Doc Marten boots, recognition made my heart skip a beat.

I looked at Leah to confirm she hadn't been hurt during the fall and found her on her knees, one hand clasped to her mouth. "Those boots," she whispered as I went to her side and wrapped my arms around her, as though it would shield her from the truth.

Abe and Elijah, still taking their own horrified assessment, looked at us in confusion, "The boots?" Elijah peered at the dead man's feet. One pant leg had risen up, exposing an empty holster strapped to his calf, its leather sheath empty where a knife had once been secured.

"Leah gives him…gave him crap about them. He got them in England when he was in the military and wore them every day since. She teased him that one day…" I stifled a sob and felt Leah's hot tears on my arms, "that one day he'd be buried in them." The last words came out in a whisper.

After a long moment, Abe broke the silence, "You think this is…"

"Vargas," Leah's whisper came out crackly as I hugged her fiercely, perhaps to offer her comfort or to distract my own emotions from surfacing.

I knew if I started crying, I would never stop. I was sick of losing people too soon. And while we're never prepared to lose anyone, I certainly never thought, no matter his current circumstances, the burly detective with his quick wit and undeniable presence could be reduced to this. Why Vargas? I cursed the earth his killer walked.

My thoughts were interrupted by the sound of approaching vehicles. I helped Leah to her feet and made sure she was steady enough to manage the stairs on her own. As the four of us emerged from the cellar, Nicoh waited quietly at the top, his position undisturbed. Despite the distance we'd put between ourselves and the hellish scene, the air to my lungs still felt constricted, as though death was suffocating me as punishment for being alive. The grim faces of the others told me they were feeling much the same: confused, heartsick…devastated.

I watched Ramirez approach with at least four other officers I didn't recognize in tow. The news would cause his world to come crashing down, too.

"What do we have here?" He developed a healthy frown as he surveyed each of our faces, his nose crinkling as he took in the smell.

"It's bad, Detective Ramirez," I said, showing incredible restraint in my attempt to be respectful of his position in front of his team.

He nodded toward the open cellar. "We obviously have remains down there, am I correct?"

As Abe and Elijah took turns answering Ramirez questions, I quietly stepped to the side and gave Leah's arm a reassuring squeeze. Her misery was palpable as she resumed chewing on a nail, ignoring the filth and grime. I knew she was thinking about Vargas and the last thing she'd said to him. I ventured a small glance at Ramirez and wondered what his last conversation had been with his friend. The Stantons had not yet revealed that detail and I knew no amount of preparation—no matter how tough the cop or the person—would soften the blow. Anxiety built as they walked through our steps—how we'd come to find the root cellar, our clearing of the area and descending into its depth—to our discovery of the body.

There was no reason for Ramirez to assume we knew the person's identity, especially considering the condition we'd found him in, so before anyone had a chance to tell him, he assigned tasks to his team and each dispersed in a flurry of activity, leaving him to enter the cellar first. I attempted to insert myself between him and the opening and nearly tumbled into the hole. Ramirez grabbed my arms and started a familiar lecture when I cut him off.

"There's something else you need to know, Detective. Something you need to be prepared for."

He glanced at me, less than amused, "I've seen a dead body or two in my day, AJ."

"I know, I know…just let me catch my breath."

"AJ," he growled, "not now."

"Please," I pleaded, garnering a look of concern from the sturdy detective who was still clutching my arm. "It's different when you know the person." It came out a whisper. "Believe me."

"You know who it is? I thought the victim's face was missing?"

"It is, but there were other…identifiers."

"Such as…" This time, I had his interest.

"His boots. His Doc Marten boots," I whispered. "As you well know, he notoriously fell under the category of 'never leaves home without them'…until now."

A look of surprise crossed his face. "You're not saying…"

I nodded, looking away…away from Ramirez. Away from the pit where our friend had taken his last breath, where his life had been robbed from him. "I'm sorry, Ramirez." It was all I could manage. And, if I hadn't previously thought a guy his size could move that fast, I was now a believer as he effortlessly skimmed the steps, skipping two at a time.

I started after him but was given a stern "Don't" by both Abe and Elijah, as the latter used his arm to hold me back. "Let him be."

"But…" I countered.

"AJ, trust us on this one," Abe replied.

For what seemed like a lifetime, there was nothing but silence. I could not bear to peer down at Ramirez. The time that passed before he emerged was excruciating. Though he did a stellar job of remaining stoic, he nodded in our direction before quietly relaying the information to each of his team members. Every one of them had known and worked with Vargas, so I couldn't imagine what they must be feeling. I only knew how I felt.

And it hurt like hell.

* * *

We gave our statements to one of Ramirez's team members—an officer whose name I don't remember—while the rest of the team worked. Long after we were told by another officer we were free to go, but elected to stand off at a safe distance until the body was removed.

Why we chose to stay, I had no idea. Perhaps to offer Ramirez moral support, even though he'd managed to maintain a cool exterior as he skillfully orchestrated the investigation. I admired his ability to remain professional and wondered if Vargas being his friend made it that much more important. Still, I thought it must be hard to separate the two and my heart went out to him.

Hours passed before a team of three artfully maneuvered the steps—careful in the way they handled their fellow officer— before placing him on a gurney for transport to the Medical Examiner's van. I could not bring myself to look at the body bag much less accept it would be the last time I would ever see Vargas —my memory of him now tarnished by blood and bone and the smell of decay. And death. My gaze found Ramirez and was surprised to find him looking back.

Before I could interpret his current expression, he waved us over then asked one of the Medical Examiner's assistants to wait before loading Vargas into the van. I wasn't sure what Ramirez had in mind and was glad Vargas' prone frame was covered, masking his violent disfigurement from view.

"I wanted to share something with you." I shuddered, perhaps

I had been wrong. Surely Ramirez wouldn't subject us to this sort of cruelty and force us to view our dead friend again? Leah gasped and clutched my arm as we inched forward. I'll give credit to Abe and Elijah though. Their expressions remained unchanged as we huddled around the gurney.

Once he was sure he had our attention, Ramirez continued, "I take it none of you actually touched the body?" The circulation in my arm dropped a notch under Leah's death grip as a revolted frown covered her face. I didn't dare tell him how close I'd come to sitting on Vargas' lap and frankly, didn't relish reliving the visual. After each of us shook our heads, Ramirez nodded. "Good answer. Then it's not surprising you didn't see this."

He raised a corner of the sheet, exposing Vargas' right arm. As he carefully peeled back the sleeve of the t-shirt, exposing the muscled bicep, a blueish-black mark appeared.

"What is that…a bruise?" Leah asked.

Ramirez shook his head. "Look closer."

Collectively, we leaned toward the gurney and stared at the marking. It wasn't a bruise at all, but a tattoo. Inked in a rudimentary fashion, the lines were jagged and uneven, weathered by sun…and time. As I squinted, allowing the details of the design to emerge, a single word formed. A name.

Grace.

CHAPTER TWENTY

"It's not him! It's not Jere," Leah breathed, squeezing my hand as a collective sigh of relief was released.

"I don't think so," Ramirez replied and while I could tell he was happy the body was not his friend's, it was still a very dead body. Meaning it told only a portion of the story.

"It could be Grace's ex, Darian," Leah added.

"We have to wait until the Medical Examiner's official report is released for confirmation." Despite the boilerplate law enforcement response, Ramirez offered a single head-nod.

A barrage of questions erupted as we absorbed the new information. Was it a coincidence Darian's build and features were similar to Vargas'? I personally didn't think so and though no one made a comment to that effect, we were left to wonder why he was wearing Vargas' boots. How had he crossed paths with the killer? Was he a decoy—meant to put us on the wrong track—or another means to an end?

More importantly, if this wasn't Vargas, where was he?

* * *

As our little convoy made its way home, I realized we'd never gotten to look inside Mort's house for clues. And now that it was an official crime scene, we probably never would.

We had left Ramirez with his team, still directing the flurry of activity. Though he'd agreed to stop by later, his presence would be for our friend Vargas and for our commitment to finding him and bringing him home. If, along the way, we pieced together the puzzle of this wandering tale, then justice would come full circle. But after that, I wasn't sure where Ramirez and I went. I'd broken his trust and he'd damaged my soul when he questioned my loyalty and called me naive. In the end, whether we came to a common ground, or if we failed miserably and came to an impasse, one thing was certain—I'd either lose my biological father, or I'd lose him.

I shook my head to clear the cobwebs but only managed to make it worse. Realizing I hadn't eaten in hours—and no one else had either—I called Leah before making a quick detour to Oregano's for pizzas.

Upon hearing my plan, she nearly drooled in my ear. "Oooh, Abe and Elijah will love you for that. You know it's their favorite when they're in town. Can't get a pie like that in La La Land." It was the most cheerful she'd been in a long while, now reenergized by the prospect Vargas was still alive.

"A little dough and cheese are a pretty wimpy offering, considering everything they've done to help us find Vargas. Who knew it would go to this extent or amount to so much drama."

"Somehow I don't think you're simply talking about Vargas."

"No, I suppose I'm not," I replied as my thoughts drifted to Clark; then to Martin and of course, Ramirez.

I let out an audible sigh.

"Want me to pick up a few refreshing adult beverages to pair with our tasty offering?" she asked. "Perhaps that would take your mind off the good, the bad and the ugly. I'll let you decide who is what."

Sometimes, it was hard to distinguish one from the other, I thought wryly. "Eh, better make it a round of Starbuck's—I have a feeling it's going to be a long night—and we don't need anything dulling our senses." In hindsight, perhaps there were parts I needed to forget altogether.

* * *

As expected, the Stanton brothers were both surprised and ecstatic after I arrived home with my haul, which included a couple of pizzookies—peanut butter chocolate chip pizza cookies, topped vanilla bean ice cream—for dessert if they remained on their best behavior.

I fed Nicoh while the others cleared a space in the living room for our working dinner. Despite licking his bowl clean, the temptation of stray pizza toppings was too great as he stealthily inched his way closer, making Leah his first victim. She squealed in horror as he snatched her piece. Of course, it was Nicoh who got the surprise when he realized she had added a few condiments to her slice. Unfortunately, one of them happened to be a healthy dose of Smoked Chipotle Tabasco.

We laughed as he snuffed, sneezed and made his best pucker-pooch face. "It serves you right, you thieving wretch." She jabbed a fork in his direction before returning to survey the remaining pizza options.

"So, rough day," I breached the topic we'd been chewing over in silence.

"Yeah, though I'm thrilled Vargas wasn't the one we found in that hole, we certainly managed to stumble upon on an entirely different can of worms," Elijah mumbled as he stuffed a pizza bone into his mouth.

"It definitely feels like we're back to square one," Abe replied.

"Were we ever off square one?" Leah countered. "If it was even a square to begin with—it sure feels more like a circle to me."

"I don't know. Let's look at this objectively." I placed the remainder of my slice safely out the reach of Nicoh's tongue before moving to the white boards. "We have three murders: Mort, Erica and Darian. The thing that ties the first two together is the book—a tell-all about the Gemini cloning project. We need to identify who has the most to gain by preventing its publication. It's obvious they'll do whatever it takes."

"So, why get Vargas and Grace involved?" Elijah asked.

"They were simply pawns, used to divert suspicion or cause misdirection," I replied. "And whether the real killer intended to make it appear as though one of them masterminded it or they collaborated as equal partners, it provided the police with viable suspects to focus their attention on.

"The killer selected them—singled them out—because each had a connection to Erica. Anyone doing a bit of quick research could have learned about her contentious relationship with Vargas and her undermining of Grace's career and personal life.

"That brings us to Grace's ex, Darian. It's too much of a stretch he just happened to match Vargas' physical description."

"I agree. Perhaps it was a way to throw more suspicion onto Grace or prevent her from continuing the book," Leah suggested. "But what I don't get is how the killer missed the tattoo."

I shrugged. "Maybe he didn't miss it. Maybe he just didn't care. Or didn't expect the body to be found as soon as it was, figuring decomp would take care of it."

"So what exactly is the killer doing with Vargas, then?" Elijah asked.

"I don't know but I'm pretty sure Vargas plays a role in the killer's end game," I replied.

"Which is what, exactly?" Abe posed a good question.

I thought for a moment before responding, "No idea but I have a feeling this impostor—whether he's a killer or not—has an insight into whatever it is. And who's responsible."

"How we find him?" Leah asked. "The real Daniels has been identified so his cover is blown. And now that the body has been found under the house he's been occupying, he certainly can't stick around."

I waved her off. "Not to worry, I think I know someone who can help track him down."

CHAPTER TWENTY-ONE

Martin didn't seem surprised by my call but when I shared its purpose, his tone was serious. "You told Detective Ramirez I was your father?"

"Well, technically, he already knew you were my biological father but I did mention you were the person I had met in the park. Meaning, he's now aware you are alive."

"I see." He took care in formulating his response. "I thought we had an agreement, Arianna. It was, after all, for your own safety."

I sighed at his attempted reprimand. "No Martin, you made a suggestion…a recommendation…whatever. I went along with it for as long as I could. At great cost, I might add. I certainly hope you can appreciate the effort I made until it was no longer within my power to withhold the information from him." I thought about Ramirez's face that day. The frustration. The disappointment. The betrayal he'd tried to hide when he'd known I was lying. "He followed me to the park, Martin. If I hadn't told him, he would have learned your secret some other way. And you may not have liked what he managed to unearth. He's very persistent when he wants to find the truth."

"I only wish—"

I cut him off. It was not a subject I cared to rehash. "Martin, it's too late for that. Dog's outgrown the doghouse. Move on. You're not really on Ramirez's radar at the moment. He's got more pressing things to deal with."

"Oh? There have been additional developments?"

"You could say that." I told him about finding the body at Mort's house.

He was quiet for a moment as he digested my news. "You were right to call me. Where can we meet?"

We agreed on a nearby dog park. Nicoh had been cooped up for days and his jaunt about the neighborhood with Clark didn't count as exercise. A trip to the dog park would give us both a much needed reprieve.

I thought I had made decent time and was going to use the extra minutes to review the old GenTech files Mort had given me months earlier but once again, Martin had arrived ahead of us.

His attention was on a pair of pups playfully nipping at one another in an energized mixture of whimsy and camaraderie. I wished things could be as effortless for us.

"Hello, Martin."

"Hello, my dear. And Nicoh." He bent to give Nicoh a generous round of scratches before I released him to join the pups. The two younger dogs welcomed him into their group and soon the three engaged in a game of tag.

While I kept an eye on Nicoh, Martin got down to business, or at the very least, what had been at the forefront of his mind. "You're quite sure the dead man found in the cellar was not your detective friend?"

"Vargas? No, we're fairly certain it wasn't." I told him about the tattoo and the missing bartender, who had also been the father of Grace's child.

"Interesting." Martin squinted as he mulled over the details.

I shifted topics. "Had you ever met Mort Daniels?"

"The newspaper reporter?" He shook his head but a gnawing feeling in my gut told me he wasn't being completely truthful.

"So you wouldn't have known he'd been replaced by an impostor—if you'd never met or talked to him, that is," I confirmed.

Martin turned to face me. This time, his reaction struck me as genuine. "When my associates need to get in touch with me, they contact me on a special phone. I believe you kids call them burners?" I shrugged, not familiar with the vernacular, perhaps indicating I was no longer in the group defined as "you kids." "Anyway, a woman contacted me—part of the arrangement with my associates. We never know who, or when. We just know that sooner or later, a call will come."

"I don't understand. How did you know she was legit? That someone didn't infiltrate your group of associates and give false information in an attempt to draw you out?"

He shook his head. "It doesn't work like that. We're very careful. There is a rotating call list. A sequence of calls must be made. Each person gives a code to the next and the recipient must return the correct code, otherwise the connection is broken. Once I supplied the correct information, the woman gave me a message that roughly translated to 'your daughter needs you' and so I showed up."

"Just like that?" It was a bit too loose for my taste.

Martin looked at the dogs and shrugged. "I had no reason to doubt her and after losing Victoria, I couldn't afford not to come."

His response gave me that same unsettled feeling I'd had earlier. Something about the way he'd relayed the information seemed contrived. Rehearsed. Martin was a scientist, after all. I doubted covert ops were part of his daily repertoire. Then again, the man had been underground for over twenty years. It did make me wonder about these associates. How could a dead man not know who was helping him? Or vice versa?

"So you're telling me you had no idea I'd called Mort Daniels and in turn, he managed to get through to you?" When he shook his head again, I added, "Sounds like you need a better set of associates, 'cause it sure seems like you've got a rat in the haystack." Again, he shrugged. "You are awfully calm for someone who's just been outed and probably has a target on his back."

"It's been part of my plan all along," he replied flatly.

"Geez, Martin." His lack of affect was driving me nuts. "Do you have a death wish or something?"

"Not at all. This new information could work to our advantage. It means we're getting close." He offered me a knowing look.

"So now you think Clark's prison break, his subsequent arrival here and the deaths are connected?" I asked because he hadn't been so sure before.

"Now I'm convinced they're connected," Martin replied.

"Do you think Clark is the killer?"

"I can't provide a definitive answer but if he didn't kill these people, he knows who did. Besides, I doubt he broke himself out of prison."

"So he has a team of associates, too, wouldn't you say?" I prodded.

"It's a definite possibility."

"How do you know your associates aren't his associates as well?" This gave Martin pause, the furrow in his brow deepening. "Do you have any idea who the impostor could be?"

"No, but it appears he's involved, too." I was disappointed by his response though perhaps I had expected too much.

"It does appear to be the case," I replied, "which means we no longer have the luxury of assuming he's an innocent bystander, hired to act as a stand-in for Mort Daniels. His hands are definitely dirty. So he's either being paid quite a lot or his motivations run as deep as Clark's." Even as I said it, the words gave me no comfort, realizing we were dealing with a person just as evil as Winslow Clark. "Let's assume this has to do with the book project Erica and Mort had in the works. Who would benefit from the project getting canned?"

"Currently?" Martin blew out an extended breath. "Any number of people."

"Then let's make a go at the short list. Could any of them be a part of your team?"

"I can't tell you that." He looked away, pressing his lips into a tight, unforgiving line.

"Because you don't know? Or won't tell me?"

"A bit of both, perhaps. That, and the unnecessary risk. To you and everyone else involved."

"You make them sound like a very serious bunch, Martin."

"Deadly serious, Arianna." His response sent a chill through my body as I saw of glimpse of a man I didn't know slip through the façade.

"Are you involved in criminal activity, Martin?" He laughed as the chill retreated and his calm demeanor returned. Still, he didn't answer. "Detective Ramirez thinks I should be suspicious about you and your sudden appearance."

"I couldn't argue with his assessment or blame him for it, either." The look he leveled on me—and held—indicated the conversation was not up for further discussion.

I dropped it and moved on, "Getting back to Clark. Any updates?"

He shook his head and sighed. "Much the same. We've been able to track where he's been, but not where he is currently."

"Why do you think he's been so quiet? I mean, it's not like I enjoy his cryptic text messages or having him break into my home to assault my dog." I glanced at Nicoh, who appeared to have recovered without any long-lasting effects, given the way he ran, chased and cavorted with the other dogs.

"I'm not sure you'll appreciate my thoughts on that."

I opened my hands. "I've got nothing, Martin. Try me."

"Well, based upon what I know about him—and knowing the same thing held true for his father—it can only mean one thing." I gave him a prompt to expound. "The quiet calm we're experiencing? It means he's busy plotting his end game."

I had drawn the same conclusion but had to ask, "How do you know?"

"Because it's what I would do."

* * *

When Martin spoke again, his tone was sad as he looked into the distance. "When Theodore pushed me off the bridge, every fragment of the life I had known went with me. And when I miraculously survived and decided to go underground, there was no turning back. It meant leaving no breadcrumbs and nothing to indicate I had been anything but a blip on the screen for a moment in time."

"But you left me behind. And Victoria. Along with our secrets."

"Yes, when I survived, it was my only choice. You see it now, don't you, Arianna?" His voice, as well as the sadness in his eyes, pleaded for me to believe him and somehow find it in my heart to forgive him for the choices he'd made. For abandoning us. "I only did what I thought was best. I had no idea the lengths Theodore would go or that he would foster the same hatred and resentment in his son—the need for vengeance and retribution. Resurrecting myself from the dead was the only way."

"The only way?" I shook my head. "The only way…what?"

"To end this," he raised his hands in frustration, "once and for all."

"But *I* have what they want, Martin." I pounded a fist to my chest. "*I* alone have the chips."

"True..." his voice was slow and calm. He'd given this a great deal of thought. "But I can offer them something you can't."

"Something more than the chips? And me dead?" I asked, incredulous. "What more could they want?"

"Oh, there's always more, Arianna."

"So when you said it was part of your plan all along..."

"I plan on offering them the icing on the cake, so to speak. What I'd be offering them...is me."

Perhaps Martin was ready to seal—or reseal—his fate, but I didn't need him prodding mine in the same direction. "And you think once they have you, they won't need me?" I shook my head. "How, Martin? I have the information."

"As do I, my dear." He tapped the side of his head, offering me a small smile, which did nothing to bolster my confidence.

"You know *everything* that's on those chips?"

He shrugged, shoving his hands into his pockets. "I know enough to make them believe I do."

"Surely you realize you're making yourself a pawn?" I was beyond exasperated and it was all I could do to not give him a good, solid shaking. "Once they get what they need, they'll kill you." Of that, I was quite certain. Then, they'd hurt everyone I'd ever cared about. Or worse. They'd make me witness it before putting me out of my own misery. This plan was sounding worse by the minute.

"It won't ever get that far, Arianna," he replied. "There are... people...who will want them dealt with."

I held no affection for Clark but the tone in Martin's voice suggested these people wanted to do a little more than have a friendly chat with Clark and his minions. "Dealt with, as in killed?" my voice crackled, as if merely speaking the words would put things—bad things—into motion. "And these people—they are your *associates*?" I raised an eyebrow.

He chuckled, realizing the conclusion I had drawn. "They are not vigilantes, Arianna. Think of them as a group of concerned citizens—individuals with the means to monitor certain types of situations and react accordingly." Another chill ripped through me as the crap-meter amped up a notch.

For now, I'd play along. "Like a neighborhood watch?"

Martin nodded. "Only on a broader scale with better connections. And funding."

"Care to share the MVPs on this team?"

"That's all you need to know."

"For now? Or forever?" I pressed.

He shook his head, putting out a hand to stop me. "That's all I can tell you."

"Alrighty then…" I was getting nowhere with the 'who' of this conversation, I needed to change tactics with him and focus on the 'what.' "You still haven't told me what you're intentions are with Clark and his cohorts? Will you…will your associates kill them?"

"Would it bother you if they did?" He raised an eyebrow at me. "After everything they have done?"

I was weary of the runaround. "Just answer the question, Martin."

He sighed. "It wouldn't be our intention, Arianna, but Clark's already chosen his path."

My laugh came out harsh. "Yeah, well, up to this point his path seems to be interfering with mine."

"And yet you worry how he will be treated in the end." It was Martin's turn to lay on the sarcasm. I gave him credit—he was pretty good at it. Perhaps I was more like him than I'd wanted to believe. The thought nearly gave me a rash.

"Not worried. I'd just like to know what type of people we're dealing with here. What type of people *you're* dealing with."

His eyes crinkled and the corner of his mouth turned up. Frankly, it annoyed me he was getting any entertainment value out of this conversation. "Why, Arianna? Are you concerned your father is into something corrupt?"

"My biological father, Martin." I corrected. The smile quickly dropped from his face. "And my concern runs more along the lines of the company you keep."

"I see." Oh, I doubted he did. Even if he'd caught a glimpse of what I was thinking, he'd not even touched the tip of the iceberg. He was still safely standing on the shore looking at the world through binoculars.

"Just so we're clear." I pointed a finger at him and called Nicoh to my side. Winded from the energetic play with his new friends, he came reluctantly but allowed me to clip his lead. "I'm all for taking Clark and his cohorts down but we do this by the book or we don't do it at all. If you or any member of your secret club takes them out, or makes them go poof, I will unleash Ramirez and his team on you like a pack of rabid dogs. Whether you're my *father* or not."

CHAPTER TWENTY-TWO

Once again, Martin had been evasive and I'd only managed to confirm things I'd already ventured a best-guess at, though it had been intriguing to learn in the years since his supposed death, Martin had made acquaintances with some very powerful, motivated individuals. Not knowing his level of involvement with them concerned me. While I knew Clark's end game, how could I be sure the one Martin's associates were playing wasn't the same?

It irritated me to admit Ramirez might have been on the money when he called me out on my naivety where Martin was concerned. Of course, when I pulled up to my house and found his police cruiser in the driveway, I decided I wasn't prepared to allow him to gloat. I looked at Nicoh, who'd slobbered all over the front seat, dashboard and console in his attempt to cool down after a hard hour of play. Seeing Ramirez's vehicle gave him a second wind and he grumbled a low moan of impatience as I collected my belongings, along with my wits and prepared for the confrontation.

Nicoh trotted into the house, while I took more time than usual to scale the stairs and greet my housemate and our guests, who were gathered in the living room, engrossed in something

Ramirez was relaying. He paused when I entered and scrutinized my expression.

"How'd it go?" he asked wryly.

I shot a glance at Leah. "You told him?"

"Don't look at me," she huffed. "The man's got super spidey senses. When he arrived and you were the only one MIA, he drew his own conclusions."

"I suppose…considering you're here…you had someone follow me." I could not face him but felt the heat of his gaze.

"I did not," he replied, his tone even. "Leah was correct, I drew my own conclusions and she didn't deny it."

"I didn't utter a single word, Detective," Leah replied indignantly, rose to her feet and placed curled fists on her hips.

"It wasn't what you said, Leah, it's what you didn't say. Your body language betrayed you."

"You keep your eyes off my body…language, Detective," she growled. "You are so on my crap list."

Ramirez appeared only mildly amused. "You mean you've downgraded me? I would have assumed I was on some sort of other unsavory list of yours by now."

"That's her department. Talk to her." She hooked a thumb in my direction.

"My lists are currently not up for discussion," I retorted, "but now that you're all here, I have a few other things I'd like to share. Of course, you could go first if you like, Detective?"

"Oh…no, no…you're house, you've got the floor. I'm dying to hear what you've learned."

He pursed his lips as I mustered my best teacher voice before detailing my conversation with Martin. I concluded with a few final thoughts on the subject, including my curiosity surrounding the identity of Martin's cohorts.

Ramirez's mouth twitched. "I hope you urged Martin to let the authorities handle this matter. That any interference by outside individuals, whether attempting to track, capture, detain Clark, or otherwise—"

I felt a lecture coming on and faked a yawn before cutting Ramirez off, "Would result in being charged with obstruction of justice. I know the drill, Detective. And yes, I did mention it to him but…"

"But?" Ramirez prompted.

"Martin's a big boy and not my concern. Whatever lines he crosses are all on him."

"Hmm, changing your tune on the old man, are you?"

Ramirez dangled the licorice rope in front of me but for once, I managed to keep my sweet tooth under wraps, moving the conversation elsewhere. "You came here for a reason, didn't you, Detective?"

My directness earned me a tight smile and an uncomfortable shifting of seats from Abe and Elijah.

"The Detective had just started sharing his latest fashion tips." Thank goodness for Leah, who always managed to make the awkward moments less awkward. Less awkward for me, anyway.

"So, what does this Fashion Policeman have to say for himself?" I crooked an eyebrow at Ramirez, who was not even remotely amused.

"I can boil my couture tips and tricks down to one word, Ladies—handcuffs." Belatedly, he realized he'd stepped into it, as Leah gave him a ferocious growl.

"Oh, Detective! You know all the right things to say to a lady." She winked and blew him a kiss.

Temporarily flustered, Ramirez coughed. "I might have used the term 'ladies' a bit loosely." He must have been tired otherwise our usual shtick wouldn't have ruffled his feathers so easily. I ventured a glance at Leah and found her grinning unabashedly. "Now that we've gotten that out of the way, I do have a few points of interest. First, I was able to obtain Erica's text and email conversations with

Daniels." He gave me a sideways glance. "What? You thought I'd forgotten?" Shaking my head, I gestured for him to proceed.

"Much like Grace's, they are in all caps and fairly nondescript. That is—until we dug up the correspondence before Daniels went missing. Here, see for yourselves." He pulled a few sheets of paper from an accordion-style file folder and spread them across the coffee table.

We crowded around the pages and based upon the diction and depth of details after Leah read a few of the threads aloud, it was plain to see a different author had crafted this email than the one who had pieced together the blocky, nondescript correspondence.

"To confirm, the *Chicago Tribune* supplied us with samples Daniels had written when he served as the bureau chief." Ramirez laid a few more sheets in front of us. Clearly, Erica's original correspondence had been with the real Mort Daniels.

"No wonder she was so agitated. Not only was she unable to get a face-to-face with him, but his written correspondence had gone from outlining the book and providing all the nitty-gritting details—to nada." Leah pointed at the radically different correspondence.

"If Erica put two and two together, maybe she tripped the impostor up or threatened to expose him in some way. Suddenly, the cat's out of the bag and bye-bye Erica." Several heads nodded in agreement.

Even Ramirez seemed mildly intrigued. "Too rough around the edges to be a working theory but it does have some teeth to it."

Leah supplied her two cents. "It sounds like something Erica would have done. She wouldn't have passed up an opportunity to make another person look bad. No matter how much she needed them."

"Unfortunately, it could have been her downfall," I added.

Leah looked thoughtful. "Especially if she started poking around."

I nodded. "She would have gone from cash cow-ess to a liability, though chances are she already was one. A liability, that is. But perhaps she served a greater purpose as long as she was alive." Having worked with the gal, Leah looked doubtful.

"Maybe they needed to find out what she knew," Elijah offered.

"Or maybe they needed her to *tell* them what she knew?" I suggested.

"Meaning, something they weren't already aware of?" Leah worked the idea like Silly Putty in her mind.

"You don't think Erica knew about Martin, do you?" Abe piped in.

"If that were the case, wouldn't it mean Mort Daniels also knew and was likely the one who told her?" Elijah countered.

"It's very likely." Leah was warming up to the idea. "AJ, what if that inside source Mort mentioned really was Martin?"

"I honestly don't know. Martin denied it when I brought it up. You have to consider what was at stake for him at the time. Not just the project but his relationship with Alison. Plus there was her pregnancy to consider. He would have been burning the candle at both ends."

"Maybe he's just that good of an actor." Up to this point, Ramirez had been quietly watching our banter.

"Yeah, AJ, he's played dead exceptionally well for over twenty years," Elijah replied.

"That is true." I was reminded of the undercurrents that washed over me each time I had spoken to him. I couldn't deny Martin had been less than honest, but about which parts?

"Of course, one thing we've got to remember, if Erica knew about Martin then Grace could have known, too," Abe added.

I shook my head, out of my league when it came to those two. "I don't know…Leah?"

She tapped her chin. "Interesting point but if Erica thought certain details could be of potential value, she would have withheld them from Grace until she'd gotten everything from them she could. That means she would have still been hanging onto them when she died. It does present another item for consideration. If Erica had known about Martin then she could have also known about you." Her eyes were wide with excitement. "And if she had identified other players, she could have been sitting on a gold mine."

I was thinking more of a land mine but didn't say it, leaving Ramirez to interject, "We can certainly follow-up with Grace but for the time-being, let's work under the assumption Erica knew something more about the Gemini project—something that got her killed. We can agree the book deal drew the players out, but there would have been other ways for interested parties to have put the nix on it. They wouldn't have had to murder three people to do it." He nodded toward our white board, where pictures of the victims were displayed. "There has to be something more to the story that would not only draw Clark out, but whoever else had a stake in the game." Ramirez moved away from the board and began pacing. "At the end of the day, those stakes have resulted in three dead people, one that's missing and others—including Grace and everyone in this room—that are in potential danger."

The room was unusually quiet for several minutes, minus the sounds of Nicoh gnawing on a rawhide bone before Ramirez continued, "On a separate note, the crime lab came back with some interesting results on one of the sources of blood found at Erica's house."

"Please tell me the initial findings were wrong and it wasn't Vargas'?" Leah pressed her eyes shut.

"While the third source has yet to be identified, some of the blood found at the scene was Vargas'. But unlike Erica's, neither his nor the unknown source were fresh," he replied.

Leah opened one eye and squinted at him. "Err…what do you mean they weren't fresh? Are you saying they've got rotten blood?"

Ramirez shook his head. "It means the blood had been extracted then frozen before it was distributed throughout the house—*after* Erica's murder."

"Which means the blood is circumstantial and could have been placed there by Erica's assailant," I offered. "What about Vargas' knife? It certainly seems plausible if one piece of evidence was placed at the scene, then others could have been to, doesn't it?"

Ramirez nodded. "We can hope law enforcement, the prosecutors, etc. will come to the same conclusion. Unfortunately, we still don't know where he is, or who that third source of blood belongs to. And like you, they're running out of leads."

"At this point we're holding out for a miracle, considering every trail has dried up," Elijah replied.

"A miracle would be Vargas coming home on his own, in one piece," Leah replied. Everyone nodded in agreement. While Ramirez's news was better than we had expected, it wasn't the ace we needed.

I shifted the conversation away from Vargas. "What about the bartender, Darian—was he just collateral damage—another means to distract the cops? If so, why was the killer so sloppy with the tattoo?"

Ramirez ground his teeth, incensed by the level of subterfuge the criminals were willing—and arrogant enough—to attempt. "It certainly helped he was of the same size and build and had similar features to Vargas. I'm sure the intent was to slow us down. As for the tattoo, it could have just been an oversight, or the killer thought he had more time to remove it."

"Or the body would decay to a point it wouldn't matter," I added.

"That too," Ramirez replied.

"What about Mort's house? We never did make our way inside after the business with the cellar." I shuddered. "Were there any more surprises found there? Any other hidey-holes?" Leah's coloring turned a lovely puce. Even though I had been the one to pose the question, I also fought the urge to dry-heave.

Ramirez shook his head in disappointment. "Nada. It had been cleaned. As in Mr. Clean."

That caught Leah's interest and returned her coloring to a more healthy shade. "Oh! A professional?" Of course, she also had a bit of a crush on Mr. Clean, despite the fact he never inspired her to do any actual cleaning.

"Would be my guess," Ramirez replied. "They are using ground-penetrating radars on the rest of the property but at last check, hadn't come across any other disturbances in the ground."

"I assume by 'disturbances' you are referring to underground death chambers?" Leah asked.

"That would be correct. And no other bodies." Another gag reflex went into overdrive.

"Well, for Vargas' sake, I'm glad to hear it, though I'm also disappointed the contents of the house yielded nothing," I replied. "Are you sure we can't go inside to see if there's something the crime scene techs missed?" Ramirez shook his head in the negative.

I was tempted to use the opportunity to point out there wouldn't have been any crime scene had it not been for our discovery, but was interrupted by the doorbell. I started to move toward it but Ramirez used his forearm to stop me.

"Hold on, AJ. Let me." He moved out of the living room

toward the front door. He hadn't given instructions otherwise, so I slipped in behind him with Nicoh on my left flank, serving as my wingman.

I heard a surprised "Oh!" as Ramirez opened the door.

After peering through the crook in his arm, I managed to squeak out my own response before receiving a glare reminding me I had been told to stay put. "Grace?"

"AJ?" Her eyes were wide as she attempted to capture a glimpse of me around Ramirez's massive frame.

Ignoring Ramirez's hard stare, I pretended he was merely an obstruction and elbowed him in the side. "Come on you big lug, don't just stand there. Let the girl in." Ramirez squinted as he formulated an appropriate retort. Considering the company, he thought better of it and stepped aside.

"Come on in, Grace. You already know Detective Ramirez but I'll introduce you to the others," I gestured toward the living room, where Leah gave her a quick hug as I introduced her to Abe and Elijah. "So, what can we do for you?"

"Oh, it's what I can do for you. I came to deliver a message to you, AJ." She looked from me to the others. I nodded, giving her the go-ahead to relay it in their presence. "A man contacted me at the office—said his name was Martin. Nothing else, just Martin. When I pressed him, he said you'd know who he was?"

I nodded. "You could say in a manner of speaking, I know Martin better than most." Ramirez's gaze pierced mine, his expression unreadable.

If Grace noticed, she made no mention. "Okay, then. Martin said it was urgent I deliver the message in person immediately— that it could mean life or death," she paused, looking at me with curiosity before continuing. "He wanted me to tell you he'd made good on his word and had tracked down the information you discussed. After doing so, he was able to make a trade for the item you've been looking for." I kept my expression neutral for the benefit of the others while my stomach did flip-flops. "He also said to tell you to expect a text message with the location of that item." I bit my lip. What had Martin gone and done now?

Grace shook her head. "Not that I understood a word of what he said, but the last part of the conversation really had me scratching my head. Before signing off, he apologized for the loss of my ex-husband and said if he'd done anything to perpetuate the situation, it hadn't been his intention." She squinted at me. "Any idea what he meant by that?"

My stomach sank as I realized Grace was not yet aware Darian had been found at Mort's. No one did, as the body had yet to be officially identified by the Medical Examiner's office. Martin only knew because I had told him and inadvertently assumed they had been married.

"Sorry, my…Martin assumed you were married." I glanced at the others. How were we going to tell her the father of her child was on a slab in the ME's office, missing most of his face after being held captive in an underground dungeon? Ramirez gave me a single head shake, indicating I was not to go there. Leah saw it and pursed her lips. Like me, she believed Grace had a right to know. I looked at Grace and found her watching our silent exchange with growing curiosity.

When none of us elaborated, she tossed in her own shocker, "Yeah, well, actually, I *was* married to Darian."

"You…were married…to Darian." My tone was flat. How could this have slipped our radar? I glanced at Leah, who shrugged, not having been aware of this bombshell either.

Grace gave a small wave and chuckled. "Oh, most people didn't know. We ran off to Vegas over one Labor Day weekend— this was before I got pregnant. His parents made us get it annulled once we got back. So the 'marriage' lasted all of six minutes. We were stupid kids, yada yada. Surprised your friend Martin even knew about it." As I looked around the room, it was clear she wasn't the only one curious how Martin had managed to obtain that little detail. "So, I hate to make this about me, but why would he think Darian was dead?"

"Err…about that. Maybe you should sit." I gestured to the couch, avoiding eye contact with Ramirez as I sat beside her and after Leah followed suit, we took turns telling her about our trip to Mort's, finding the root cellar and the body of man who bore the tattoo "Grace."

She took the news remarkably well and her response was as telling as it was surprising, "Honestly, I wouldn't wish something like that on anyone—I almost hate to say it—but for people like Erica and Darian, when you start dancing in the Devil's playground, at some point, he's gonna start collecting a cover charge."

I couldn't disagree with her. Only in my world, the Devil sends his minions to do the dirty work.

CHAPTER TWENTY-THREE

Heading off any further discussion, Ramirez called for a patrolman to escort Grace back to her office. She was relieved when we suggested the officer stay with her while she worked, but reluctant about missing an opportunity to press me for more details surrounding the cryptic message she'd been asked to deliver. Unfortunately, as much as I liked Grace, I wasn't prepared to divulge my relationship with Martin or the specifics of the item he had referenced—if not for her own safety, then for the rest of ours.

Once she was safely on her way, Ramirez turned to me. "I'd like to know what Martin meant."

"So would I," Abe added.

If I could have rolled my eyes without drawing attention I would have. I'd known I wasn't going to dodge this line of questioning forever. "Martin suggested offering himself to Clark so he would leave me alone. Personally, I think it's a stupid plan." I shrugged.

"He shouldn't be attempting anything in the first place," Ramirez growled.

"I'm not going to argue with you, Detective, but what do you expect me to do about it? Like I told you before, Martin's a big boy." This time I did roll my eyes. The sneer I received for my effort told me it was not appreciated.

"What do you think he meant about returning the item you were looking for?" I shrugged, hoping that would suffice but Ramirez was dogged. "You said Martin's associates had been able to track Clark but hadn't nailed down his location?"

"Yup, that's what he told me." Ramirez jingled his handcuffs, apparently in no mood for brevity.

"Then how did he manage to make contact in such a short time?" He gritted his teeth.

I released an exasperated breath. "I don't know, Ramirez. Maybe rather than worrying about where Clark was, he concentrated on where he'd been." The last bit made him look like he gulped down a glass of sour milk.

"Perhaps you should try calling him." It wasn't a suggestion.

I shook my head, suddenly aware of the others carefully watching our volley. "I don't think so, Ramirez. If Martin went to the trouble of asking Grace to deliver the message, we should stick to his plan and wait for the text."

"What do you guys make of that, anyway?" Leah asked. "Don't you think it was pretty risky for him to contact her using Grace? And why?"

Something made me wonder if it wasn't to ensure all the players were safe before he put his plan in motion. Made sense, considering Ramirez had provided security for Grace and the rest of us were already together. I wondered how Martin knew Ramirez would be with us to do so. I shook my head at my own stupidity—Martin had his associates watching Ramirez, too.

It was difficult keeping all the players straight, especially considering I didn't know who any of them were. Or how many there were. Remembering what I had said to Martin about the rat in the haystack, it also made it difficult to figure out which side they were on. What if there weren't any sides? What if there were only pawns to be traded? Everything had a price. And a cost. Something to be gained and something to be lost.

Suddenly, I knew what Martin had done.

"Oh, Martin…no…" I muttered, more loudly than I had anticipated, drawing a round of stares. "I know what he's trading."

Before I could explain, my cell phone alerted me to an incoming text message, the sender unknown.

Four sets of eyes were on me as I read it aloud, "Look outside."

"And?" Leah prompted.

I shook my head, my voice coming out a whisper, "There's nothing more." But there wouldn't be, would there…unless…

Surprising everyone, I ran to the front door and like one of those bumbling idiots fresh out of a campy horror movie, threw it open and raced out, ignoring Ramirez's warning growl behind me. Heavy footsteps told me he wasn't far behind. Not to be deterred, I ran down the steps, toward the end of the driveway. Even his shocking display of profanity did not distract me. If I made it through this day, I'd make him pay for it later.

"AJ!" Ramirez yelled as I broke into a full sprint, running toward what, I had no idea.

I only hoped I looked more like an Olympic runner barreling to the finish line than a bad imitation of Steve Martin in *The Jerk*. Had it been Leah, she would have taken either scenario as long as her hair looked good while she was doing it. I chuckled, amused by the thoughts I used to distract my mind until they caught up with my body.

And that's when I saw it. A giant mass covered in burlap and bound together by thick rope, just beyond the shrubs at the end of the driveway, where the pavement met the street. Had I not known better, it looked as though I had received an oversized shipment of Idaho potatoes.

Panicked, but filled with enough adrenaline to fuel a race car at the Daytona 500, I crossed the mental finish line and dropped to my knees, tearing at the knots with my bare hand in an attempt to work them free. Before I could finish the first, Ramirez was next me and together we tore at the restraints. Abe and Elijah joined us while Leah clung to an agitated Nicoh. It was hard to ignore the dark stains that mottled the material and the smell that permeated from within. I could hear my heart beating as sweat trickled down my face. I tried not to focus on the horror in front of me. Work the knots, I silently chanted to myself. Don't look at the blood. Work the knots.

After several minutes of getting nowhere fast, Ramirez broke from the group, ran to his cruiser and pulled a utility knife. Tossing his phone to Leah as he passed, he shouted for her to call 9-1-1. I moved back as he worked the knife against the rope, fraying it until it snapped. Free of restraints, we scrambled to uncover the burlap-covered heap.

Leah released an ear-splitting scream when a lump of bloodied flesh was revealed. An arm. I moved toward what I assumed would be the head and flipped back a section of material, bracing myself for the worst. Still, horror washed over me and I let out a horrified wail when I digested what had once been a ruggedly handsome face.

Vargas' eyes were swollen shut and a flap of skin had been ripped from his cheek, exposing bone. His lips were cracked and dried with blood, partially from dehydration, partially from the assault. As we removed the remainder of the material, we found him bound in a fetal position, secured with more rope. Ramirez carefully worked the bindings while I gently pulled them away from Vargas' skin, wincing as flesh peeled.

"They're bound so deep," I murmured, my voice shaky.

Ramirez's voice comforted me as he whispered in my ear. "Just take it easy, AJ. You're doing fine." As I removed the last binding, Abe and Elijah helped us roll Vargas onto his back. It was all I could do not to survey his wounds, bleeding through torn cotton and denim. Several bones appeared to be skewed at odd angles and his bare feet showed signs of disjointed, if not broken bones.

I tore my gaze from Vargas' unmoving form, pressing my head on his chest, not caring whether I became coated in the same blood, sweat, grime and muck. I could barely hear it but it was there—a tiny, frail rhythm of heartbeats.

"He's breathing." My lip quivered and tears streamed down my face as the emotion I'd been withholding washed over me. I let them fall. Their heat burned my cheeks and still, I welcomed them. "Call 9-1-1!"

"Already done!" Leah shouted. Her eyes glinted with tears and hope. She quickly dabbed them away. "Backup's on the way, too, Ramirez."

The detective nodded as he assessed the damage. Vargas had been badly beaten. Angry cuts lashed every piece of flesh that was exposed and his clothing was reduced to bloody shreds. He was filthy and given the musty, rotting odor that rolled from him, it was clear he'd been cooped up for a while. I was betting he'd been in Mort's cellar at some point.

Looking at all the blood, I began to wonder if perhaps some of it wasn't Vargas', but the dead bartender's. I shuddered, my eyes drifting to meet Ramirez's. If I'd hoped for comfort, he was fresh out, his eyes black and fists clenched as he thought of the monster he would seek out, whatever the cost.

The driveway soon swarmed with activity, as both law enforcement and medical assistance arrived. After giving my statement and ensuring Vargas was being well cared for, I firmly grasped Nicoh's lead and treaded up the street, away from the sounds. Away from the nightmares.

"Just going around the block. In need some...fresh air," I

shouted over my shoulder, refusing to look back at my friend's haunted, sullen faces when they called to me, as though the path ahead would offer an escape from what I'd left behind.

When would I ever learn?

No sooner than I had cleared the end of the block, my cell phone buzzed. I half-expected another adjective-filled reprimand from Ramirez.

"I'm still within line-of-sight, Detective. Surely you can see my ponytail bouncing?" I tried keeping my tone even but came off sounding more irritated than I had intended.

"Now that's an offer I've definitely been looking forward to," the voice oozed into my ear, like a vat of slugs. Only this slug had a name.

Clark.

"What do you want?" I avoided turning around—no need to put the others on alert—instead using my peripheral vision to peer from side to side.

Clark huffed, "What? No friendly kiss hello? At the very least I would have expected you to ask about the moldy prison bologna on white."

I snorted, processed animal parts—ridden with mold or otherwise—were too good for the likes of him. "A lot of people are looking for you, Clark."

"By people, I assume you mean Ramirez?" It was his turn to emit an amused snort.

I shrugged, as though he could see me. "And others."

He laughed, that same annoying sound I remembered so well. "If you're referring to Ramirez's porky friends, it looks like they have their hands full with other matters."

"I thought you were too busy breaking out of prison and ruining lives to care about the police, Clark? Maybe you're the one who's gone all soft and doughy?"

He laughed, the sound grated on my already impatient nerves.

"I have missed you, Arianna Jackson. But then again, you weren't really talking about Ramirez and the doughboy set, were you? You were referencing your dear old dad and his wiley friends."

My tone was flat, I would concede nothing. "My father is dead, Clark. My mother, too, thanks to your handiwork."

"Come on Arianna, did you really forget who you were dealing with? Stop babbling. That's not the daddy I was talking about, and you know it."

"If you say so."

"I say Marty and his friends are too darn slow. And old. It's probably time for me to put Papa Bear out of commission. He's been a bad boy for far too long. And honestly, I'd thought you'd be pleased, Arianna."

I kept my tone neutral. Clark had always been quite a braggart and loved to talk. If I was going to have to hose slime out of my ear for a month having to listen to this annoying piece of shoe gum, I might as well get something useful out of it. "Pleased about what?"

"Pleased he was dead, obliterated, once and for all. He didn't save your sister, after all. And his presence will only ensure your demise." His tone turned congenial, almost pleasant, "Why not help me? We could team up, take him down together."

I laughed harshly. "What? Like the Wonder Twins? I think I'll pass. But, for the sake of old times, let's say you're right about Martin Singer…"

A snort pierced my eardrum. "Give me a break, Arianna, we've already established that."

"Perhaps you had. Getting back to your…offer. What do you care about an old man?"

He scoffed. "I could care less if he had ceased to exist as originally planned the day he plunged off that bridge."

"The day your father helped him off the bridge," I clarified, just to be sure we kept the playing field even. Not that I was a huge advocate of Martin's but the events of that day on the bridge had been no fault of his own.

"'Helped'…now *that's* an interesting way to phrase it. And interesting you would have drawn that conclusion. Perhaps I've underestimated you?" I had no clue what he was mumbling about. Then again, Clark was like that when he was full of himself. In my experience, that tended to be most of the time.

"So, if you could care less about whether he 'ceased to exist,' then why are we talking about him? Why do you care what he does? Or with who?"

"Knowledge is power, Arianna. And those with the power…"

I feigned a yawn. Geez, where I had I heard that before? "Been staying up late watching too many of those self-empowerment infomercials again, I see."

"Fine, Arianna," Clark was annoyed, his tone flat, "let's get down to business. Martin has something I want. Something he took from me and my father. And now that he's popped out of his gopher hole, I expect him to return it." He paused for a moment before continuing, "Of course, in using you to draw him out, I had no idea I'd end up getting a two-for-one."

"Go on," I prompted.

"I figured I'd have to use you as collateral but then Martin showed up and offered me a better deal."

"I'm still listening, Clark."

"Turns out, Daddy wanted to make good with his little girl, so instead of making a trade for you—the trade I'd assumed it would take—"

"He made it for Vargas."

"Now *that's* Daddy's girl." I heard a clapping sound in the background and wished I could force my fist through the receiver. Perhaps Apple could work that into an application and call it the iSlug.

"And now that you've got your copsicle back, I'm calling in another favor."

"From me?" I couldn't wait to hear this proposal.

"If you don't want to lose another parent, you'll give me what I want."

I groaned inwardly. He could mean only one thing: the chips. Martin had served himself up to save my friend, thinking the knowledge he had would suffice. Instead, he'd signed both of our death warrants.

"How much time do I have to decide?"

Clark snorted, "If that cop reaches the ER and I don't see your shining face, it's bye bye Marty."

"But, they're already gone, Clark. There *is* no time." I raked my hand through my hair, my mind racing.

"That's why I always come prepared, Arianna." This time, the voice I heard wasn't in my ear.

It was behind me.

As I turned, something was pressed into my back and as I fell to the ground, Nicoh let out an unearthly whine.

As darkness swelled around me, I pleaded with my captor, "Please don't kill my dog."

I was rewarded with a cruel, unforgiving laugh.

CHAPTER TWENTY-FOUR

Despite feeling like I'd been hit by a Humvee, I found nothing bound or broken when I awoke on an unforgiving concrete surface. The pinprick of light overhead did little to illuminate my surroundings but after hitting my head, realized I had propped myself in the corner of two wood-paneled walls. I jerked as something touched my right shoulder. Looking up, I found it belonged to the handle of a broom, hanging alongside several other gardening tools. The area smelled musty, a combination of old dirt and fertilizer.

Searching for my cell phone, I wasn't surprised to find it missing. I hoped Clark hadn't ditched it. Or worse, was using it. I bristled at the thought of that jerk racking up minutes. I looked at the broom and made a mental note. It might just come in handy.

The sound of breathing told me I wasn't alone. I felt the ground and came into contact with something furry and long—a tail. Familiarity washed over me as I found Nicoh's chest. The rise and fall was shallow but he was alive. I moved to his muzzle and found his breath warm and tongue damp as it lolled against my hand. Relief washed over me—my brave boy had been spared.

"I love you, Nicoh," I whispered, before leaning back on my haunches and cautiously rising to my feet.

I didn't get far before ramming my shins into various unmovable objects. Sucking in a deep breath and collecting every ounce of superpower I could muster, I counted the steps I had taken. If my calculations were correct, the open space I had traveled was roughly sixty by ninety feet.

Now if I could only see my surroundings. The flashlight app on my phone certainly would have come in handy but that was long gone. I couldn't reach the light source but it appeared to filter in from the outside. I knew it hadn't been light out when Clark had accosted me. Had I been out of commission for that long? Something about the way it fluoresced struck me. It was similar to the lights on the security cameras the Stantons had just installed. Horror washed over me as I realized I was being filmed. The thought of Clark watching me was both revolting and maddening.

I grabbed the broom handle and jabbed at the spot, which yielded me nothing. I half-expected Clark to come on via intercom—channeling his best *Wizard of Oz* voice—but the beady eye continued to stare. I flipped the broom over so that the bristle side was up and offered a sneer before positioning it over the light.

After taking an inventory of the other gardening tools left at my disposal, I decided Rake and Shovel were my new best friends. Not that I had anything against the hoe—despite the fact they always seemed to get the bad rap and ended up on the raw end of the deal—I selected the shovel as it suited my current needs and continued to survey my surroundings, limited as they were.

I had yet to locate an entrance to the space and selected the wall—or what I assumed to be a wall—farthest from where I had started. Inching forward, I used Mr. Shovel as my tour guide to unmovable objects. I soon found the expedition to be a fruitless one, not having determined where the door was, much less a suitable escape route. I returned to the corner and plopped down to contemplate my next plan of attack, which entailed whapping the business-end of Mr. Shovel against the wall housing my new besties. The sound…echoed.

After giving my new friend a pat on the head for good behavior, I began rapping my knuckles against various sections of the wall. Finding it hollow, I moved to the other side of the corner and was rewarded with the same result. Was it possible I was somewhere someone could hear me?

Like a crazed lunatic, I yelled for assistance while using my weight to bang Mr. Shovel against every surface within reach. Suddenly, the ground shifted. Only, it wasn't the ground. It was the walls. Moving. Up. Light filtered in, illuminating my feet and ankles as they creaked upward. I grabbed Hoe and Rake and together with Mr. Shovel, we flattened ourselves on the ground, preparing for whatever awaited us.

I squinted as my eyes adjusted to the harsh fluorescence. My escape route quickly evaporated into another wrong turn as I took in the smug expression of the form looming in the distance. Scrambling to my feet, I dropped Hoe and Rake in the process, but managed to secure a firm grip on trusty Mr. Shovel. I looked for cover but Clark had already spotted me. He perused me from head to toe in way that made me want to gag and punch him in the throat.

I took the opportunity to survey him in kind, noting his tousled locks were blonder than they had previously been, which made his ocean-colored eyes even more piercing. His attire was also uncommonly casual. I hadn't thought a black t-shirt and Levis would have occurred to him. Of course, the last time I'd seen him, he'd been sporting a designer suit belonging to another one of his victims—his brother.

"Tell Paolo I love the new do." Clark preened like a peacock when he noticed I was squinting at his perfect highlights.

"What did you do to him?" My voice cracked from dehydration but the tone was clear. If he dared harm a follicle on Paolo's perfectly gelled hair, I would rip Clark's blonde strands out one by one. And fully enjoy it. Didn't he know how hard it was to find a decent stylist in this town?

Clark clucked, dismissing me with a hand. "Not to worry, Paolo's still Lord of the Salon, overcharging clients for his services and up-selling them with unnecessary product." He shook his head in disgust, while I snorted. "By the way, Arianna, looks like those ends are due for a bit of a trim. Too bad I informed Lord Paolo you would be otherwise occupied. Indefinitely." He tapped his chin. "Of course, perhaps he thought you and I were off to have ourselves a little tryst."

I snorted in disgust. "Not even if you dipped me into a fryer and made me into a deep-fried mushroom."

"That could be arranged, my dear," Clark replied, his smile laced with malice.

"Where are we?" Looking around, I noticed several old projector parts and film reels. Remnants of cameras and light casings had been tossed into piles, while more faux walls and risers were haphazardly strewn in every direction.

"Old public television station," Clark's tone was congenial, as though we were old friends. We were not. "Went out of business many years ago. My father bought it 'as is' in an auction sometime after that, figuring the space would come in handy."

"Handy for a safe house," I replied. No wonder Martin and his team had a hard time tracking him down. If memory served, a few of the old stations had been located in warehouse districts scattered throughout the metropolitan Phoenix area, meaning we could literally be anywhere.

"Homey, isn't it?" Clark waved his hand like a game show

hostess presenting the latest prizes. "Your guest accommodations were the home and garden set. I thought you'd see the humor in it, given the lack of green thumb at your own abode."

I ignored his last quip, no matter how on the mark he might have been. "I would have thought the Phoenician or the Biltmore, the Scottsdale Princess at the very least, to be more your speed."

Clark laughed. "Shows how little you truly know about me, Arianna. I adapt. Like a chameleon."

"More like you spread, like a bad rash," I muttered.

"Getting down to insults already?" Clark wiggled a finger at me.

I shrugged. It was what it was. "How did you manage to snatch me away from the others?"

He snorted, as though the answer was obvious. "Getting you away was easy. Your detective boy toy was distracted with other priorities." He tapped his chin. "How does that make you feel? Always playing second fiddle?" he asked coyly, attempting to get a rise out of me. We had played this game before and it was getting stale. Clark had that effect on me, like a hangnail or a kink in the neck after a bad night's sleep. Only this particular kink never goes away.

"Ramirez was taking care of his friend, no thanks to you. Why did you have to drag Vargas into it, anyway? Erica, I could understand—but why him?"

Clark snickered, amused by my earnest query. "Always putting the cart before the horse, Arianna. When will you learn?"

I bowed my head, keeping my tone as even and as genuine as I could muster, "Educate me then." I swiveled the shovel on its head as I slowly made my way back to my two other besties. I promised to give up gummy worms for a year if Clark didn't notice my retreat. Sour Patch Kids, if I lived.

Clark hummed a few bars of Dr. John's "Right Place, Wrong Time" in response, causing me to groan. I had once enjoyed that song. Now I would need therapy every time I heard it. I cleared my throat, hoping to distract the bile that was creeping its way up, as well as force Clark back to the present. Or at least into his own body.

"Ah, where were we?" Clark smiled, taking in my discomfort. "You were asking why Vargas was such an enticing…guinea pig. No pun intended." He put a finger to his lips, tapping it. "Actually, a pig is a pig no matter the jig."

I gave him a dry look. He wasn't Dr. John by a long shot. But Dr. Seuss? Not even in the same ballpark.

"Vargas was merely…a happy coincidence." He looked thoughtful. On him, it was downright creepy. I used it as an opportunity to shimmy back toward Hoe and Rake. "Don't think I'm not seeing that, Arianna." He laughed but as his eyes met mine, a chill went up my spine. "Creating a statewide manhunt for a cop had not been on my bucket list but wow…those metro police of yours, they really take the ball and run, don't they? I merely put the bait under their noses and they were off like starved rats. Of course, it would have been thrilling to see that outcome, had they managed to catch him." He chuckled; then sighed, disappointed at having missed the opportunity.

"Why break onto my property, drug Nicoh and steal Leah's cell phone?" I asked. "Why go to all the trouble?"

"Trouble? That was child's play. I simply wanted to let you know I was around. Everywhere. Watching. That I could get to you and those you cared about. Any time. Any place. Though I should have disposed of that pesky neighbor of yours. Susie, is it? Annoying old bird. Attractive, yes, but a little on the dry side for my taste." He snorted out a laugh.

"So, why am I here?" I asked through gritted teeth.

"That should be fairly obvious," he replied. "I want those chips, of course." Taking in my look, he snickered. "What? Did you think Marty's offer—to exchange himself for the formulas—

would suffice? I'm surprised even you believed his line of bull. As if the formulas alone would have been worth all this effort." He gestured to the surroundings.

I blinked, unsure of what to make of his comment. "If not the formulas, what?"

Clark shifted off the riser and bent to grab what appeared to be a power brick with switches. "Why don't you ask Daddy Dearest yourself?" He flipped a switch on the device and a spotlight lit the area a hundred or so feet to my left. Its harsh light fell on one thing.

Martin.

I gasped. Though disheveled, he didn't appear to be harmed. It was the contraption he was rigged to that had me panicking. Martin's frame had been used to lift the fabricated home and garden set, judging by the pulleys that lead to his waist and ankles. A second set of pulleys circled his neck and while they hung loosely on the ground, one look at the controller told me it was how Clark had managed to keep him under control. Any warning from Martin could have been deadly, for all of us.

"What have you done, Martin? I told you this wouldn't work."

"Hush, Arianna," Martin's voice was gruff as he shot me a look that could have singed my eyebrows.

Clark was clearly enjoying the reunion. "What's the matter, Marty? Baby girl's got your number? Apparently, she isn't the only one. You're losing your edge, old man."

"I have nothing to say to you." Martin sounded as angry as I'd ever heard him, which wasn't all that often. Still, from what little I knew of the man, he didn't have the patience to deal with Clark's animated behavior. It was one way I was a chip off the old block. Unfortunately, he was no better at hiding his emotions and Clark quickly saw Martin held little regard for his antics.

"Oh? Perhaps you'd prefer chatting with an old friend?" Clark snarled, using his controller to tighten the reins. Martin's face reddened at the pressure against his neck, leaving Clark to chortle in delight. I started to cry out in protest but something in Martin's eyes willed me to stop. Clark ignored us and made a call on an ancient walkie talkie he'd pulled from his back pocket.

When he saw me eyeballing it, he shrugged. "Place is a fortress. Even I can't find most of the entrances and exits." The grin forming at the corner of his mouth said otherwise.

A door creaked behind me. I squinted as our new visitor made his way through the quagmire of props. Finally, the stranger emerged from the darkness. As my mind caught up with my eyes, my heart chimed in with a sharp jolt, causing me to gasp.

Clark bowed. "Hello, Father."

CHAPTER TWENTY-FIVE

The moment he entered, Theodore Winslow's steely gaze trained on Martin and the two appeared to be in a mental stare down. Nicoh took the opportunity to sit upright, looking a little drunk and discombobulated from whatever concoction Clark had popped him with. Though it was hard to dislike the man any more than I already did, the abuse he continued to inflict upon my canine companion reserved him a very special spot in Hell. My mental meanderings were distracted by Theodore, who swiftly moved toward Nicoh and began securing him roughly.

"Hey! There's no need for that!" Theodore ignored me, using a rope to tie Nicoh to a nearby pallet. Nicoh howled and thrashed but in his sluggish condition was no match for the man's deft handiwork. After ensuring Nicoh was restrained, Theodore stood and started making his way toward me. I backed up a few inches, nearly stumbling in the process. After miraculously catching my balance, I grinned at the three men and feigned as much enthusiasm as I could muster. "So, who's going to make the introductions?"

Clark snickered until his father gave him a sharp look. It was easy to see Clark was on a short leash with the older man. This could prove interesting, if not beneficial. One look at Martin told me he had surmised the same thing.

"I believe you are well aware of who is who," Theodore replied after a long moment, though the blackness in his eyes told me formal introductions were off the table "It's been a long time, Martin." Theodore studied his former colleague. "Time has been good to you."

"Doesn't appear you're any worse for the wear either, Theodore." Though Martin kept his tone congenial, the look he returned was anything but.

Theodore snorted. "Times could certainly have been better." To this, Martin said nothing and the two continued to glare at one another.

"I can imagine this is a far cry from the good old days at GenTech," I muttered sarcastically, drawing an angry look from Theodore.

"What would you know about it?" he snarled.

"Err, I simply meant—"

"Arianna, I think it's best if you let Theodore and I handle this." Martin attempted to chastise me but if I let the two of them continue their silent standoff, we'd soon be as dusty as the equipment in this place.

So I did what I always do when given advice I don't care for. I ignored it. "Getting back to my original question, Clark," I glanced at him, his eyes still fixated on his father and Martin. "Why am I...are we here? It's certainly not to hold a multiple family reunion. I didn't even have time to bake a pie or whip up a batch of my famous potato salad. Though, in hindsight, it probably wouldn't have fared well under these conditions with the mayo and all—"

Theodore cut me off, "Though she has difficulty staying on point, much less getting to it, she reminds me of Alison." He looked at me with something just past the wrong side of creepy

—admiration.

"She is a lot like Alison, despite her upbringing." I didn't care much for Martin's tone, or his innuendo.

"My upbringing, which is absolutely no business of yours, was just fine. As for my shortcomings in getting to the point, the three of you have been sidestepping it quite nicely. So let's get down to it, boys. Why are we here and what do you want?"

"Definitely like Alison," Theodore murmured, with more affection in his voice than my gag-meter allowed. Martin must have felt the same, given the look he shot at Theodore. Clark looked strangely befuddled, perhaps not used to being the odd man out. "We're here, Arianna, to conclude old business. Clean the slate of old debts." I shook my head in disgust—these guys held onto old baggage for way too long. "Martin took something that belonged to me…belonged to all of us, really."

"When you say 'all of us,' are you referring to the proverbial us or something else?" I asked.

"I mean the other scientists at GenTech, as well as to the world at large, Arianna," Theodore replied. "Technology that would have revolutionized the way we look at human life, at evolution and the universal gene pool." I felt a yawn coming on and kicked myself for failing to ask for the Wikipedia version.

Fortunately, Martin interrupted what was quickly becoming a lecture, "It's easy to allow the truth to be blurred by time, Theodore, but the fact of the matter remains—I didn't steal Gemini. I was saving it from being manipulated and corrupted by wanton greed and fantastical visions of a superhuman race. You and I both know the pressures we were under—even to get meager funding—the hoops we had to jump through, the promises we were forced to make and eventually the results we would have been expected to produce." Martin shook his head, despite his former colleague's attempt to interject. "No, Theo, when you're honest with yourself—when you dig deep and find the truth you once knew—you will realize I did what was best for everyone."

"You did what was best for *you*, Martin. You didn't even bother consulting me. We were colleagues...friends even at one point." Clark blanched at his father's admission, not having considered the enemy he'd known since birth had once been an ally to his father.

"No, Theo. I saw what you were doing. Knew what you were up to when you hushed the others in the corridors or in the lab late at night when you thought I was with Alison. The greed had gotten to you. I could see it in your eyes—the promise of fame and adulation in the scientific community. The promise of power."

"And a fat bank account," Clark added, receiving a wicked glare from his father. "Seriously, Father! This...man took everything you worked for and ran—"

"Silence, Winslow! I do not need you to tell me what he's taken. Or what it has cost me." Theodore turned to Martin. "It wasn't what you thought, Martin, it wasn't like that at all, especially not after we had formulated the plan...that day at the bridge—"

Martin cut him off sharply, surprising us all by the venom in his voice. Had Theodore been about to reveal something he hadn't want me to know? "It's a moot point now, isn't it Theo? So, now that you've got me here, let's finish this."

It was my turn to interrupt. I wasn't as eager to rush to my death. "Whoa, guys! Before we get down to your business"—I didn't really want to know what that entailed, given the lengths Clark and his father had gone to over the past several months —"could I pose a few questions? You know, just for my own edification? It's not going to matter in the end but I'd like to clear a few of the things rattling around in my brain."

Martin started to speak but Theodore raised a hand. "I think the girl deserves some answers. She's been made a pawn in this, though none of it was her doing." Some might have thought the man had a soft side but his unforgiving sneer and the black vaults of his eyes told me Theodore had no soul. I wondered what he had to gain by drawing out the game. I looked at Martin, his expression grim and caught a glimpse of something he hadn't intended for me to see.

Fear.

Now Theodore really had me curious. What would terrify Martin more than his own death? Realization washed over me.

The truth.

I clutched the handle of Mr. Shovel and managed to get within a foot or two from Hoe and Rake then posed my questions before Theodore could change his mind.

"So...Mr. Winslow—"

"*Dr.* Winslow." Theodore sniffed, giving me a look of impatience. I glanced at Martin, who rolled his eyes.

"Err, my apologies, *Dr. Winslow.* It's obvious the Feds did not arrest you in Florida. So who is sitting in that prison cell on your behalf?"

It was Clark who answered, though his father looked less than pleased. "It was just some vagrant I found in our travels who looked a bit like Father. He was whacked out on drugs at the time, until Father and I took him in, got him sober and provided him with food, clothes and a roof over his head..." I wanted to gag, both of them looked as though they remembered the time fondly, believing they had actually helped another human being out of the kindness of their cold, dead hearts.

"And let me guess, he was so appreciative, he agreed to become one of your minions...one of your precious flock," I commented dryly.

"You can call it what you want." Theodore could have cared less about my opinion, much less convincing someone like me of his methods. I was beneath him. And for the time-being, he was just toying with me. "The man was most appreciative of our offerings and once he was able to become a productive member of society—"

"You forced him to repay your generosity by setting him up to take the fall for you?" I interjected.

Theodore didn't appreciate being interrupted nor questioned and from his sharp look, certainly was not accustomed to it. "I was going to say, he knew a sacrifice had to be made to support the cause. He was a willing participant."

I snorted. "Your cause? Exactly what cause is this? You brainwashed him, like you did the person who helped break your son out of prison."

"Friends of the cause are very loyal." Nothing I said appeared to affect or deter him. "Winslow was being held for crimes he had no control over."

I quirked an eyebrow. "You're not suggesting he had no control over killing my parents?"

Theodore shook his head and gave me a look one would garner on a simpleton. "I assure you, he did not have anything to do with killing Alison. And, as you can see, Martin is quite alive and well."

I gritted my teeth. Had it not been for the circumstances—and my need to ferret the truth out of these two—I would have allowed Mr. Shovel to give him a free tooth adjustment. "Those are not the parents I am talking about, Dr. Winslow. And I think you know it." Theodore responded by pursing his lips. "As for assessing guilt, he admitted to killing them. And the pilot of the plane. And Victoria, my sister. As well as her parents. Oh, and there was his brother—" Theodore blinked in surprise. "Oh, what? *Winslow* didn't share that little tidbit with you?" I laughed, my tone rough as Clark started to speak.

Theodore raised a hand. "That was an unfortunate hiking accident. As for the others…the evidence was fabricated by the police to make my son look guilty."

"Oh? And just how do you explain his confession?"

"Coercion, by the same incompetent fools," Theodore sniffed.

"I meant his confession to *me*." My patience was wearing thin with this dog and pony show.

Still, Theodore shook off the notion. "A misunderstanding, Clark was under extreme pressure. You threatened him."

I threw back my head and laughed. "Wow. You are delusional, aren't you? Clark was certainly right when he said you'd lost your marbles."

"I said no such thing!" Clark's face reddened as his father cast him a murderous glare.

I waved a hand. "Whatever, I digress…so this homeless guy *volunteers* to take your place in prison. Months later, some of the other appreciative members of your cause break Junior out. Just how did you manage to facilitate that?"

Theodore sniffed. "We have eyes and ears everywhere and when I put out the request, things happen. Our network of friends is vast. And that's all I am willing to divulge. Certainly you can appreciate the anonymity of one's confidants, Martin?" He slid a coy glance in his former colleague's direction. Martin looked away, causing Theodore to chuckle. "Still holding it close to the vest, I see. You'd think after all this time, all that I've—"

"Arianna still has questions that need answering, Theodore," Martin's sharp tone made us turn and look at him but whatever burr Theodore had put in his craw, the emotion did not reach his face. It occurred to me Martin was trying to direct the conversation away from himself. I wondered why it mattered.

I wasn't thrilled with Martin's attempt at misdirection and hoped I'd have an opportunity to get to the bottom of it later. Of course, I wasn't exactly getting the answers I needed from Theodore and Clark either.

"Err…yeah, thanks, Martin." He nodded, an awkward movement given his current predicament. I turned to Theodore, his appraising look still on Martin as though deciding something. "Did you know Mort Daniels before you took over his life?"

Theodore's gaze never left Martin but he appeared thoughtful. "I never met Daniels personally but others at GenTech had, and all were aware he was collecting information about the cloning projects at GenTech and Alcore. After he retired and moved here, we kept an eye on him and eventually, he seemed to have dropped it altogether."

"It was his pet project though, wasn't it?" I asked.

"Oh yes, that part was true but he'd been out of the game for so long…"

I picked up as he hesitated, eager for him to proceed. "So you were caught off-guard when he contacted Erica Stone and began discussing a tell-all about Gemini. Why do you think he became so interested again, after all those years?"

"You really don't know, do you?" I shook my head and Theodore shot Martin an annoyed glance. "It was your sister, Victoria. She'd done her own research and when she came across his name, she contacted him to compare notes and determine whether he could lend anything to what she'd already learned."

"But that was long before she came here—before your son murdered her and left her for me to find." I glared at Clark, who was contently picking at his manicure.

"Victoria and Mort had never met in person prior to that, all their correspondence was done by phone or email. After he contacted that…woman about the book, we knew he wasn't going to let things rest," Theodore replied.

"And that's when you knew you had to intervene," I added.

"As I mentioned, we'd been keeping an eye on him for years. We knew his routines, his daily patterns and things of that nature.

All we had to do was find a suitable replacement, tie up loose ends and the situation would have been under control."

"You appointed yourself as this 'suitable replacement.' Isn't that a bit of a coincidence?" I asked.

Theodore shrugged. "We were of the same body structure, same general coloring and after studying his mannerisms, dying my hair, adding colored contacts, along with a few other modifications, I easily slipped into his role."

"So by tying up loose ends, you mean Erica—someone who would have known you were an impostor and realized the subterfuge sooner or later."

"Yes, the people Mort Daniels was associated with had to be dealt with, along with other matters."

"Did these other matters include his research?"

Theodore nodded. "We had to get our hands on it to understand the full extent of what we were dealing with."

"After you found out, he was removed from the picture —permanently."

"Another accident…" He glared when I clucked my tongue, a reminder of the mutilation Mort and Erica had endured before their *accidents*.

"Huh, there sure are a lot of accidents around you two, Theodore. Must be terrible, to be part of such an accident-prone family?"

Theodore slid a look at Clark, whose lips curled into a small snarl. Apparently, they had no more love lost for their own family than they did anyone else's. What a pair.

"Yours appears to be no less accident prone, Arianna. Perhaps you should ask yourself the same question." I ignored Clark's comment, returning my attention to his father.

"So you took on Mort's persona in the interim. What went wrong? What suddenly made Erica a liability? A loose end?"

"That girl was a nuisance from the start and far more clever than anticipated. We'd done our research on her, too, but she was a more formidable opponent than we'd initially given her credit for. Once her mind was set on something, her greed fed her tenacity, which drove her persistence," Theodore replied.

"The way you talk about her, she sounds more like a promising recruit for your cause than someone who needed to be eliminated." I added a thick layer of sarcasm to Theodore's admiration sandwich.

He pursed his lips. "I take it you didn't know Erica Stone very well."

I shrugged. "I knew enough, my best friend used to work for her."

"Then you should understand Erica was her *own* cause. When she didn't get exactly what she wanted precisely when she wanted it, she became—"

"Like you said, a nuisance. So, why not just make sure she had the information she needed—edited, of course—and send her on her merry way? Certainly there were ways to fulfill her demands?"

Theodore shook his head. "It was never going to be that easy. She got snoopy and managed to catch of glimpse of me, as Mort, and once she'd seen the GenTech photos…"

"Erica put the pieces together and the gig was finally up. Erica not only recognized you as the impostor but realized you weren't where you were supposed to be—in your comfy prison cell. And when she confronted you about it, she'd finally worn out her welcome and her usefulness," I replied.

"Her usefulness?" Theodore quirked a brow at me.

"Surely before you eliminated her, you wanted to find out exactly how much she knew about the project, beyond whatever Mort had shared with her? She was a journalist after all, and despite the fact she manipulated others into doing her bidding, she wouldn't have merely taken Mort at his word, nor would she have trusted she'd gotten the full story from him. Erica may have been many things but she was thorough, too. She wasn't about to put her name on a book without having all the facts. And I mean *all* the facts. Enough to blow the public's socks off and perhaps even blow a few of you guys out of the water, especially when she realized who you really were." I glanced around the room, both Martin and Clark seemed less than interested, though given the twitch at the corner of Martin's mouth, he wasn't pleased with the way things were going. Why was that, exactly? "Anyway, you decided she had to be…contained. Before she got out of the Tupperware and ran off with the lid. I hate it when those things go missing."

Theodore looked confused by my analogy but shrugged it off. "Something like that."

"So rather than paying her off or asking her to join your little club"—both Theodore and his son snorted in disgust—"you agreed to meet her, only you surprised her by showing up at her house—where you extracted the threat. Quite literally. A bit barbaric but I guess it got the point across." My comments were met with bland stares and oblique silence. "Convenient, too, after Vargas had already threatened to rip out her tongue a few hours prior, in full view of at least a dozen of his co-workers. Though I have to ask, if you went to the trouble of eliminating Erica—weren't you concerned Grace Turner might do the same thing? Considering she was doing the lion's share of Erica's work on the book, she could have easily obtained the same information Erica had. Even with Erica out of the way, she could have been equally dangerous." While I knew Erica had likely kept certain details to herself, including the juicy morsels that could have given her leverage and a fatter payday, I wanted to hear Theodore's rationale.

He shook his head. "Grace had other factors that made her…pliable."

"You mean made her a likable scapegoat." Might as well call a spade a spade.

"Perhaps it seems that way but her situation, particularly the one involving the custody of her child, definitely made her more manageable." I hoped he wasn't alluding to hurting a child, had things not worked out so fortuitously. Who was I kidding—this was Theodore Winslow and his son we were talking about.

"Especially once her ex out of the way," I replied wryly.

Theodore ignored the tone but looked thoughtful at the notion. "It probably relieved a huge burden off her mind." Even up to this point, I noticed he never fully accepted responsibility for murdering the bartender, much less Erica. Perhaps another tactic —plausible deniability—if he didn't say the words, it wasn't true.

Or was there another reason?

"However, despite being more manageable, you also succeeded in making Grace a suspect in the murder of her boss," I added.

"A backup in case the detective didn't work out." Clark belatedly realized he had spoken out of turn when his father glazed him with a stare reserved for dog crap on the bottom of one's shoe.

"How did you get to Vargas? Or the bartender? Did you know about Vargas' altercation with Erica at the police station, or was that just another happy coincidence?" I asked.

"There's no such thing as coincidences, Arianna. Like I said before, we have eyes and ears everywhere. While Vargas could have been easily manipulated—to get him where we wanted when we wanted—the altercation certainly put him right in the middle of the action."

"Meaning the evidence you fabricated in Erica's apartment." Theodore shrugged. "Cat's got your tongue? Sorry, no pun intended. Let me elaborate for you. You commandeered Vargas' suburban after rendering him unconscious, extracted his blood, froze it for later, dribbled some across the crime scene—added in a bit of Darian's for good measure—then used Vargas' knife to do the deed. But you also went to the effort of making us believe he was dead—using Darian as a body double—despite keeping him alive. Why? And don't tell me Junior here got squeamish about killing a cop." Clark responded with a grin so rabid, he looked like he could have gnawed on a raw T-bone.

"He was useful for other reasons," Theodore replied, ignoring his son's fervor at the mention of murdering a cop.

"To distract Ramirez and draw me out?"

"Among other things, which I am not prepared to discuss," Theodore replied, his tone flat.

"Okay, let's talk about the bartender then. Was he just a diversion, or part of a greater plan?" I asked.

"I thought we had already discussed his level of participation." Theodore was clearly bored.

Tough gummy bears.

"To keep Grace pliable? Nope, not buying it, Doc. If that were the case, the Clark Bar here wouldn't have done such a bang-up job of blowing a hole in Darian's distinguishing features." Theodore leveled a glare at his son that had me wondering if he wasn't considering a shorter leash for Junior. Nothing like the present. "Yeah, nice job, Clark. Considering Darian's size and build was similar to Vargas', you could have kept the police in the dark for a while, had it not been for the tattoo."

"What tattoo?" Gotcha. Clark's voice almost squeaked, like the wooly chew man toy Nicoh destroyed at PetsMart during our last visit. If only Nicoh could do the same to Clark. Then again, wiping that annoying smirk off Clark's face?

Priceless.

I played it off, waving a hand at him. "Ah, never mind that now. How else do you think they would have been able to identify him so quickly?" I released an obnoxious snort. "Getting sloppy, Junior."

"Stop calling me that, you wench!" The spittle from his outburst landed on my cheek. Where was a wet-nap when you needed one?

I moved my hand in a calm-down gesture. "Hey now, there's no need to get rude just because I've got your number. Besides, only Leah gets to call me that but for future reference, the correct title is Margarita Wench."

"Shut up!" He was at a full-boil now, dropping the controller and advancing on me like a raging bull.

Theodore quickly interceded, stepping between the two of us. "Enough, Winslow! I don't recall inviting your commentary."

"I didn't realize I needed permission," his son spat. Future father and son baseball games were obviously out of the question.

I glanced at Martin and found him staring intently at me. As Clark and his father exchanged a mental battle of wills, he nodded ever so slightly in the direction of Nicoh before mouthing a single word. My eyes widened in surprise as I looked at Nicoh's contraption—awkward and cumbersome—but not unmovable. I gave Martin a small nod of understanding.

All I needed to do was create a distraction.

"Sorry to break up the family squabble but why exactly are we all here again? I'm still not totally clear." Both father and son turned to face me, their looks venomous. Oops, perhaps I shouldn't have interrupted family time?

Clark snorted. "See, Father? I told you she wasn't all that bright. That cow of a sister of hers got all the brains."

"How dare you talk ill of the dead, Junior, my sister was not a cow," I glared at him and enunciated each word through gritted teeth. "And I may not be the brightest color in the crayon box but I'm also not the person who botched the murder of an innocent man." Clark started toward me, but his father placed a firm hand on his chest to prevent him from throttling me. "Anyway, it was my understanding Martin made a trade, fair and square. Detective Vargas for himself. Seems like someone reneged on that deal, Dr. Winslow. I get that you've had Junior here keeping tabs on me, breaking into my house, poisoning my dog." Theodore frowned at Clark then looked at Nicoh. "Oh, you weren't aware of that part? Whatever. I'm assuming you were trying to draw Martin out by hazing me. But why do you even need me or the chips when you already have Martin?"

Clark stepped toward Martin and snickered. "Come on Marty, why don't you do the honors of telling her?"

I shrugged. "Tell me what? What is it Martin is supposed to be telling me?"

Theodore looked at his old colleague and shook his head in disappointment. "She really doesn't know, does she?" Martin pursed his lips.

"I knew the old man was holding out," Clark growled. "Some things never change, huh, Father?"

"No, son, it appears they do not." Theodore scowled at Martin.

Clark continued, "Just using her as bait, while pretending to be long last daddy come to save the day—"

"Shut up!" Martin's eyes suddenly went wild as he spat out the words. "Ignore them, Arianna. Typical rantings of madmen."

Clark turned to me, his voice earnest, "Have I ever lied to you, Arianna?" I tilted my head. Clark had a point, if you overlooked the whole killing part—which I didn't—he'd technically never lied. Several months ago, he had said he would kill me. And here he was. Again. I gave him credit for persistence. He certainly had Martin rattled.

"Would someone…anyone, like to tell me what's going on here?" I looked from Theodore to Clark to Martin, challenging any one of them to do the deed.

It was Clark stepped to the plate, whether the action had been warranted or not. "Seems like Daddy Dearest hasn't told you the truth about the chips he implanted in you and your sister."

"If you're talking about the formulas for Gemini it's old news, Clark," I replied, unimpressed.

"That's rich." Clark appeared to be the only one amused by my comment, given the way Theodore and Martin were launching visual daggers at one another.

I gripped the handle of Mr. Shovel in frustration. As usual, Clark could never just get to the point. Everything was a production. All part of his little drama. "If you've got something to say, then spill it. This song and dance should have been left in the 1980s," I growled. Nicoh wasn't the only one who could show teeth when needed.

Clark scoffed, "A ten-year-old could have reproduced those formulas."

"Yeah, well, a lot of ten-year-olds are smarter than most adults I know. So, other than the formulas, what exactly are we talking about?"

"Oh, I'm sure Marty will concur what's on those chips is far more valuable than some outdated formulas." Clark laughed. "Just as I'm sure he knew the minute he implanted them, he'd sealed your fate." When I didn't respond, he added, "Look what happened to Victoria."

"Oh, no, you can't put that blame on anyone but yourself, Clark. Not your father. Not Martin. Not your secret club members. *You* brutalized and beat her to a pulp. And dumped her like trash." My voice sounded foreign, if not a bit crazed.

The venom I wanted to unleash on him had risen to the surface, refusing to stay tucked where I had buried it for months. I feared it made me too much like the monster standing before me. Too much like his father. And perhaps, much too much like Martin. All of them repulsed me. Human lives were flesh and blood with thoughts, emotions and souls. Not playthings to be manipulated or destroyed simply because it suited their needs. Clark may not have been the worst of them but he was part of the environment these men had created.

"Tell him, Dr. Winslow. Victoria would have been more useful alive than eating worm dirt. Had he not acted so hastily, so savagely…like the selfish, spoiled, undisciplined little boy he's always been, you probably would have already had the chips by now." I stared straight at Theodore and had my answer.

Though soulless, his eyes could not lie.

Clark saw the truth, too, and suddenly his life came unraveled.

And just my luck, it did so…right on me.

CHAPTER TWENTY-SIX

Clark converged with such momentum and sheer rage even Theodore couldn't prevent him from launching into me, knocking me to the ground. I heard Martin call out and Nicoh howl but Clark was a wild man, quickly regaining his balance and rewarding me with a hard kick to the gut. Followed by another to my ribs.

A scream echoed. It took a few seconds to comprehend it had been mine. There was shuffling, scraping and yelling but the thumping of my heartbeat was the only sound I recognized as pain surged through every nerve. Clark was unrelenting and only after the fourth kick—this one landing squarely on my right kidney—Theodore managed to corral his frenzied son in an awkward bear hug.

"That's payback for your friend Leah." Clark was breathless from the energy he'd exerted as he struggled to free himself from his father's grasp. I was surprised the elder man was able to detain him for as long as he had, though perhaps having a son like Clark required a stronger arm than most. "I've waited quite a while to dish out that punishment and considering she's not here, you make a suitable stand-in. Not quite as satisfying I might add, but still delicious." He laughed before hawking a spitball at me.

"You kick like a little girl, Clark," I huffed. "And spit like one, too." Blood oozed from my mouth as I snorted, dripping rivulets onto the ground. Clark struggled and cursed under his father's weight but Theodore maintained his grip. For the moment, I was thankful, if not a bit impressed.

Suddenly, I registered movement off to the right.

Martin.

In Clark's zeal, he'd left the controller on the riser just within Martin's reach. During our altercation, Martin had managed to unhook himself. His wrists were still bound with a threaded bike lock but the slack allowed him to move each arm separately. He yelled my name and upon catching my eye, glanced at Nicoh.

I turned to the canine and belted out the word Martin had mouthed to me earlier, "Mush, Nicoh, mush!"

Theodore had inadvertently created a crude sled when he'd attached Nicoh's lead and mid-section to the pallet and now the canine's ears perked as he used his weight to shift the platform. Gaining momentum, despite the slickness of the concrete floor, he heaved the contraption forward—toward our captors.

Too bad Theodore and Clark had treated us poorly, I mused, as Nicoh got his revenge and pounced upon both men, using the full force of an Alaskan Malamute followed by the makeshift dog sled. Clark took the brunt of the blow and was thrown to the ground upon impact, his head connecting with the concrete in a satisfying thump. Theodore was knocked off balance, which allowed Martin to charge in from behind. Using the extra span of bike lock chain as a noose, he pulled it taut against the other man's windpipe. Theodore gasped as his hands scratched and clawed at Martin's head. Martin used the man's imbalance to take him to the ground, subduing him with the chain. Theodore emitted a sickening, burbling rasp as he struggled for air and finally slipped into unconsciousness. Martin continued to apply pressure, his demeanor unnervingly calm, as though the act brought him peace.

I forced myself to look away and screamed in horror. Nicoh was lying on his side partially covered by the riser. After colliding with Clark and his father, he had landed on the rake, now embedded into his side. Blood wept from the wound as I strained to listen for signs of life. Tears surged from my eyes when I heard the muffled gurgling of his labored breathing.

I wanted to comfort him but Clark was conscious and despite being woozy from the impact, still looked murderous as he snarled at the wreckage and the prone canine. Fighting through the pain, I struggled to my hands and knees while holding a hand against my injured ribs, as though the effort would meld them back into place. Mr. Shovel had managed to get himself stuck under the mess but I spotted Hoe and as I struggled to my feet, ripped it from beneath the rubble, stalking toward Clark.

He was panting and bleeding from the back of his head, as well as from the other injuries to his chest and midsection. Blood spittles erupted from his mouth as he laughed at me, amused by the girl with the gardening tool bearing down on him.

"Given the way you look right now, I'd say I won this round, Arianna."

I snorted but quickly had to fight the urge to react to the pain the gesture caused. "This is hardly a competition, Clark."

"Don't you get it? Life *is* a competition. Every day we fight to cheat death."

I shook my head. "No one cheats death, Clark."

"Ah, but that's where you are wrong, every day we live—we may be fighting the inevitable—but our survival means we've won." He hadn't struck me as a glass-half-full kind of guy but I went with it.

"Even though we lose in the end." This time, I posed no question.

"Only if you see death as a loss." Clark shrugged awkwardly, wincing from his injuries. I was happy to see he wasn't impervious to the pain.

"And you don't?" I asked.

"It depends on what you do with the time you have—the battles you've won, the challenges you've overcome—"

Who was this guy? Tony Robbins' evil twin? "The number of lives you take and are able to get away with?" I replied sarcastically.

Clark ignored my tone. "My life is my own to live. I make my own challenges and rewards and therefore, my own victory over death."

"But you interfere with other's battles and challenges in doing so. Your victories actually destroy their opportunities and their lives," I replied through gritted teeth.

"They have the same opportunities to survive, they just choose a safer path," he huffed, indignant he had to explain what seemed to be common sense for him. A dark comedy was more like it. Or a satire.

"So you're saying it's their own fault they didn't cheat death longer?" I scoffed.

Clark shrugged. "They made choices that put them on a losing path."

"Or perhaps just a collision course with a sociopath," I replied dryly. My attitude, or lack of agreement was not lost on him but he would not allow it to dissuade him. His ego and delusions of grandeur were too great, eclipsing even those of his father's. Would Papa Smurf have approved of his son's little soapbox moment? Or would he have realized it for it was? He'd created a monster that had no bounds. And no loyalty. Clark would eventually kill his own father, if the notion appealed to him or suited his needs.

"We all do what we have to—to survive. And to achieve victory, there must also be sacrifice," Clark replied.

"But the blood is not yours, Clark."

"Isn't it?" he growled. "You don't think I've made sacrifices?"

I gave him a single head shake. "Not unless these 'sacrifices' were a means to satisfy your ends."

"And *that's* why it's a competition, Arianna. In the end, it all comes down to life or death. Who possess the strength and the will to do what it takes." Every conversation with this guy was circular. The point he missed was in cheating death, he had also cheated life. At some point, that scale would have to be balanced. "Just out of curiosity, are you going to do anything with that gardening tool? Or are you just going to stand there and bleed all over me?"

"In a hurry, Clark?" I inched Hoe closer to his throat, so it had a front row seat to his carotid artery. "No worries. Where you're going—or should I say, going back to—you'll have plenty of time to pontificate how great of a player you've been in the game of life. You can even throw a few tea parties with your prison buddies to celebrate those victories. You are, after all, already familiar with all the activities they enjoy doing. Maybe you'll even find a few like-minded individuals to play Scrabble with. Or better yet, Twister." I grinned and when the taste of blood filled my mouth, I was happy to share my hideous smile.

Clark's lips curled into a snarl. "I'll twist your scrawny neck if you don't shut up." Hmmm, hit a nerve, did I? As if reading my thoughts, he managed to contain himself long enough to grit out, "All your incessant chirping interrupts me from deciding how to eliminate you. Permanently." His smile cracked the mercury right out of the creep-meter.

"Oh?" I toyed with Hoe, using Clark's neck for balance. "I thought you *needed* me, Clark. Martin, too? And, why was that again? You started telling me when—well, when Martin kicked Daddy's keister." Speaking of Martin, he'd been noticeably silent after wrangling with Theodore, which had me worried. "Been pretty quiet over there Martin, you doing okay?" I didn't dare take my eyes off Clark.

Martin replied, his voice weary, "Just trying to maintain control over here…"

He started to say something else but Clark surprised me by grabbing the back of my leg, forcing me off-balance and plunging me forward, along with Hoe. A sickening crunch echoed through the warehouse and Clark's eyes went wide as he gasped and gurgled, crimson spewing from the freshly made crevasse that had been his throat, coating me like a shawl as I made my downward journey. My battered frame connected with his, forcing the air from my lungs until there was nothing but blackness and silence.

I captured a final glimpse of Clark as consciousness eluded me. It turned out I had been wrong.

The hoe hadn't gotten the raw end of the deal after all.

CHAPTER TWENTY-SEVEN

Time had no relevance.

No hours.

No minutes.

No seconds.

Subliminal blips on the screen, only they weren't persuading me to buy cars, cologne, liquor…or love.

They were random glimpses.

Of Life.

And Death.

Glimpses of Clark's horrified expression as Death won the final match.

Glimpses of Martin, speaking soft and low. Brushing bloody, sweaty hair from my eyes. Squeezing my hand. Whispering my name.

Glimpses of activity. Commotion. Screeching. Crashing. Footsteps in a frenzied shuffle—like runners escaping a stampede of angry, charging bulls—followed by obscure voices. When had I been transported to a death metal concert?

One voice in the distance—a child's lullaby in comparison—familiar but worried.

Ramirez.

Time, sound and sight intertwined until I welcomed the blackness that beckoned me and offered the solace I sought. Still, something tugged at the back of my mind, begging me to return. I pushed it away, not wanting to remember.

As darkness took my hand, a persistent nudge made its last attempt and the memory slipped through. In it, a sickening crunch. A man's frame slumped, his neck contorted. And though the life behind them had extinguished, even in death, his soulless eyes stared on.

* * *

Hospitals.

Does anyone enjoy visiting them, much less waking up in one? I hadn't been given much choice in the matter, thanks to Clark's assault. While my stomach and kidneys were still mad and not at all shy about telling me just how they felt, my two cracked ribs—now known as Death Wishbone 1 and 2—were a constant reminder of the importance of playing nice in the school yard. Or not. Then again, Clark had probably never spent much time mastering that art.

Faces swarmed around me like faded watercolors. I could not move my arms but could feel the warmth of others enclosing my hand. My throat was dry and lips were cracked. Someone dribbled a bit of liquid into my mouth, like a small bird fetching a worm or tiny insect from its mother's beak. I pressed my lips together and winced as they chafed.

A small chuckle erupted to my right. "You'll get used to it." I exerted a great deal of effort turning my head and found my ears had not deceived me.

Vargas looked like a cross between a zombified soldier of death and one of Dr. Frankenstein's rejects, with a bad case of road rash tossed in. My head was swimming as I took in the road map of stitches and surgical tape that did little to mask the angry gashes and bruises that had once been his face.

"I really hope I'm not looking in a mirror," I rasped, drawing a round of chuckles from the others in the room, which included Leah, Abe, Elijah and Grace.

"Nah, this stuff's not for amateurs," Vargas teased, grunting as he shifted uncomfortably in his wheelchair. I noticed it was his hand that held my right. Except for the IVs, it was hard to tell where his began and mine ended, the bandages barely patching together skin and bone. I started to retort but felt a squeeze on my left.

"He's right you know." Despite her beaming smile, I saw the worry in my best friend's eyes as she took me in. "This time, anyway." She reached across and squeezed Vargas' free hand, resting on the edge of the bed. An unexpected look of tenderness passed between them.

Abe patted my leg. "Glad to have you back with us, Ajax. For a while there, we thought you were gone for good this time."

"Of course there was no way we were going to let you leave us with that unruly canine of yours," Elijah added, winking at me.

"Nicoh..." My heart and stomach did simultaneous flip-flops as I remembered the last time I had seen my big boy. "He...he... saved me..." I stuttered, tears welling in my eyes.

Leah clutched my hand. "He's gonna be okay, AJ. The rake did some damage but the vet got in there in time, did his magic and patched him up. And while he's currently mad about being poked and prodded, he'll be back to a hundred percent in no time."

I attempted to nod but the movement made me woozy. "I wasn't sure..." I replied quietly. "He was so still..." Again, tears burbled as the memory surfaced.

"Of course, it will be a while before he's eating cookies off the counter or chasing Mrs. Grimley's cat out of the bushes," Leah offered me a quick wink and smiled, "which means you and I'll will have to step up and do our part...on the cookies, anyway."

I chuckled but the sound didn't translate as I'd expected and the group worked hard not to wince.

"Hey Grace, is that you over there?" She looked less disheveled than the last time I had last seen her—in her smart red business suit and heels—hair pulled into a sleek up-do. The bags had diminished from beneath her eyes and her pale pallor was now flushed with a healthy pink.

She stepped forward and placed a small stuffed dog on my bed. "Hey you...I know it's not the same as having Nicoh here but I thought this little guy was a reasonable facsimile and could keep you company until you get out."

"How are you?" I asked after relaying my thanks.

"You're the one in the hospital and yet you're asking how I'm doing?" She chuckled, shaking her head. "I came to thank you."

"Thank me?"

"If you...and Leah...and well, all of you hadn't gotten involved..." She looked down. "Let's just say, things could have gotten messy."

"The police would have eventually figured everything out," I replied.

"Maybe, but it was you. You wouldn't let it go and now the monsters who killed Erica and Darian and Mort Daniels. And kidnapped Detective Vargas"—she looked shyly at the detective —"have been identified. And gotten what they were due." I inadvertently shuddered and looked away—if she'd known what I'd done, would she have felt the same? "Anyway, I wanted to thank you. And I don't want to seem morbid but something positive did come out of all this." She paused, a tiny smile forming at the corner of her mouth. "My ex's parents—the ones who have custody of my daughter? Well, since Darian's death, they've reached out to me and we've really had a chance to sit down and talk about things. And while we're not there yet, we're talking about visits, possibly shared custody. Anyway, it's promising."

"That is wonderful, Grace. I'm truly happy for you." If something good could come out of this tragedy and the mess Clark and his father had created, then Grace should definitely be on the list of people to benefit. "How about work?"

"I'm still filling Erica's position until they find a permanent candidate," Grace replied.

"You'd be a fine replacement." Leah patted her former co-worker on the arm.

"Oh, I don't know about that. It would be strange." Grace shook her head.

"At least give it some consideration," I added and everyone nodded in agreement. "In the meantime, what's going to happen with the book?"

Her eyes perked up at the mention of it but she patted my leg. "I've taken up enough of your time, AJ. There are a lot of people here who want to see you. Besides, we can talk about that later." She gave me a hurried wink and after thanking me again, made her exit.

"What do you suppose that was all about?" Elijah asked.

I slid a glance at Leah. "Who knows," I replied, changing the subject as I perused one face to the next. "So what else have I missed?"

"Err, you should probably talk to Detective Ramirez about that." I could only stare at my friend—typically the first to divulge every juicy detail—as she shifted uncomfortably.

"For once, the voice of reason." I hadn't realized he'd been in the room until the group parted and suddenly there he stood, arms crossed, leaning casually against the door jamb.

"Come in and join the fun, Ramirez," I managed to scratch

out, while the peanut gallery barely managed to withhold their chuckles.

"Actually, why don't we leave you two to talk?" Abe nodded at his brother, before leaning down to kiss me on the forehead.

"Yeah, we've got to get back before Anna completely takes over," Elijah replied.

"I hate to tell you this but I think she already has." I laughed.

"True, true," Elijah sighed but his smile was wide. "She sends her best. By the way that obnoxious display of roses was her doing, though we managed to deliver them."

"Uh, huh. Girl's definitely got taste. And class. Tell her thank you and I hope to see you all soon."

"You'd better behave yourself. She still expects you in L.A. to help with the wedding plans. She wants her photographer to be in top form, after all," Abe teased.

"Like I said, girl's got good taste." Both Stantons laughed and shook hands with Ramirez and Vargas before leaving.

Leah released my hand and shifted off the bed. "Ready to go, gimpy?" She looked at Vargas, who mocked-growled. The guy was completely smitten with my best friend.

He squeezed my hand as she maneuvered his wheelchair. "You take it easy, Ajax." As Leah rolled him away, I had a feeling he was talking about more than nursing my wounds.

Ramirez remained in place long after Leah and Vargas retreated down the corridor to his room, tossing insults back and forth all the while, just like old times. I tried to laugh but the movement caused me to wince and though I fought to hide the pain it inflicted, the detective's sharp eyes missed nothing.

"Smarts, doesn't it?"

"Just getting used to all this gift-wrapping." I gestured toward the bandages and IVs.

"Still, must have been a rude awakening to find yourself in this condition." His tone was sarcastic but his gaze was more than a little intense. "I have to wonder what you were thinking, running off like that?"

"What?" I scoffed. "You think it was part of my grand plan to get blindsided by Clark; then beaten to a pulp?" I wanted to throw my head back and have a good laugh—show him how ridiculous that notion was—but my injuries had other ideas.

"Your actions suggest you have a death wish. Do you?" He searched my eyes.

I squinted. "What exactly are you getting at?"

"Things around you tend to die." When I grimaced, he raised a hand to clarify. "Or at least, that's your perception. I honestly don't know, perhaps you don't feel like you deserve to live, because they didn't? That somehow, their lives were more important and that you're not worthy of being the last one standing?" He shrugged; then began to pace. "Why else would you take the risks you do? Certainly not for the sport of it."

I thought back to my last conversation with him. "No, Ramirez, I do not have a death wish. But I also don't like seeing my friends and family hurt. Or worse. There's already been so much loss."

He raised an eyebrow. "And so it's Ajax in her Wonder Woman suit and lasso, off in her invisible jet on a solo mission to take down all forces of evil?"

"Actually, I'd like to think of myself as a grown-up version of a Powerpuff Girl armed with my Chemical X, high ponytail, mischievous Alaskan Malamute and spunky best friend."

Exasperated, Ramirez shook his head. Clearly, he didn't watch the Cartoon Network. "Chemical X or not, you take risks—absurd risks—which could end up not only hurting you but the people who love you." I bowed my head so he couldn't see the tears welling. "What would Leah do without you? You're the only family she's got. And Nicoh?"

"And you?" His silence spoke volumes and when he would

not meet my gaze, I changed the subject. "All this heavy stuff is making my brain hurt. Would you mind if we discussed what happened when Clark snatched me? And perhaps you could fill me in on what happened…after? I'm a bit fuzzy on some of it." Boy was I.

I yawned and suddenly, the biggest peanut butter fudge shake couldn't have kept me awake. Perhaps this impromptu sleepiness was some form of subconscious avoidance technique. Whatever it was, within a few short minutes, despite my attempts to keep my eyes open I lapsed into that dream land, where only happy memories awaited me.

Ramirez was waiting when I woke, sitting in a corner chair, reading a *People* magazine.

"Catching up on the latest gossip, are we?"

Ramirez smirked at me over the top of the well-endowed celebrity gracing the front cover. He looked as though sleep was a thing that existed in the past, his eyes tired but still alert.

"As if I know who half these people are. Or care. What was I supposed to do? You fell asleep. One might draw the conclusion it had to do with the company."

I yawned, wishing I could scratch the itch on my nose but the IVs had other plans. "Nah, it was nice everyone could make it. They certainly didn't need to—"

He put the magazine down and stood but remained at a safe distance. "I wasn't talking about everyone, AJ."

"Urrr…what was it we were talking about before I zonked out?"

Ramirez ignored my side-step. "You were going to fill me in on what occurred after we found Vargas."

"Right. So what have I already told you? "

He shook his head. "Not much. At least not much more than your constant reference to the 'ho.' " He smirked, using his index fingers for emphasis.

I chuckled. "The hoe is not a person, Ramirez. It's a gardening tool." He shook his head in disbelief. "What? You've never worked with garden tools before?"

Ramirez grunted out a harsh laugh. "I know what a hoe is, AJ. The question is, what does it have to do with anything?"

My face flushed and my stomach stirred with what could only be described as a flurry of bumblebees as I remembered the look on Clark's face. And the flood of crimson. "The hoe killed…I killed Clark."

"No, AJ. He was killed in an accident." An accident? This was news to me. Ramirez caught my surprise and elaborated, "An entire set from the abandoned television station landed on him."

I shook my head and winced. "That's not what killed him, Ramirez. Believe me, I got him with the hoe first. He was… spurting blood…everywhere." I started shaking and though Ramirez moved to comfort me, he stopped short when I waved him off. The walls were already closing in without having him dote over me.

He sighed. "I'm sorry, AJ, but there was no hoe at the scene. At least not when we got there."

"That's impossible," I whispered, my mind reeling through the events. I was sure it wasn't playing tricks. I hadn't dreamt the whole thing.

Ramirez evaluated my expression. "Maybe you'd better start at the beginning." He patted the foot of the bed, careful not to venture closer. "Just take your time and please breathe, will you?"

I shook my head, giving him a small smile and once I'd drawn a few cleansing breathes—with extreme discomfort—I told my tale, top to bottom, left to right, front to back. Just the facts, ma'am. When I finished, he was quiet for a long while. Too long, even for a cop.

"Say something," I whispered.

He rubbed his chin as he carefully formulated his response.

"All right. There appears to be several…inconsistencies between what you have just told me and what we found when we arrived on the scene."

"I'm sure Martin corroborated what I told you." I shrugged. "He saw the same things I did."

Ramirez shook his head. "That's the thing, AJ, Martin's one of those inconsistencies."

I raised my head off the pillow. "Come again?"

"Martin wasn't at the warehouse when we arrived."

"How did you know where to find me?"

"I received an anonymous call. A man told me where to find you and Nicoh and hung up." When I raised an eyebrow, Ramirez elaborated. "He called you both by name."

"And you're thinking it was Martin." It wasn't a question. He shrugged, noncommittal, causing me to sigh. "Tell me what you found. Did you see Clark snatch me?"

"I saw you get thrown into a black Escalade. Leah had gone with Vargas to the hospital, so Abe, Elijah and I took pursuit. We temporarily lost sight of it as we weaved in and out of an industrial park and after we spotted it again, we realized the driver had used the distraction to swap out vehicles." I wondered how they'd known it had been a decoy and Ramirez did not disappoint. "Plates were the same but the first vehicle had a trailer hitch with a crease in the bumper molding. Anyway, we eventually lost that one, too and had to assume they'd snuck into one of the warehouses."

"And once you lost them—what? You waited to get the call?"

"No, we didn't just wait until we got the call," he growled. Apparently, the detective was feeling a bit touchy despite the fact I hadn't intended for the comment to have been taken that way. "We went back to your house and looked for clues. I talked to the other officers, neighbors, etc. to see if they had noticed anything suspicious but they hadn't. Your neighbor Susie is horrified now that she knows what really happened to Nicoh and that she chatted it up with a ruthless killer." Words couldn't remove that image from my mind, though the look Ramirez tossed me came pretty darn close.

"What? I certainly didn't tell her. Nicoh is like a teenager at a Justin Bieber concert when it comes to her homemade doggie treats, not to mention she's one of the best neighbors a person could have. Do you think I'd want her moving on account of my penchant for attracting the unwanted attentions of murderous psychos?" Ramirez nearly broke his jaw chewing that one over before I quickly added, "Present company excluded, of course."

He waved it off. "Not you. I think Leah let it slip but she wouldn't confirm when we asked her. Did pretty much the same circle dance you tend to do, though."

"I learned it from her," I replied, pleased by the level of smugness I'd managed to conjure.

"I'd believe that," he replied, though his expression suggested I'd been a willing participant. "Getting back your question. We got the call and when we arrived at the abandoned warehouse, you and Nicoh were out front. No one else. We were checking you out—Nicoh still had the rake embedded in his side—when we heard the crash. I had called for backup while we were en route, along with a couple of ambulances but they hadn't arrived yet, so Abe, Elijah and I went in. Place was a booby-trapped maze. We were surprised the whole place didn't come falling in on us."

"I'm sure old Theo had something to do with that—it probably made purchasing the property all the more worth his while."

"I don't doubt the booby-trapping part—the place was a dump to begin with—but Theodore Winslow didn't own it. In fact, had it not become a crime scene, it was slated to be torn down by the real owner within a few months."

"Huh." Clark had lied to me after all. "Guess you guys

wouldn't have found us had it not be for that anonymous caller." Another testament to how close I'd come to death's door.

Ramirez ignored my comment. "We made our way through that minefield of a television junkyard until we found Theodore and his son. It appeared as though the rigging from one of the sets gave way while both were underneath."

I reconstructed where we'd been positioned during those last few moments. It was possible both men had been in the vicinity when the structure fell. But crushed? Improbable. Certainly not without some serious staging. "Were they…dead?" I managed to squeak out.

Ramirez nodded. "Both sustained massive trauma when the structure collapsed, obliterating Theodore Winslow's windpipe and severing his son's head." Despite what the evidence suggested, I was still convinced I had inflicted Clark's fatal wound. What happened afterward just ensured he stayed that way. "Of course, we need wait for the official report but…" he shrugged, the facts being what they were, before taking in my impassive expression. "You're still thinking about the hoe."

"Yeah, that…and other things." I had yet to mention the memory I had before slipping into darkness.

"You care to share these 'other things' with me, AJ?" Ramirez searched my eyes and for a moment, I was afraid they would betray me.

I looked at my hands. "I don't know. Just images mostly. There was so much going on and I was out of it at the end. I certainly don't remember leaving the building." He nodded, not completely convinced. "And considering Nicoh was injured and I didn't have much in the way of defense other than a hoe and a shovel, our odds of getting out of there unscathed were slim."

"AJ, there was no shovel, either."

I snorted. "Surely you're not suggesting Martin took the hoe and shovel, but left the rake?"

"He saved Nicoh's life when he left the rake in place. Nicoh would have bled out if Martin had removed it."

"You realize how ridiculous this sounds, don't you? Martin, who was probably injured himself, not only manages to get me out but Nicoh out as well, with a rake impaled in his side. He then reenters the building, repositions Clark and Winslow, releases the mechanism holding the set in place and then has the wherewithal to remove evidence?" I huffed.

Ramirez heard me out before speaking. "It's not all that ridiculous. Not if Martin was trying to protect you by ensuring you were in the clear. You did handle the shovel too, did you not?" My expression was a dead giveaway. "I thought so. Sure does seem like Martin's going out of his way for you, AJ. Now why do you suppose that is?"

I shrugged, not really wanting to have this discussion, though I did wonder where Martin had put the tools, given the time frame. And, how had he known where to put them. Or better yet, where to put them so the police wouldn't find them. When I looked up, I found Ramirez studying me and tried my best to remain nonchalant. "No idea. Making up for lost time, I suppose. Plus, he thinks it's his fault Theodore and Clark came after me in the first place as a ploy to draw him out."

Ramirez wasn't convinced. "A convenient response, especially when you're the one with the chips everyone's hot for."

"Are you suggesting he wants the chips for himself and with the other two out of the way, things have worked out quite nicely for him?"

He shrugged. "I know you've been contemplating whether to hand the chips over to him but you should think long and hard before doing so. In fact, I would advise against it. It could be to your own detriment. You're safer with them than without."

I snorted, gesturing to my current predicament. "Yeah, real safe, Ramirez. Real safe." He pursed his lips. "Did it ever occur to you Martin might be the only one who can ensure the information on the chips is safe from people like Clark or Theodore? Or whoever they were working with?"

He didn't respond immediately but something I'd said had gotten under his saddle. "There's something else I wanted to tell you about Vargas. When he was held captive down in that pit, he was forced to watch Darian's execution."

I gasped as horror rolled through me. "Clark forced him to watch—"

Ramirez shook his head. "It wasn't Clark. Or Theodore."

"There's a third man," I inadvertently uttered.

"Looks that way." It wasn't what he'd said but the way he'd said it.

"What? Don't tell me you think it was Martin?" He continued to work his jaw, providing me with my answer. "You actually think he could have been in cahoots…with them?" My voice went up a perilous octave. Ramirez raised a hand, encouraging me to tone it down before the hospital staff brought in a crash cart.

"I think Martin knows more than he's letting on—that his connection to Theodore and his son was more involved than any of us realized—and that it was in his best interest to have them out of the way. I believe they were a means to an end and you were the tool he needed to facilitate that end. I have nothing linking him directly—whether he personally executed Mort, Erica or Darian—but indirectly, I doubt his intentions were as innocent as saving his daughter."

"What about the others Clark and Theodore were working with?"

"There's no proof there was anyone else, AJ. Just as there is no proof Martin had any associates helping him. How do you know it wasn't just the three of them all along and when Martin saw an opportunity to double-cross the others?" Ramirez paused, allowing me to draw my own conclusions.

I felt my face reddening in fury, though several of the same questions had been swirling around in my brain and gnawing at my gut. "I can't believe you can so easily come to this conclusion, Ramirez. Even after he traded himself for Vargas and saved Nicoh. And me."

"From where I sit, it changes nothing. Regardless of what he's done as of late, I still don't trust him." He shook his head. There would be no reasoning with him and when it came to Martin we were at an impasse. He must have been reading my thoughts or perhaps, I had been wearing my emotions like a comfortable, old pair of Chuck Taylors. "Anyway, you should draw your own conclusions about Martin."

I quirked an eyebrow. "Are you assuming I haven't?"

"I think you're still on the fence. Your mind is telling you one thing, your gut another and your heart…" his voice trailed off as his eyes took in the sunset from the limited view of my hospital window, as though he wished he could be anywhere—anywhere but here.

I urged him to finish his thought. "What does my heart say?"

"Your heart says…" he paused, shaking his head and when he finally replied, his voice was filled with sadness and disappointment, "it doesn't really matter anymore." He turned away, placing a hand on the door.

My lip trembled. I wanted to call out to him, to beg him to take it back. Once again, tears emerged and I couldn't speak. Ramirez did it for me but they weren't the words I'd hoped for.

"And AJ? You're going to need to repeat what you just told me—leaving nothing out and I mean nothing, including the part about Martin—to Detective Chavez." He easily slipped back into his detective role, like a suit of armor that had been custom-designed. It pained me to realize he found solace in it and not in our relationship. It was, in effect, his escape from it.

"Your partner?" I managed to choke out.

Despite the shakiness of my voice, Ramirez still would not turn to face me. "He's waiting outside to take your formal statement. And a piece of friendly advice: if Martin contacts you in any way, you need to encourage him to come to the station, as well as contact Detective Chavez immediately."

"You're not staying?" I asked, my voice hopeful.

"No, AJ, I've done all I can," he paused, his voice barely a whisper and for a moment I thought he would continue. Instead, he silently opened the door and walked out of my life.

At that moment, I realized while my fractured ribs would eventually mend, the piece of my heart I'd reserved for Ramirez had shattered forever.

CHAPTER TWENTY-EIGHT

Once my story had been told and told again, I cried myself to sleep. It was something I hadn't done since my parents died. The tears scorched my cheeks but I welcomed their pleasant diversion from the bitter, savage chill that nipped at my bones.

When I dreamt, it wasn't of the horrors I'd witnessed or the pain I now felt. It was of sunshine kisses...of smiling faces...and laughter. Images filtered by on a hazy cloud, like random snapshots in a photo album. The past danced with the present and mingled with unrecognizable fragments. The future, perhaps? All I knew was that I felt safe and as long as I stayed, nothing would threaten to steal my warmth, ever again.

Something told me I couldn't stay locked in my cocoon forever and once the images had melted away, I emerged from my sanctuary. Feeling a familiar hand clutching my own, my heart did a little pitter patter.

"Ramirez?" I let a yawn escape as my eyes fluttered to adjust to the darkness of the room.

"No, sweetheart, he's gone." My heartbeat slowed in disappointment.

"Martin?" My throat was rough from sleep and tears long cried out.

"Yes, my darling…" His face was hidden by the shadows but his voice was gentle and soothing. "Why don't you have a sip of water?" I felt the cup against my lips and though it was room temperature, I shook off a chill.

"Where have you been, Martin?"

"I tried to get here sooner but that detective of yours is quite persistent, as are your friends—who waited tirelessly for you to awaken."

"You were here, then?"

"At a safe distance but yes, always near."

"How did you manage—"

"The duty nurse stepped away."

"I had to tell them everything, Martin," my voice cracked as I muffled a sob.

Martin patted my hand, his voice reassuring, "Of course you did, my darling."

"Why didn't you stay? They don't believe me. At least, not about everything."

"In due time, they will."

"But, Martin…they need to know…you saved me."

"No AJ, you saved yourself. I merely moved you and Nicoh out of harm's way."

"You saved his life by not removing the rake."

"Because he's important to you," his tone was earnest.

"He is…very, very important." My voice cracked, thinking of my big beast. I wanted nothing more than to scratch his muzzle and tell him I loved him. Had I told him I loved him that day? I swallowed hard and turned to where Martin sat, wishing I could see his face. "Did you kill him, Martin? Did you kill Theodore?" I sucked in a deep breath. "After I killed…after the struggle with Clark, I thought I heard…"

Martin cut me off, his voice firm but gentle, "Theodore died a long time ago, Arianna."

"I know the two of you shared quite a history." Recalling the scene at the warehouse, neither father nor son had appeared to be surprised by Martin's sudden manifestation or that he looked so fresh after being dead for nearly three decades. There was also Martin's lack of venom when interacting with the man he'd supposedly not seen in all those years—the same man who'd murdered the mother of his newborns and had attempted his own demise. In fact, Martin had been quick—too quick—to shut Theodore and his son down. "He even alluded to circumstances surrounding that history—they both did—though they never quite managed to divulge any specific details." And now the only man left standing who could reveal those details was sitting before me. Silent. One was left to wonder why. "Did he help you disappear, Martin? Is that what he was trying to tell me? Is that how he knew you were alive?"

Martin sighed, his voice weary. "It's not that simple, Arianna."

"The truth never is, Martin."

"Theodore and Clark were bad men—men with no conscience, no souls."

"What kind of man are you, Martin?"

It took him a moment but he finally answered. The strain in his voice told me it pained him to do so, "One who has seen and done too many things to recall what it was once like to differentiate black from white."

"The Gray Man." My response bore no judgment, merely an observation. A conclusion.

He chuckled. "So it would seem."

"Does the Gray Man's inability to differentiate the black from the white also give him the capacity to murder innocents?"

"By innocents, I assume you mean Erica Stone and the bartender?" he asked, his tone contemplative.

I nodded. "And Mort Daniels."

"Even the Gray Man…even I have limits, Arianna. While I may have traipsed across one line or the other, I am not without morals, or without a soul."

"So the answer is no?"

"The answer is no."

"On all the above?" This time, there was only silence. As usual, there was no clear-cut answer with him and while I believed he had not killed Erica, Mort or Darian, I wasn't convinced he hadn't had knowledge that would have spared them. With Martin, it seemed as though there were always contingencies —truths within the truths. He'd kept things close to the vest for so long he probably couldn't remember what those were.

"You were never really going to tell me about yourself, were you, Martin?" I'd known the answer before I'd asked.

"Some things are better left alone, just as they are, which sometimes means leaving them in the past," he replied.

"I am part of that past," I countered.

"I said *some* things, Arianna."

"Does that include the chips? You've been awfully careful not to ask me about them," I hesitated, "but you want them, don't you?"

"Unfortunately, Mort Daniels brought the Gemini project back into the limelight, sharing it with Erica and perhaps even this girl, Grace," his displeasure was palpable as he bit out the words, "which now makes it extremely dangerous for you to have them."

"So, I assume you want me to hand them over. To you," I replied dryly.

"It would be your decision," he replied, "but it would be for your own safety. And for the safety of the ones you care for."

"Some decision," I responded.

He chuckled again. "The tough ones—the ones that mean something—always are. The rest…"

"Just fodder?"

"Exactly."

I nodded. "May I have some time to think about it?"

"Of course," he replied and if he was disappointed, his voice didn't betray him.

"A couple things have been puzzling me—how did you know about Vargas?"

He might have been a skilled actor but his confusion sounded sincere. "I'm not sure I understand what you mean?"

"Back when I told you about my friend who was in trouble and missing, you asked if it was the Tempe Homicide Detective, despite the fact I hadn't mentioned it was a *cop* friend. It could have just as easily been Leah, or another friend altogether."

"Surely I heard it on the news." His tone wasn't as convincing this time around.

I shook my head, though he probably couldn't see me either. "No, Martin. The police had just started searching for Vargas. The news media hadn't even been alerted much less associated him with Erica's murder."

"Oh? I'm not sure, then. Why do you ask?" I noticed he had released my hand. If only I could see his face.

"Just something Ramirez said," I replied, nonchalant. "Vargas was forced to watch as Darian, the bartender, was shot…executed. I assumed it had been Clark but Vargas insisted it was neither Clark nor his father, but a third man."

"Huh…I had no idea." A tiny tremor filtered in, but was gone just as quickly.

I clucked my tongue. "No, of course you didn't. But then, now that I think about it, Clark never mentioned it. And if I've learned anything about Clark, he wouldn't pass up an opportunity to blab about his feats. As for old Theo doing the deed? From what I saw, he would not have done his own dirty work when he had a son that was so proficient at it." I shrugged. "Anyway, I guess we'll just have to assume it was one of their minions, who managed to escape into the sunset."

"Looks that way." His voice was now devoid of emotion—the switch had been flipped into the off position—apparently, the father-daughter session was over. I wasn't going to get answers to any of the other questions either—like how he'd finally managed to track down and make contact with Theodore or his son, or how he'd known Grace had been married to Darian. Not today, anyway. "I hear the nurse coming back. We'll talk more about this later? Once you're out of the hospital, of course. In the meantime, you'll give some serious thought to what we discussed regarding the chips?"

"You can count on it, Martin."

Martin slipped out as silently as he had entered, leaving me to contemplate the truth behind the truth.

And the foundation of lies it had been built on.

EPILOGUE

I was released from the hospital a few days later and of course, assigned to a regiment that required limited movement. For once, I decided obedience was in my best interest. I'd like to think Ramirez would have been both proud and probably a bit amused by the state of affairs in my household. Leah had brought Nicoh home from the vet with strict instructions which included the threat of an e-collar, should he choose to deviate from them. In the end, we were both vying for prime real estate on the couch while Leah served as our surly nursemaid.

Honestly, she didn't seem to mind, as it allowed her to unleash her bossy streak. Plus, with her manning the snacks, it meant she got to pick her favorites. At one particularly cantankerous moment, she threatened to bring out the cocktail weanies and while that might have had Nicoh salivating, I opted for being a good little patient. Though I'll admit, I did fantasize about getting even with her one day.

As we'd settled in one night, I noticed she had a mildly amused look about her.

"Spill it," I growled, praying Spam Surprise wasn't on the menu. Again.

She did her best to maintain a poker face—even using Nicoh to distract me—but he was immersed in his own bowl of popcorn and could not be bothered with the absurdities of humans, so all she received for her efforts was a disgusted canine snort.

"Abe and Elijah left us a special little parting gift." I motioned for her to continue before I became part of the couch. "All right, all right! They made a few tiny 'modifications' to the security room."

I groaned, whenever she used finger quotes for emphasis, I knew we were in trouble. "How tiny?"

"They converted it into a small panic room. Of sorts." She winced, as though I would risk tossing my box of Junior Mints at her. "I'll give you a tour once you've gotten the clear to give the couch back its cushion."

I smirked at her as she prattled on about the Stanton brother's architectural prowess in regards to security—at least, that's what I hoped she was talking about—in addition to the various benefits of having such a feature. I couldn't deny I was intrigued by the concept, but was more curious about the intention.

Had Abe and Elijah designed a panic room to keep the baddies out? Or to keep us in?

Apparently, my reputation as a trouble magnet had continued to precede me but before I had a chance to ponder another one of life's little mysteries, my phone tinked at the sound of an incoming text message.

From Martin.

Have you made a decision?

My thoughts drifted to the information I had received earlier that day. Before I gave Martin an answer, I'd needed to know why the chips were so important. If they were worth killing and dying for, would they be safe in Martin's hands? Or in the hands of his unknown associates?

I had to be sure, once and for all, so that morning I had

contacted the geekiest person I'd known—a computer, audio visual and security expert who went by the alias Tony B. After swearing him to secrecy, I had relayed all the sordid details surrounding the Gemini project, including the ones involving Victoria and me. When I finished, he was eerily silent.

"Tony?"

"I'm here, just calculating the likelihood—given your track record—that you're going to get both of us killed if I do this."

"Oh, is there an app for that?"

Tony snorted. "Yeah, I wrote it."

"Give it to me straight, what are my…our odds?"

"Less just say they are not in our favor and leave it at that."

"I didn't need an app to tell me that," I joked.

"It never hurts to know what you're facing though," he replied, "even when writing your own death warrant."

"Hmm…a realist. Always good to have one on the team." He was silent. As a self-proclaimed hermit—I'd never actually met him in person—I doubted he'd want to be associated with anyone's team, whether going to his death or not. "Anyway, you want me to messenger these over?"

"Same place," he replied. "And AJ?"

"Yeah, Tony?"

"I may be a genius but I'm not a miracle worker. Nor am I a super hero. So, even if I'm able to extract something off these suckers, I can't save your bacon once the information is out there."

"It's okay, Tony, you do your geeky best, take care of your own bacon and leave the super hero stuff to me." A snort reverberated in my ear, followed by the sound of a dial tone.

It turned out Tony B. was both a genius and a miracle worker, as he got back to me within hours of taking delivery of messengered package. He wasn't one for bursts of emotion but his findings warranted a bit more than he managed to exude.

"You're not going to like this," were his first words.

"It can't be any worse than what I've already cooked up. It's like Sauerkraut Sunday back in the day at the Jackson household —you knew it was coming but you could never escape the stench." My analogy was met with awkward silence. "Just give it to me straight, Tony."

"It was pretty simple getting the data if you had both chips. Each chip contained a code needed to unlock the information on the other. You just had to do it in the right sequence." Much like Martin's arrangement when he contacted his associates. Clever? Or paranoid? "Once paired together, I was able to access the comprehensive data."

"So, one's like the table of contents and the other contains the chapters?"

"A bit more complex than that but generally speaking, you're in the ballpark." His tone indicated I wasn't even in the same time zone. "Anyway, the chips contained the formulas for the project— as you'd expected—along with the dates, times, names of bene-factors, patients and donors, including details about the off-spring and their adoptive parents. Quite a dossier on your family tree, in case you're interested."

"Err...yeah, maybe later. Surely there was something...more? Something worth killing for?"

"I believe I just mentioned it."

"Come again?"

Perhaps it was the connection but I was pretty sure I heard a head-slap. "The names, AJ. It all comes down to the list of names."

"The benefactors? The donors? The children? The adoptive parents?"

"*All* of them, AJ. The list is quite a doozy. You'll never guess whose names popped up." This time, Tony B. sounded almost human.

"Do I really want to know?"

"Oh, I think you'll find it very…educational."

"Go on…"

"Two of the products of Gemini turned out to be local boys. The first is your pal, Jeremiah Vargas, and the second, Congressman Bob Fenton." I gasped. What were the odds? The congressman was married to Ramirez's ex, Serena. Vargas was his best friend. "And that's not even the best part—they're brothers."

Too speechless to respond, Tony B. took it as a sign to proceed and continued to rattle off other several high profile names—politicians, entertainers, athletes—even a few miscreants, including a recently decommissioned drug czar, as in dead. Most of them had more than enough reason to ensure Erica's book never saw the light of day. Some even had the means to guarantee it. And just when I thought things were starting to get complicated, Tony B. graciously tossed in another wrinkle.

"Of course, this is where it gets *really* interesting." Good old Tony B., always saving the beast for last. "Turns out the benefactors had a board of directors, for lack of a better term. Anyway, the Chairman of the Board, so to speak, was also the scientist who spearheaded the consortium—someone whose name I think you're more than a little familiar with…" His revelation sent the world toppling off its axis, where it landed squarely on the right toe of my favorite vintage Chucks.

"Earth to AJ! Have you even been listening to a word I've said?" Leah's exasperated expression told me I'd missed out on more than a few pertinent details involving the Stanton's modifications while I'd taken that mental sidebar to revisit my conversation with Tony B.

I sighed and looked at Martin's message one last time, before flipping the phone over and shoving it out of the way with the toe of my injured foot.

Leah looked at me curiously, having seen the message from where she was sitting. "Aren't you going to respond to that?"

I nabbed the remaining gummy worm just as Nicoh's tongue was zeroing in, popping it in my mouth with a satisfied grin.

"I believe I just did."

~ The End ~

ABOUT HARLEY

Harley Christensen lives in Phoenix, Arizona with her significant other and their mischievous motley crew of rescue dogs (aka the "kids").

When not at her laptop, Christensen is an avid hockey fan and lover of all things margarita. It's also rumored she's never met a green chile or jalapeño she didn't like, regardless of whether it liked her back.

For more information on the author and her books, please visit her at www.mischievousmalamute.com.

OTHER BOOKS BY HARLEY

Mischievous Malamute Mystery Series
Book 1 ~ Gemini Rising
Book 2 ~ Beyond Revenge
Book 3 ~ Blood of Gemini
Book 4 ~ Deadly Current
Book 5 ~ Gemini Lost
Book 6 ~ Fatal Bonds
Book 7 ~ COMING SOON!

Six Seasons Suspense Series
Book 1 ~ First Fall
Book 2 ~ Winter Storm